The Inevitable Love

Laney and Luke

The MacFarlands
Book Four

By SJ McCoy

A Sweet n Steamy Romance

Published by Xenion, Inc

Published by Xenion, Inc.
First paperback edition January 2023
www.sjmccoy.com

Cover Design by Dana Lamothe of Designs by Dana
Editor: Kellie Montgomery
Proofreaders: Aileen Blomberg, Traci Atkinson, Becky Claxon.

ISBN: 978-1-960017-04-8

Dedication

For Sam. Sometimes, life really is too short. Few oxo

Chapter One

Laney tapped her foot as she waited by the baggage carousel. The Bozeman airport had changed a lot over the years. There were three carousels now – that hadn't been the case when she used to live here. Then again, how many years had it been since she'd left? She moved away straight after high school. She took her hat off and ran her hand through her hair, wondering if the way that the airport had changed was just an indication of how *everything* changed. What was she thinking? Moving back home had seemed like a good idea just a couple of weeks ago. Now? Now that she was here, she wasn't so sure.

She rolled her eyes as she listened to the two guys standing next to her talk. They were tourists – it seemed that about ninety percent of the people on the flight from Denver were. These two were worrying about driving in the snow.

"We could get a hotel near the airport for tonight," one of them suggested. "Maybe it'll be better tomorrow."

Laney watched as his companion walked toward the windows and peered out.

She rolled her eyes again when he came back and said, "That might not be a bad idea. It's icy out there."

"What about you?" the guy standing closest to her asked.

She turned and raised her eyebrows when she realized that he was talking to her.

The second guy grinned at her. "Are you staying close by? Can you recommend a hotel?"

She shrugged. "I have no idea about hotels. I'm driving."

The first guy jerked his chin toward the windows. "It's gnarly out there. If you like, we could all share a cab. There has to be a hotel nearby."

Laney shook her head. "No thanks. I'm fine driving. There's an information desk over there." She pointed to the desk, where a line was already forming – no doubt those people didn't want to drive, either.

"You should come with us. It doesn't look safe out there – and all we can see is the airport parking lot, and I'm sure that's been plowed."

She had to laugh. "Where are you guys from? Have you never driven in snow before?"

"We get snow sometimes, but not like this."

"Well, I grew up here. I'm used to this. I'll be fine." She turned away from them; there was still no sign of the bags coming out, so she headed for the car rental desk. There was no line there; she may as well take care of that rather than stand here listening to these two.

By the time she had the paperwork taken care of and the keys to her rental car, the bags had started to arrive. She was relieved to see hers and went to grab it. The two guys were still there, and one of them made to get it for her, but she took care of it herself.

When she stood back, he gave her a rueful smile. "Independent woman, huh?"

She laughed. "Just a woman. I appreciate the offer, but I don't need it. You guys have yourselves a good vacation."

By the time she exited the rental car lot, the snow was really coming down. The outside temperature gauge read fifteen degrees – nothing out of the ordinary, but she couldn't help smiling at the thought of the tourists bundling up in huge coats, hats, and scarves.

The highway was slippery over the pass, but nothing too bad. She was confident in her ability, but she wasn't reckless; if the roads had really been bad, she would've spent the night in Bozeman just like the tourists. By the time she was over the other side, the snow was letting up.

Now that she was here, she wondered what everyone would have to say. She probably should've told them, but then again, it was nobody's business but her own. She hadn't wanted to make some big announcement that she was moving back – she wasn't a hundred percent sure that this was an actual move yet. There were a few things she wanted to figure out before she made the commitment.

The most important thing she wanted to be sure of was that her sister, Janey, was good with it. For years, their relationship had been … not strained, they loved each other too much for that … maybe shaky was the right word? It seemed as though they were back on a solid footing since Janey married Rocket, but Laney wanted to play things by ear for a while. If having her back home was going to make Janey uncomfortable, then Laney wouldn't stay. No way would she ever do anything to hurt her sister – despite what people might think.

The other detail she needed to get a handle on before she committed to the decision to move home was … No. He wasn't a factor. He couldn't be. She was over him. Whatever feelings she'd had for him were … She wished she could say that they were gone, but that'd be a lie. The truth was that she still wanted … still wished … but whatever her feelings might be, they were those of an eighteen-year-old girl – the girl she no longer was. Everything she felt for him might have been a big part of the reason that she moved away – but all these years later, she wouldn't let those feelings stop her from coming home.

She slowed as she approached the exit for Livingston. She was going to stay up in town tonight. She'd rented herself a little place out at Mill Creek for the month, but she couldn't get in there until tomorrow. She hadn't told anyone that she was coming, but she planned to hit the town tonight – see who was still around. It might not be the wisest move given the way that gossip spread like wildfire in the valley. Whoever saw her tonight would probably somehow get word to her family that she was here before she did, but that was fine. They were used to her – and if they weren't, they should be.

She took the exit, and a big smile spread across her face as she headed down Highway 89; it felt damn good to be back. She put her foot down as she headed south out of town. She'd have to turn around at some point and come back up to get to her hotel, but for right now it just felt good to drive the old familiar highway.

Luke leaned his head back against the headrest and blew out a sigh. It had been a long day, and he was ready for it to be over. He could head back into the station now, but he knew that if he did that, Deacon would likely give him shit. His brother had been riding his ass hard lately. It wasn't as though Luke didn't understand why. As the sheriff, Deacon was hardly going to show him any favoritism. He had to treat all his deputies the same. To Luke's mind, though, Deacon was going a little too far in the other direction. Sure, he hadn't been as focused at work lately as he usually was. Maybe he'd been hanging out at Chico too much – partying a little too hard –

but he was still good at his job. Deacon was just pissed at him because he wanted to see him settle down.

He came back to the present when a vehicle flew by the spot where he was parked in a pullout on the side of the road. He made a face; it was a local truck, and he wasn't going to start dishing out tickets to the locals. They weren't the problem. It was the tourists who were a danger to themselves and to everyone else on the road. They either drove like grannies because they were afraid of the snow, or like idiots because they thought they were invincible.

He pulled out his cell phone and shot a text to Tanner. Tanner had one of his rare nights off from working at Chico tonight, and the two of them planned to hit the bars in town.

Luke: What time do you think you can get up this way?

He watched the display for a few moments, wondering if Tanner would reply, but he'd no doubt be busy with the horses. Sometimes, Luke envied his friend that.

Tanner ran the stud on his family ranch, spending his days working with horses. There was a time when they were kids that Luke had spent all his days right there on the MacFarland ranch with his buddy. But that was a long time ago now.

Tanner had joined the Navy, while Luke himself had gone off to the police academy. He'd always wanted to follow in his brother's footsteps. He loved his job – it was just that he was going through a rough patch lately. He didn't even know why. Nothing had changed. Then again, perhaps that was it, nothing had changed in his life for longer than he could remember. He worked, he hung out with Tan and his brothers, he hung out with Deacon – and his soon-to-be wife, Candy, and that was about it.

Candy was a welcome newcomer in his life. Perhaps that was part of what had him so unsettled. Deacon had been single for years after his divorce. If Luke had thought about it at all, he thought that Deacon would be forever single. But Candy had come along and sweetened him up. Luke loved her, but he had to admit that he was a little envious of what she and his brother shared. Sure, he dated, he'd had a few relationships, but he'd never had anything like what Deacon and Candy shared. To be fair, he hadn't thought he wanted it. Well, not since …

The sound of his cell phone beeping shook him out of his thoughts, and that was a good thing. He'd do better to chat with Tan and figure out what they were doing tonight than to let his thoughts stray anywhere near Laney MacFarland. Nothing good ever came of that. He looked down at his phone.

Tanner: Not sure I'm going to make it tonight, bud.

Luke: Yeah, you are. You might be a bit later, but you'll make it.

Tanner: Okay, you twisted my arm. But don't wait for me. Head over to The Mint whenever you're ready. I'll text you and let you know when I'm on the way.

Luke: Okay but don't leave it too late, you don't want me to have all the fun.

Tanner: No worries. You know me. I'll make up for lost time whenever I get there.

Luke smiled. Tanner wasn't joking about that. He had a good time no matter where he went. He was just one of those guys; everyone loved him – especially women.

He looked down at his phone when it beeped again in his hand. It wasn't Tanner this time.

Deacon: You might as well come back in. Shift's almost over.

Luke eyed the message suspiciously. It wasn't like Deacon to cut him a break — not lately, anyway.

Luke: Do you want me back in there for something?

Deacon: No.

The curt reply didn't do much to reassure him, but then another message popped up.

Deacon: If you must know, Candy says I'm being hard on you lately. I don't like to think that you're sitting out there in a blizzard just to avoid me. Come on in.

Luke chuckled. There was no question that Candy was sweetening his brother up.

Luke: Thanks. I appreciate it. See you in a … Shit! I might be a while. Some crazy tourist just blew by doing at least ten over.

As he pulled out to follow the Jeep and turned on his siren, he saw the words *Be careful* flash up on his phone. No matter what little rough patches they went through, he never doubted that his brother cared.

He switched his full attention to the road as he quickly caught up to the red Jeep, which had immediately slowed when the driver spotted him. It rolled along at five under the speed limit until it reached a place where the shoulder widened.

Luke nodded to himself as he pulled up behind it. The driver might be a tourist — the Jeep was a rental; the Bozeman plates and barcode sticker in the rear window announced that detail to any observant eye — but at least they had sense enough to find a safe place to stop.

He turned up his collar and put on his hat. The snow was getting heavier again, and the wind had picked up. He was going to do his best to keep this short, if not sweet.

As he approached the vehicle, he could see that the driver was wearing a cowboy hat. Maybe he was wrong – maybe this wasn't a tourist after all. Yes, they'd been speeding, but he'd seen no indication that they weren't in full control of the vehicle. Perhaps he could let them off with a warning, whoever they were.

The driver's window rolled down when he got close. Luke decided to give the driver the opportunity to talk themselves into or out of a ticket based on their responses.

However, when the driver turned to him, he knew that it would be his own responses that determined how this encounter went. And he wouldn't be able to respond until he got his reaction under control – his heart was racing, and he could feel the blood rushing through his veins, pounding in his ears.

Laney MacFarland sat there staring at him, her hazel eyes huge and rounded with shock. A slight flush touched her cheeks, and she bit down on her bottom lip.

Luke just stood there, staring back at her. She was still as gorgeous as ever – no, scratch that, she was even more beautiful now than she'd ever been as a girl. Her long, blonde hair fell around her shoulders. Her lips were pink and plump as she pressed them together, looking … uncertain.

The silence dragged out for a few long moments before Luke managed to pull himself together.

"Laney."

Her gaze searched his face as she nodded. "Luke."

Damn, he'd been hoping that she might give him more to go on – if she'd said anything more than his name, he might have a clue as to what she was thinking. Was she still mad at him? Did she hate him? Had so much time gone by that she just didn't care anymore? Was he just a guy from the past?

They continued to stare at each other. She wasn't giving anything away.

Laney's knuckles were white as she gripped the steering wheel. This could not be happening! She hadn't even been in town for five minutes – hadn't even checked into her hotel yet, let alone moved into her rental. She'd thought that she would have until tomorrow before she had to face her family, and hopefully much longer before she had to face Luke Wallis.

And yet, here he was, standing next to the Jeep looking even hotter than she remembered him – and to her, he'd always been the sexiest guy on earth. She swallowed. He probably didn't even care anymore. She wasn't sure that he ever had. If she stood out at all among the women he'd been with in his life, it would only be because she was his friend's little sister.

She tried waiting for her heart rate to return to normal, but it didn't look like that was going to happen anytime soon.

She risked a smile. "You're going to freeze to death if you stand there staring for much longer."

Her words seemed to shake him out of his stupor, and he smiled back. Damn! There was just something about that smile that melted her insides. It always had. Even when she was a little girl, she used to do everything she could think of to make him smile at her. He and Tanner weren't that much older than Janey and her, but Tan used to try and run them off whenever Luke was over. They were his annoying kid sisters, after all. But Luke … Luke always had a kind word for her – well, no, he had a kind word for Janey as well. But it seemed like he saved his smiles for her.

"What are you doing here?"

Her heart sank. She should probably be grateful that he wasn't immediately issuing her a ticket, but she was more disappointed that he hadn't said something more welcoming.

She let out a short laugh. What was she thinking? She knew better than to hope for anything when it came to Luke. At best, he was one of her brother's friends. At worst, he was just some guy she used to know – a mistake from the past.

"Well, thanks! It's great to see you, too." If that was the kind of greeting that she was going to get, there was no way she was going to share anything with him. "And I guess the honest answer to your question is speeding."

His eyebrows drew together.

"You asked what I'm doing here," she explained.

"Oh, right. Yeah, well." He peered out at her from under the brim of his hat, and his light blue eyes met hers. "That wasn't what I meant. I meant ... It's good to see you, Laney."

His words knocked all the air out of her, but she didn't have the time to respond.

He continued, "But yeah, you want to slow down. It's slippery out here."

She nodded. So, he was going to talk to her like a deputy and nothing else? Oh well.

"Sorry."

He raised his eyebrows, but she didn't know what he was waiting for.

"Do you want my license and the papers for the car?"

"No, Laney, I don't. I just ... I just want you to ... be safe."

"No ticket?"

"No ticket. You just get on home safe. How long are you here for?"

She swallowed. "I'm not sure yet." That was the truth. She didn't know what he'd think, say, or do, if he knew that she was thinking about staying.

He started to back away from the Jeep and touched the brim of his hat. "I hope you have a good visit."

Her heart sank as she watched him go. No matter how much she hoped for more, Luke just didn't see her that way. That one time? He saw it as a mistake. He must, there was no other explanation for his behavior since.

"Thanks."

Chapter Two

Luke hung his hat on the hook by the door when he got home. He shrugged out of his coat and walked straight to the kitchen. When he got there, he braced his hands on the countertop and hung his head.

He was still reeling from seeing Laney. He wished their encounter had gone differently – but what the hell was he supposed to do? He hadn't been prepared, but even if he had ... what would he have done? He'd just have to lie low for the next couple of days, or however long she was here. No doubt Tanner would fill him in on the details later.

With that thought, he pushed away from the counter and headed upstairs. He was going to take a shower, get ready, and go out. He needed a drink.

He was glad that his stop back into the station had only been brief. His shift had been over by the time he got back there, and he'd only seen Deacon in passing. He didn't want to think about what his brother might have to say when he found out that Laney was in town.

After his shower, he looked himself in the eye in the mirror as he shaved. If he were given to talking to himself, he might ask whether he really planned to lie low or whether ... No. Too much time had gone by. Laney would always be the one who got away. He might get to thinking every now and then that maybe he should do something about it, but he probably never would. How could he? She might be all grown up now, but she was still Tanner's little sister. More than that, she was also Ford and Wade's little sister, and the two of them had made it clear that she was off-limits. Yes, that might have been in the days when she was still jailbait, but he couldn't imagine that their opinion on the matter would have changed even over all these years. It was just an unspoken rule – you didn't go after your buddies' sisters.

And if the thought of Tanner, Wade, and Ford wasn't enough, there was always their oldest brother, Cash. The thought of how Cash would react if he found out what had happened should be enough to put Luke off even thinking about Laney ever again.

It should be enough, but it wasn't. He'd never stopped thinking about her, he doubted he ever would. He tightened the towel around his waist when the memories flashed through his mind. Images of Laney – Laney laughing, Laney pulling him down into a kiss as they danced. He closed his eyes and could still smell her, could still feel her naked body under his that one time …

He shook his head to clear it. That one time should never have happened. Even as he tried to convince himself of that, he could hear her breathing his name as he lost himself inside her. Damn. He had to put her out of his mind. It was a mistake. If he loved her, he loved her as a sister, not as anything more. They couldn't have anything more. And besides, it wasn't as though she wanted anything more from him. If there'd been even one time in all the years that had passed since then that she'd given him any indication that she wanted something more, he would have manned up. He would have faced his friends – her brothers – he would have done whatever it took to make her his. But she hadn't. Not once in all the years since she moved away had she done anything to make him think that she wanted him. For all he knew, she treated him the way she did because she was embarrassed by what they'd done.

When he was dressed and ready, he went back to the kitchen but a quick glance in the fridge and the cabinets proved what he'd already known; he didn't have anything in the house worth eating.

He took his phone out and sent Tanner a quick text.

> *Luke: I'm going over to The Mint now. I'm going to eat there. Let me know when you're on the way?*

He was surprised when a reply flashed up almost immediately.

> *Tanner: Give it about fifteen then order me a burger? I got done early. I'm on my way.*

Luke frowned at his phone. Laney hadn't been home often over the years, but whenever she was here, he felt guilty. He felt guilty right now as he wondered whether Tanner had seen his sister and she'd finally confessed to him. Was that why Tanner was on his way to town already when earlier he'd said that he'd be late?

He grabbed his keys and wallet from the counter. He was being paranoid, and he knew it. Tanner had just finished work earlier than expected. That was all. He hoped.

His shoulders relaxed a little when he walked in through the doors of The Mint, and the warm wave of familiar sounds and smells washed over him. He needed to put Laney out of his mind, and this was as good a place as he could think of to do it.

He smiled and nodded at friends and neighbors as he made his way to the bar, but when he was almost there, he stopped in his tracks. Laney was sitting on one of the stools, chatting with the bartender. What the hell was she doing in here? How was he supposed to put her out of his mind when she was right here, looking ... no, he couldn't let himself focus on how damn good she looked.

He only hesitated for a moment. His instincts might be screaming that he should avoid her but for all he knew, Tanner had arranged to meet her here. He told himself that his feet were carrying him toward her because Tanner would find it odd if he were at the other end of the bar avoiding her. But the truth was, she drew him to her like a magnet – she always had.

Nixon, the bartender, greeted him with a chin lift. "Hey, Luke! Have you seen who's back in town?"

Laney spun her stool around and met his gaze. Her hazel eyes seemed to glimmer, but he couldn't get lost in them again. They couldn't just stand and stare at each other like they had out on the road earlier.

He smiled. "I have. I didn't expect to see you back up in town."

She tucked a strand of long, blonde hair behind her ear and looked away. "Yeah. I haven't made it down to the ranch yet."

Luke gave her a puzzled look. "You haven't?"

She let out a short laugh. "No. If you want to know the truth, they don't even know that I'm here."

"Why?"

"Because I haven't told them."

He smiled through pursed lips. "Okay, that's the obvious reason. Want to tell me the not so obvious one?"

He loved the little smile that tugged at her lips. They used to play this game when they were kids – she would give the most obvious answer to any question he asked so that he would have to ask another. There was a time when he believed that she did it just so that he would stick around and talk to her longer.

Now, she shrugged. "I'm not so sure that I do want to tell you, but I might as well. I haven't told them that I'm here because I don't know if I'm going to stay."

He cocked an eyebrow, not sure that he understood. A few years back, after a big blow-up with their dad, she'd vowed that she would never set foot on the family ranch again until he died. She relented last year when her sister, Janey, got married on the ranch. But he could understand that she might not want to stay there. But from the way she said it, it sounded like she meant something else. Could she possibly mean ...

Nixon grinned at him as he set a beer down on the bar in front of him. "Get this, Luke. We might be getting our favorite cowgirl back."

Luke met Laney's gaze again. His heart was hammering in his chest. What did getting her back mean? He didn't ask – he didn't dare. He just waited for her to explain.

She looked away before turning back to him. "I'm thinking I might move back."

He felt as though all his energy drained out of his body down through his feet and into the floor. He grabbed the stool next to her and hauled himself up onto it, not sure that he'd be able to remain standing.

"You're coming home?"

"I'm thinking about it."

Nixon set another beer in front of her. "What can we do to persuade you?"

Luke's heart felt as though it might beat right out of his chest when she shot him a sideways glance.

"I don't know, Nix, I'm just gonna play it by ear."

Luke studied her as she took a long swig from the bottle. For a moment, it seemed like the most important thing in the world to somehow convince her to stay. Not only to stay, but to stay and finally give him a chance. Deacon had told him for years that he would never meet another woman like Laney, and even if he did, she wouldn't be the one for him. Unlike Luke, Deacon maintained that all the MacFarland boys would be thrilled if their sister ended up with him.

When Nixon moved away down the bar to serve other customers, Laney turned and met Luke's gaze.

"Don't worry, if I do stay, I won't embarrass you."

He sat back in his seat as if she'd delivered a physical blow. "Embarrass me? What do you mean?"

She let out a short, bitter laugh. "Don't, Luke. You know damn well what I mean."

"No, Laney. I don't. Please explain."

She blew out a sigh and turned to face him. "You know, one of these days, we're going to have to talk about it. Whether I come back to stay or not. I'm tired of this shit, Luke. It was years ago. I get that you never wanted anyone to know. I get that you never wanted me …"

"What?!" She thought that he didn't want her?

"Oh, come on!"

"Laney! What the hell?" They both turned to see Tanner, who had just come in and was yelling across the bar at his sister.

Luke's mind raced as he watched the two greet each other. He was struggling to catch up. She thought he didn't want anyone to know? Well, she was right. He didn't. But only because they would think that he took advantage of her. How would he ever have been able to explain to anyone that he was the one at her mercy? Even if she wasn't aware of it – and given what she'd just said, she couldn't be aware of it – Laney held a power over him that no other woman ever had. For all that he'd tried to deny his attraction for her, and tried to ignore her advances to him, what happened between them had been inevitable.

After a few moments, Tanner wrapped his arm around his sister's shoulders and grinned at him.

"Did you know about this?"

Luke smiled through pursed lips at Laney. Apparently, he'd known for longer than Tanner, but that didn't mean he wanted to explain how he knew.

Laney rolled her eyes. "He's known since this afternoon."

"What, you call this guy now and let him know that you're here, but you don't tell your family?" asked Tanner.

Laney laughed. "No. This guy pulled me over for speeding earlier."

"You gave my little sister a ticket?"

Laney loved the way the lines around Luke's eyes crinkled as he laughed. She didn't remember those lines. They hadn't been there when they were younger, and she'd hardly spent any time around him in the last few years. He'd looked sexy as hell in his uniform earlier, but now, dressed more casually in jeans and a snuggly-looking sweater, he looked even hotter.

"I did not give her a ticket. I was about to …" He glanced at Laney. "But when I realized who she was …" He seemed to hesitate before he continued, but then he smiled at her and held her gaze as he said, "I was just so damn glad to see her, and so happy that she was home, that the thought of giving her a ticket was the furthest thing from my mind."

Laney swallowed. Tanner took his words at face value, but she felt like there was more to them. Just before Tan had arrived, she'd told Luke that, if she stayed, she wouldn't embarrass him by telling anyone what had happened between them – she'd even tried to let him off the hook by saying that she knew he never wanted her. But the way he was looking at her right now felt as though maybe he did.

Had he really been glad to see her – happy that she was home? All he'd done was stare and ask her what she was doing here.

Tanner was laughing. "That's lucky for you, Luke. Can you imagine how much shit everyone would give you if you'd given her a ticket the minute she arrived?" He turned back to Laney. "And how come you didn't let us know you were coming?"

She shrugged. "I didn't want to make a big deal out of it."

"Well, we do. How long are you here for? If you'd let us know, we could have figured out getting everyone together."

She laughed. "That's what I meant about not making a big deal out of it."

"But it's not often that we get to see you," said Tanner. "We have to make the most of it while you're here, because who knows when we'll see you again."

"That's kind of the point, Tan. I'm thinking that I might stay."

"Seriously? Stay as in move back here?"

"Yep."

Tanner grinned. "So, where are you staying?"

Laney was aware that Luke was watching her carefully as he waited for her answer.

"I'm staying here in town tonight."

Tanner made a face at her, and Luke laughed. "That's the obvious answer; want to tell us the not so obvious one?" he asked.

She shot him a small smile, loving that he still remembered the way they used to play that game. "Okay, I'm at a hotel here in town tonight because I rented a place out at Mill Creek, and I can't get in there until tomorrow."

"Well, at least at Mill Creek you'll be closer to the ranch," said Tanner.

"Yeah, I wanted to be close by but obviously not on the ranch."

Tanner grinned at Luke. "You'll have to keep an eye on her for us."

Laney's heart raced as she looked at Luke, wondering what her brother meant.

Luke met her gaze as he said, "I'd be happy to." There was something about the look in his eyes that made all the muscles in her stomach and lower clench tight.

She pulled herself together. "Why? Where do you live now?"

"I had a place by the river just south of town for the last few years, but I just rented a place at Mill Creek, too."

Tanner spoke before she had the chance to process that. "Which place did you get, Laney?" he asked. "I didn't think there was anything for rent around there – not after Luke scooped up the Bennett place."

She swung back to look at Luke. "You got the Bennett place?"

He chuckled. "I did. All their kids have been gone for a good few years now, and Haley finally convinced Walt to move to Austin to be closer to them."

Laney shook her head in wonder. The Bennett place was only small compared to most of the ranches in the Valley, but it was a decent spread and a perfect set up for horses.

Tanner laughed at the expression on her face. "If you stick around, and you're nice to him, I'm sure Luke might let you go over there and check it out – maybe even rent you the barn if you plan on staying."

Her heart leaped into her mouth. The thought of going over to see Luke's new place, of renting the barn from him, took her back through the years, back to being the girl who had worshiped him, who had been so totally in love with him that she couldn't even see sense.

That girl would have done anything to be with him. Things were different now. Now, she was a woman, and she knew better. Now, what she would have to do was whatever she could think of to avoid being alone with him. Between their encounter on the highway earlier and the few minutes that she'd been around him tonight, she already knew that if she allowed herself to be drawn into his orbit, the outcome was inevitable.

Chapter Three

Luke's plate was empty, which meant he must have eaten, but he had no recollection of it. His mind was still reeling as he watched Laney set down her fork and dab her mouth with a napkin. He'd thought about her a lot over the years – there weren't many days that passed when he didn't think about her, if he was honest. But one thing he'd never thought – never dared to imagine, was that she might one day just show up like this and announce that she was moving home. *Might* be moving home. He had to remember that. She'd said she'd rented the place at Mill Creek for a month – not that she was definitely here to stay.

She wasn't sure if she *wanted* to stay yet. Part of him wanted to do everything in his power to convince her that she should stay here in the valley and give him a chance. Another part of him – he wasn't sure if it was the sensible part or the cowardly part – hoped that she might decide to leave again once the month was up.

He watched her lips move as she talked to Tanner. He couldn't hear what she was saying, he could only watch those plump, pink lips, enthralled. He knew how full and soft those lips were. He knew how they felt pressed against his own. How they felt moving over his chest and on down …

He cleared his throat and shifted in his seat, aware of the heat in his cheeks.

Tanner gave him a puzzled look. "You okay, dude?"

He cleared his throat again and avoided Tanner's gaze as he answered. "Yeah, sorry, I just swallowed …" Damn! That was the wrong word to use. He coughed to cover the fact that his cheeks must be even redder now. "Something went down the wrong way." He closed his eyes and grimaced. That explanation was no less damning than his first attempt.

He kept his head down so he wouldn't have to look either of them in the eye. He straightened up in a hurry when Tanner kicked him under the table. There was no way Tanner could know what was going on inside his head, but that didn't stop Luke from feeling guilty as hell.

A little of the tension left his shoulders when Tanner caught his gaze and winked. Luke's heart started to pound. Did Tanner know? Had he somehow figured things out? Was that wink his way of saying that he was okay with it?

Luke's hopes were dashed when Tanner inclined his head slightly toward the bar. "Is all that coughing for show? Are you just using it as an excuse to keep your head down, hoping that she doesn't spot you?"

Luke's heart sank when he saw what Tanner meant. There were two girls standing at the bar. Two girls who'd been at Chico last weekend. Tanner had been more than happy to escort one of them back to her room. Luke, on the other hand, had managed to extricate himself from the clutches of the other one. That probably wasn't fair; she was a nice enough girl. Nice enough to make out with – he wasn't denying that.

He just hadn't wanted to spend the night with her. It wasn't as though he had some higher moral standard than his friend – there'd been plenty of weekends when the two of them had left Chico together in the morning after thoroughly enjoying a night out. But this chick … last weekend … he just hadn't been feeling it.

He risked a glance at Laney. Had he somehow known? Known that she was coming? He'd taken more than his fair share of women home for the night – well, at least back to their room for the night – but last weekend, he hadn't even wanted to try chasing something he knew he'd never find in the arms of another woman.

Shit! Laney was eyeing the girls at the bar, too. Her eyes narrowed when she looked back first at Tanner, then at him.

She held her hands up and looked down at her plate. "Hey, don't let me keep you. I'm only here to eat." She chewed on her bottom lip as she looked down at her plate again. "I know how it goes. Don't let me keep you from your dates."

Luke was grateful that Tanner laughed out loud. *He* had no clue what to say and he sure as hell didn't feel like laughing.

"Come on, Laney! They're not dates. They're …"

Her lips pressed together into a thin line before she spat out the word, "Hookups?"

"No!" Luke exclaimed at the same time that Tanner laughed again and said, "Exactly."

Luke's heart pounded even harder in his chest as he watched Laney cover her eyes with her hand. For one terrible, beautiful moment, he thought he saw pain on her face. But that hope was short-lived.

When she looked back up, she smiled brightly. "Well, don't let me keep you. I wouldn't want to cramp your style." She pushed her chair back from the table. "And besides, I don't need you guys cramping mine, either."

Tanner grabbed her wrist as she made to stand. "Oh no, lady! I know you're all grown up and an independent woman and all that good shit – and I respect that, really, I do," he added as he let go of her wrist when she glared down at his hand on her.

"I respect the hell out of you, Laney-Lou, and I know you have every right to do whatever the hell you want, with whoever you want. But you can't say shit like that in front of me, and you sure as hell can't *do* anything about it while I'm sitting here."

Luke wanted to duck for cover when he saw the old, familiar fire shooting from Laney's eyes.

"You know what? Maybe moving back here isn't going to work out after all."

"Aww. You know you don't mean that. How about we all stay here, the three of us? Those girls were at the resort last weekend. That's all." Tanner swaggered his shoulders with a grin. "You can't really blame me for them showing up here. I didn't invite them." He chuckled. "But you can hardly blame her for wanting more."

Luke followed Tanner's gaze and saw that the girl he'd been with was waving at him. As Tanner waggled his fingers in a wave back, Luke was relieved that her companion didn't seem so pleased to see him.

He tried to sneak a sideways glance at Laney, but she caught him – and glared at him.

"It's fine. Go. I don't mind."

"Hey." He couldn't help it; he reached across and rested his hand on her arm. "Don't go lumping me in with him. I didn't…"

Tanner laughed. "He's not lying, either. I think this guy is losing his touch. I had a very enjoyable night at the resort, but this guy turned back into a pumpkin and slunk off home at midnight."

Luke had never been so happy that he'd cut a night short or turned a girl down as he was when he saw Laney's shoulders relax, and a little of the fire dim in her eyes. He couldn't know for sure that it meant that she cared – but he had to take it as a good sign.

Laney had to look away from where Luke's hand rested on her arm. Just the feel of his long, strong fingers touching her felt like he was branding her skin with his heat. But she shouldn't let him affect her that way – she couldn't allow it, not if she was going to stay.

She didn't want to look at him or Tanner, anyway. She knew that the relief she felt at hearing that Luke hadn't spent the night with one of those girls must show on her face. It was stupid. She knew damned well that he would have had his share of women over the years. But that didn't mean she wanted to come face-to-face with one of them – or worse, watch him go off with her for a repeat performance.

She forced a smile as she pushed her chair back from the table, determined to leave this time. "Seriously, I was planning on an early night anyway," she lied. "I've been traveling all day; I'm going to head home soon."

She looked at her brother. "That chick's got her eye on you; she looks like she's ready to pounce as soon as she sees the opportunity. I'd hate to give her the wrong impression."

As she'd known he would, Tanner looked over at the girl, then he waggled his fingers in that little wave that just aggravated Laney, but that seemed to work magic on the women he cast his spell over.

"If you're really going to call it a night, little sis ..."

"I am. Go on." She couldn't help laughing.

Her laughter stuck in her throat when Tanner turned to Luke. "What do you say? Do you want..."

"No. Hell no!"

Laney was surprised at the vehemence with which Luke shook his head – surprised but relieved. It was one thing to watch Tanner swoop in on his conquest, knowing how he'd be spending the rest of the night. She didn't know if she could stand to watch Luke do the same thing.

She was relieved that it sounded like she wouldn't have to watch him leave with that girl, but he would undoubtedly go over there with Tanner, and she didn't want to see that either.

"I'm going to head out." She felt bad that she hadn't paid for her dinner, but she knew that Tan wouldn't let her anyway. She'd just have to treat him next time.

She hurried away from the table, not wanting to know how the rest of Luke's night would go.

She'd almost made it to the door when Nixon called to her from behind the bar. He was a good guy; they'd been friends in high school. She was tempted to ignore him, but when he called again, she relented.

"What's up, Nix?" She changed track and went to the end of the bar where he was leaning, grinning at her.

"Tell me you're not leaving? I thought you were going to close the place down with me."

She had told him that earlier, but that was before she'd known that Luke was going to be here. She shrugged and tilted her head to where Tanner was now talking to those girls. "I'm not sure I want to stick around and watch that."

She was surprised by the gleam in Nixon's eyes when he leaned a little closer and smiled. "So, how about you sit at the bar and focus on me, that way you won't see them."

Wow. Nix was a good-looking guy, but she just didn't see him that way. As she was wondering how to tell him that, all the little hairs on the back of her neck stood up. She knew Luke was behind her, even before he spoke.

When he put his hand on the small of her back, it felt like every little hair on her body joined the ones on her neck in standing to attention – or perhaps what they were really doing was straining to get closer to him.

She swallowed as she turned to look at him, and a wave of heat coursed through her veins when he smiled.

"Hey. Can I hang out with you? Tanner's locked on target, and I don't want any part of that."

Laney couldn't unscramble her brain enough to form words. Instead, Nix spoke.

"That's okay, Luke. Laney's fine here with me. You don't need to pull stand-in big brother duties. I can take care of her."

Laney had to squeeze her thighs together when Luke's fingers dug into her hip. She couldn't resist sneaking a look at him and was stunned by what she saw on his face.

Did he really think that he needed to protect her from Nix? He should know better than that. Even Tanner and her other brothers didn't get so wound up that they looked like they wanted to punch a friend just for suggesting they'd keep an eye on her.

Nix looked as surprised as Laney felt. He held his hands up and backed away from the bar. "Jesus, Luke, don't look at me like that. I get the point. I'll get you guys a beer."

Laney looked from Nix to Luke and back again. She hadn't been planning to hang around for a drink with Nix; was she really going to stay here with Luke?

When he took his hand away from her back to pull up a stool for her, a shiver ran down her back at the loss of his heat.

He climbed up on the stool next to hers and spun it to face her. Just as he opened his mouth to speak, Nix came back and set two beers on the bar in front of them.

"I meant what I said, Luke. Laney can hang out here with me; I'll walk her back to her hotel later."

Laney had to wonder what Luke's problem was; his jaw set in a hard line as he shook his head. "That's okay." When he turned to look at her, his light blue eyes met hers in an intense gaze. "We've got some catching up to do."

Laney swallowed hard. She and Luke hadn't done any catching up since she left the Valley all those years ago. What did he think they had to say to each other now?

She was barely aware of Nixon moving away to serve other customers. She felt as though Luke had her pinned in her seat with his gaze.

"What's going on, Luke?" Her words came out in a breathy whisper. She really shouldn't want to reach out and trace her fingers over the hard line of his jaw, but she did – she wanted to trace her fingers over other parts of him, too. But she pulled herself together and waited for him to answer.

He shook his head slowly. "Sorry, I just … I couldn't … Dammit, Laney. I…"

They both turned at the sound of shouts coming from the area by the pool table. Laney rolled her eyes; some things didn't change – a fight had broken out.

Luke picked up his beer as he got down from his stool, then he handed Laney hers. "Come on, I'm off duty tonight. I don't want to get caught up in that shit."

She took the beer and started following him toward the door but hesitated when Nixon called after them.

"You don't have to go, Laney. That'll be over in a couple of minutes. Stay and hang out, I'll take you home later."

She didn't know what had gotten into Nixon, but more than that, she didn't know what had gotten into Luke. He shot Nixon a hard glare and grabbed her hand, tugging her after him before she had the chance to stop and talk about it.

When they were out on the street, she finally pulled herself together and pulled her hand out of his.

"What the hell, Luke? What's going on? What are you doing?"

He stopped walking and turned to face her. His Adam's apple bobbed before he spoke. "I needed to get you out of there."

She laughed. "I've been around enough bar fights in my time. I can handle myself."

His eyebrows drew together. "I didn't mean that."

"What did you mean, then?"

He folded his arms across his chest and fixed her with a hard stare. "You know what Nixon was after, right?"

Wow! She couldn't believe that he would try to get in the way. Not that she was interested in Nix, but that wasn't the point. "And you stepped in to block him? What the hell, Luke? I did my best to give you a clear path back there – with that girl. And you do the exact opposite?"

"Are you saying you wanted to go home with him?" He ground the words out through a clenched jaw.

"No, I'm not! But that's not the point. The point is that I'm a big girl now. I'm perfectly capable of getting myself home."

All Luke's anger seemed to dissolve, and he let his arms fall to his sides. "I know, Laney. I'm sorry. I fucked up, okay? Let's get you back to your hotel."

She had no idea what was going on with him, but she wasn't going to argue. She just nodded and set out at a brisk pace toward the hotel. Luke fell in step beside her, and they walked in silence. When they reached the parking lot, she turned to look at him.

"I can take it from here, thanks."

"No. I'll see you inside."

She opened her mouth to argue but thought better of it. It'd be better to just get this over with than stand here fighting with him.

"I'm not just Tanner's little sister, you know. I'm a grown woman who's perfectly capable of taking care of herself," she told him as they walked across the lobby to the elevator bank.

"I know."

When the elevator doors slid open, she was surprised when he stepped inside with her.

"I don't doubt that you can take care of yourself – I was more worried about Nix taking care of you."

"What's wrong with him?"

"Nothing, he's a good guy."

Laney held his gaze for a long moment until the elevator juddered to a stop. He followed her as she headed down the corridor toward her room. When she reached it, she turned to look at him again.

"So why would it be a problem if I wanted to spend the night with him?"

Her heart raced as she watched him run his hand over his face. When his arm fell back to his side, his gaze locked on hers. "Because he's not me."

She just stared at him. Her mind couldn't manage to unscramble the words. He stared back at her, and she couldn't help drinking in the sight of him. He'd filled out over the years, not around the waist, but in the shoulders. He was taller, too. There was a harder edge to him than she remembered. The truth hit her right between the legs – in the years since she'd left, he'd become a man – and he was *all* man.

She struggled to make herself focus on what he'd said. He had a problem with Nixon wanting to take her home ... because ...?

She couldn't believe that he meant what it seemed like he did. But he nodded slowly. "Yeah, Laney. I'm saying that I couldn't stand to watch you go home with Nixon – or anyone else for that matter – anyone other than me."

Her knees felt as though they might buckle under her. How long had she dreamed about him saying something like that to her? Probably her whole life was the honest answer.

She turned and swiped her key card in the door. It felt as though her whole life had narrowed down to this moment. She knew it was probably a dumb move, but she wasn't going to let that stop her.

"Do you want to ...?"

"Don't ask me to come in with you."

Her racing heart thudded to a halt, and she wiped her palms on her jeans. She didn't understand what was going on. Had she misread him completely?

"Don't ask me to come in – because if you ask me to, I will."

He reached out and hooked his finger under her chin. All the breath rushed out of her lungs as he stepped closer and looked down into her eyes. "What I'm saying, Laney, is that you need to be sure you want me – because if you take me into your bed again, I won't let you go so easily this time."

Just as she'd thought she was about to melt into a puddle at his feet, his words broke the spell. "Let me go? What do you mean let me go?" she demanded. "You didn't let me go. You were glad to see the back of me. Don't mess with me, Luke. That kind of talk might work on the tourists, but you're not going to get away with bullshitting me."

His gaze locked on hers. "Don't talk crazy, Laney. If I was trying to bullshit you, I would have kept my mouth shut and let you take me inside."

Her whole body quivered at his words. Take him inside? Sure, he meant inside her room, but the way he phrased it … No. She couldn't let herself go there.

She couldn't let herself remember that he'd been the first man she ever – or that if it had been up to her, he would have been the only one.

The look on his face made her want to rip her heart from her chest and hand it over to him. He was looking at her the way he had all those years ago – looking as though he wanted her, as though he cared, as though she was something special to him. But she knew better now.

"So, what *are* you saying?"

His gaze dropped to her lips, and her tongue darted out instinctively to wet them. She knew what was coming – it was like cellular memory, something her body remembered no matter how hard her mind had tried to forget.

His finger tilted her chin up to meet him as he lowered his head. His other arm slipped around her waist and pulled her against him until she was crushed against his chest.

"What am I saying?" he breathed against her lips. "I guess the best way to say it is this."

Her arms found their way up around his neck as he claimed her mouth in a hot, hard kiss. She opened up to him, her body unwilling to deny him, even while her mind reeled.

It felt as though that kiss stripped away all the years that had passed and took them right back – back to the time when she thought she'd discovered her future in his arms. She didn't want to think, she just wanted to get lost in how it felt.

When he finally lifted his head, his eyes shone as they looked down into hers. "I've missed you, Laney."

She bit down on her bottom lip. "I've missed you, too. But …"

He gave her a sad smile. "I know. I'm sorry. I shouldn't have, but I couldn't help it."

"What now?" Her heart thundered. If he said he wanted to come in with her, she'd let him, gladly.

He shook his head. "Now, like I said, you have to decide if I'm what you want."

All she could do was stare at him. How could he not know that he was all she'd ever wanted?

He leaned in and pressed a quick kiss to her lips before stepping away.

"Go on, go inside. I'll see you soon."

She'd never thought of herself as the kind of girl to meekly do what a guy told her to, but she obeyed without question. And before she knew what was happening, she was staring at her closed hotel room door, double locking it – in an attempt to make sure that she wouldn't run after him.

Chapter Four

Luke hung out in his cubicle, nursing his coffee, and trying to look busy. He'd rather not run into Deacon before the morning meeting. He'd done well at avoiding his brother for the last couple of days – ever since Laney had come home. But he knew that his time was running out. He'd seen Deacon talking to Laney out on the street this morning, when he arrived at the station.

Deacon had always known how Luke felt about her. He'd never been able to hide much of anything from his brother. Even when he was still in high school, Deacon had counseled him that he should be honest with her brothers. But Luke just hadn't been able to make himself do it.

If it were just Tanner, he might have told him. But Ford and Wade had both been super protective of Laney and Janey. Janey, they protected in a more literal sense. She was softer – sweeter, if you wanted to call it that. Laney, they had protected in a different way. She'd always been a bright light; she was fun, and feisty, and outgoing. She attracted guys without even trying. Luke couldn't blame all the assholes who'd tried to hit on her when she was just a kid. He'd understood why they did it, even if he couldn't allow himself to do the same.

Well, he hadn't allowed himself, except that one time. He closed his eyes, listening to the steady thump of his heart. Whenever he thought about Laney it felt as though everything came in to hyperfocus. He could hear his heart beat, feel the air around him, see every detail with crystal clarity – just as he had that night that they'd been together.

"You'd better get a move on." Undersheriff Townsend's voice brought him back to reality. "Everyone's already in the briefing room, and you don't want to be late. Deacon didn't look too happy when I saw him come in."

Luke's heart sank. That must have been after Deacon spoke to Laney outside. For a moment he wondered if maybe she'd said something to him. Would she ask Deacon to tell him to back off? No. That wasn't Laney's style. If she wanted to tell him to go to hell, she'd be sure to do it herself. He was just being paranoid because he hadn't heard from her since he left her at her hotel room.

He still didn't know what had come over him. He'd kissed her! After so many years of trying to keep what they'd done secret from her brothers, he'd just come straight out and kissed her before she'd been back in town even a day. More than that, he'd told her that if she gave him a chance, he wouldn't let her go again so easily.

"Are you okay?" Townsend asked.

"Oh… Err… Yeah. I'm coming."

He managed to find a seat right at the back of the briefing room, but that did nothing to save him from Deacon's steely gaze. Luke wasn't going to hide from him. He stared back at him, knowing that there was a lecture in his near future, and that there was no point trying to avoid it.

He was surprised when Deacon's expression gentled a little and he gave Luke a small nod before turning to address the room.

Luke didn't even bother to file out with everyone else once the meeting was over. He didn't see the point in making Deacon hunt him down. He just sat, still nursing his coffee, as the stragglers stopped to talk to Deacon on their way out.

When the room was finally empty but for the two of them, Deacon came and sat on the desk in front of him.

"Want to talk about it?"

Luke let out a short laugh. "Does it matter?"

Deacon's eyebrows drew together. "You tell me. Does it matter? Are you still as hung up on that girl as you have been for the last twenty years?"

Luke blew out a sigh. "I think we both know the answer to that question without you having to ask it."

"Yeah. I think we do. Which takes me back to my earlier question – do you want to talk about it?"

"What do you want me to say?"

"I'd like you to say that you finally got your shit together. That you're happy she's home, and that you're finally going to do something about it."

Luke finally looked up to meet his brother's gaze. "I'd like to say that, too."

"Why don't you, then?"

Luke shook his head slowly. "I don't even know …" He couldn't finish that sentence. He'd been about to say that he didn't know if Laney wanted him. That might have been true this time last week. It might even have been true while they were in the bar the other night, but the way she looked up at him outside her hotel room, the way she kissed him back – he knew.

She wanted him. The trouble was, he didn't know what she wanted him for. If it was like before – if she just wanted him for a night, he didn't know if he could survive that again.

Deacon was watching him closely. "If you're still worried about what her brothers will have to say, you need to get over it. Sure, they might be shocked at first, but they'll get over it. Yeah, they want to protect their sister, but you're like another brother to them – you always have been."

Luke let out a short, bitter laugh. "Exactly. That's what bothers me."

"Come on. *They* see you as a brother. Laney never has. The way that girl used to look at you … She thought the moon and the stars rose and fell with you."

Luke gave him a wry smile. "I never had you down as the poetic kind."

Deacon chuckled. "Yeah. Me neither, I guess you can blame Candy for that. But you know what I mean, Luke. I just want to see you happy, and the only time I've ever known you close to happy was back then – with Laney."

"I do okay. I'm not miserable or anything."

"I'm not saying you are. I wasn't miserable before Candy came along, either. But now? Now I know what happy really means."

Luke couldn't help smiling at that. "I know. It's awesome."

Deacon grasped his shoulder. "It is, and I want the same for you."

"I saw you talking to her this morning. What did she have to say?"

"Nothing much. Just chit chat, you know. She's always been wary of me."

"No. She's not wary of you. She loves you."

Deacon smiled through pursed lips. "She loves *you*. She always has. So, for fuck's sake, can you do something about it – and get it right this time?"

Luke chuckled. "Running out of patience are we, big brother?"

"Something like that. You only get one life, Luke. The more of it you waste, the less of it you'll have left to enjoy. I'll tell you now, if you let that girl slip through your hands again, you'll regret it for whatever time you have left on this earth."

"I told her that she needs to think about if I'm what she wants."

Deacon shook his head. "I don't think she needs to think about it, Luke. I think she knows. I think she's always known that you're what she wants. What she doesn't know is if she's what you want. Don't put it all on her. Let her know, show her. Back then you were more worried about what her brothers would think than about the way you made her feel."

Luke frowned. "I wasn't… I didn't…"

Deacon held his gaze for a long moment.

"Shit! I wasn't! I just didn't want them giving her a hard time."

"You didn't want them giving *you* a hard time."

"No, I mean yeah. I'm not denying that but… I didn't want her to have to… Shit!" Deacon was right – he had spent more time back then worrying about what Tanner and the others would say than he had thinking about how Laney was feeling.

"Seems to me that you and Laney need to do some talking."

Luke sucked in a deep breath and let it out slowly. "Seems to me you're right."

"Well, you've got the weekend off. I suggest you make the most of it." Deacon smiled. "In the meantime, can you get your ass to work?"

Luke got to his feet and was surprised when Deacon pulled him in for a quick, one-armed hug. He cleared his throat when he stepped back but didn't know what to say.

Deacon just nodded. "You know where I am when you need me."

~ ~ ~

Laney took a quick walk down Main Street when she came out of the property management company's office. She'd been back for a few days now, but this was the first time that she'd been up to town since that first night – the night that Luke had kissed her.

She wrapped her arms around her middle as she hurried back to the Jeep. He'd kissed her! She was still holding that thought close, even while she tried to figure out what it meant – what it could mean. She'd spent the last few days alternating between dizzying happiness, absolute confusion, and simmering anger. Even now, she still didn't know what the appropriate response was to what had happened between them after they left The Mint.

She'd had enough going on that she'd managed not to obsess over it too much. But on the drive up into town this morning she hadn't been able to think about anything else. Of course, she'd been thinking about him as she walked past the Sheriff's office. Seeing Deacon had been wonderful. She loved that man. Even the thought of him made her smile. It was easy to admit that she loved the older Wallis brother – it was the younger one who'd always left her confused.

When she got back to the Jeep, she climbed inside and sat there for a few moments, wondering whether she should do anything else while she was here in town. She checked her watch, but it was still early – far too early to entertain crazy thoughts about stopping by to see if Luke might be free for lunch.

She started the engine and headed back down the valley. There were only two people who knew about her history with Luke, and she was hoping that she might find one or both of them if she headed home.

She slowed as she approached the bakery; she doubted that Janey would be there this late in the morning. She'd most likely be at work by now, out doing her rounds, or in the clinic tending to sick critters. Then again, she did seem to find every reason she could to stop in for a cup of coffee and to see her husband, Rocket. And even if Janey wasn't there, Frankie might be. She spent even more time in the bakery than Janey did – hanging out with her fiancé, Spider.

The parking lot was still full when she arrived. If they were rushed off their feet, she wouldn't hang around. She braced herself before she pushed the door open. After all this time, having every eye in the place turned in her direction took some getting used to again. She was hardly the shy or timid type, but since she'd come home – since seeing Luke, and that kiss – she felt strangely vulnerable for some reason.

"Laney!"

She grinned when she saw Frankie waving at her from one of the big booths in the back. Although her smile faltered a little when she saw that Frankie was sitting with not just Janey, but also Wade's wife, Sierra, and Candy and Libby, too.

She could hardly turn around and walk out, but she'd always struggled with groups of women, even women like these, who she knew and liked.

Well, she didn't exactly know Candy yet, but from what she'd seen of her, she liked her. And from what everyone said, she was a real sweetheart. Laney had to believe that was true, since she'd managed to not only win over, but also sweeten up, Deacon.

She smiled around at them all when she reached the table. Janey grabbed hold of her hand. "Hey. I'm so glad you're here. I'm sorry, I should have thought to let you know that we were all meeting up this morning."

Laney forced her smile to stay in place. She had no right to be disappointed that Janey had forgotten her. Janey had a whole life that didn't include her, and she had for years.

"No worries, sis. I wouldn't have been able to join you anyway. I had to go up to town."

She jumped when a deep voice spoke beside her. "What can I get you?"

She turned and smiled at Janey's husband, Rocket, although she didn't let her gaze linger for too long. He was one good-looking guy, but no way would she ever let on that she thought so. He was her sister's husband, and given the history between Janey and her …

"Just a black coffee, please."

Rocket nodded and winked at Janey before going back behind the counter.

Frankie had moved over and was patting the space in the booth beside her. "Come on, Laney. Sit your ass down and tell us what's going on with you."

Laney had to laugh. That was typical Frankie. And she'd love to catch her up, but she wouldn't do it in front of all the others.

Sierra gave her a small smile, but it didn't reach her eyes. Laney liked her, but she got the impression that the feeling wasn't mutual. Sierra was sweet and kind to everyone, and no less so to Laney herself, but there was just something missing. It was as though Sierra didn't trust her for some reason. Laney smiled back. She could probably guess what that reason was; Janey and Sierra had become good friends when Sierra moved here. She probably felt protective of Janey – as most people did.

They might be twins, but she and Janey were pretty much polar opposites. Everyone – including Laney – loved Janey to pieces and wanted to look out for her. Laney, on the other hand, was more than capable of taking care of herself. People knew that, and somehow, it seemed to make them think that she was hard … or something. Who knew? And she wasn't feeling sorry for herself. She was just …

She looked back at Frankie, and then checked her watch. "Shit. You know what? I totally forgot that I shouldn't be here. I'll catch up with you some other time, huh?"

She turned and hurried back out, only realizing when she was back in the Jeep that she hadn't even picked up her coffee. Oh well. She'd have to make her own when she got back to the house.

Luke covered his yawn with his hand as he walked back out to his truck at the end of the day. He stopped in his tracks when he heard someone laughing at him.

"What's up, Luke? Are they working you too hard?"

He smiled when he saw Wade making his way across the parking lot toward him. "Nah. It's been a pretty easy day. I don't know why I'm yawning."

If he were honest, he knew exactly why he was yawning – he hadn't been getting much sleep since Laney came home. He spent most of his nights lying there, tossing and turning, feeling like he was living a double-edged hell in his own bed. On the one hand, he was tormenting himself wondering what Laney would say to him when they spoke again – wondering if she'd ever give him a chance, while also wondering if she'd even given his words another thought. On the other hand, it was torture to know that she was staying in a house just a couple of miles down the road. She was sleeping in a bed all alone, within his reach for the first time in more years than he cared to count. How easy would it be for him to jump in his truck and drive over there? What would she say, what would she do, if he were to bang on her door in the middle of the night and demand that she let him in?

He gave himself a mental shake and forced himself to focus on Wade, who was still talking.

"... what do you think?"

Luke felt bad that he had no clue what Wade had been saying. "Sorry, run it by me again?"

Wade laughed. "I knew you'd zoned out on me. It was the mention of her name, wasn't it?"

"Whose name?" he asked, feeling guilty without even knowing why. Wade was the most laid-back of the MacFarland brothers, but still…

Wade gave him a knowing smile. "Do you really need me to tell you? I'm talking about Laney."

Luke forced himself to stand still, even though he wanted to shift his weight from one foot to the other. He knew all the tells of someone with a guilty conscience – and shiftiness was a major give away.

"It's okay. You don't have to say anything if you don't want to incriminate yourself. But do me a favor, and don't go torturing yourself, either?"

Luke's head snapped up at that, and he met Wade's gaze. "What do you mean?" He asked too quickly, and he knew it, but there was nothing he could do about it.

"Don't worry, I don't think anyone else knows. But I've always known. The way you used to look at her gave you away. And you know what? I respect that you never did anything about it."

Luke's hopes had been starting to rise, but the possibility that the brothers might give him their blessing was snatched away before he'd fully glimpsed it. How would Wade feel if he found out that Luke *had* done something about his feelings for Laney? He didn't think he wanted to know the answer to that question.

Wade laughed. "Don't look so shocked. I didn't figure it out for myself. It was just that back then, Josie always wanted me to do more, be more affectionate, or something. One time, she told me that she wished I would look at her the way you looked at Laney. I had no clue what she was talking about, until I started paying attention."

Luke met his gaze, not knowing what to say.

Wade grasped his shoulder. "And since she's still not comfortable coming out to the ranch, I figured that you won't mind if we all get together at your place on Friday night."

"What?!"

Wade laughed. "You really weren't paying attention, were you? We all want to get together. We'd rather not go out – I want to bring the kids – but we all live on the ranch, and Laney's not comfortable there. So, I'm inviting us all over to your place. Are you going to tell me that you've got a problem with that?"

Luke smiled. "Nope. No problem at all."

"Well, okay then. In that case, I'll leave you to it and I'll get on home to that little lady of mine."

"How is Sierra? How are the kids?"

"They're great. And you'll get to see them yourself on Friday. Don't worry about food, and booze, and stuff; we'll bring everything we need."

Luke had to laugh. "I'm not that bad; I can host you guys."

"I'm not saying you can't. Just that you shouldn't have to since we invited ourselves. Or at least, I'm landing the whole clan on you."

"I don't mind."

"Yeah, I had a feeling you wouldn't." Wade's expression grew more serious. "I'm easy to win over. I always have been – you know that. You'll have to figure your own shit out with my brothers, though. And I might be easy, but if you hurt her …" He didn't finish that sentence. The look in his eyes said it all for him.

Luke simply nodded. Wade wasn't looking for an answer.

Chapter Five

Laney stood in front of the windows, looking out at the mountains. She'd lucked out being able to rent this place for a whole month. The house wasn't much, that was probably why it wasn't already booked up with tourists. But the view, the view was something else. Granted, it wasn't quite as spectacular as the view from the ranch, but she still got to see the mountains – her mountains. And it seemed fitting, somehow, that she could still see all the familiar peaks that had provided the backdrop to her childhood, just from a different perspective. After all, she had a very different perspective on pretty much everything these days.

She wandered back through to the kitchen, barely taking her eyes off the mountains. She had to drag her attention away so that she could focus on pouring herself a glass of wine. She'd been drinking too much of the stuff since she arrived. She could blame her friend Deb, who now owned the wine store up in town. It had been great to catch up with her and to see how well she was doing. But it was hardly Deb's fault that Laney still hadn't figured out what she could do with herself here.

Her life had been so busy back in Kentucky. She'd been working her ass off as a trainer with one of the big racing stables for the last few years. She'd worked her ass off since she moved out there when she was eighteen. When her contract had come up for renewal this time, she'd thought that she'd enjoy taking it easy for the month that she planned to be home. She'd thought that moving back was what she wanted – and that she'd be able to just relax and hang out with her friends and family while she figured it out. So far, though, things weren't working out that way.

Yes, she'd seen her family, but they were all busy getting on with their own lives, as were her friends. And as for relaxing…? Yeah, that wasn't working out too well, either.

She knew who she had to blame for that one. How could she relax when she couldn't stop thinking about Luke and what he'd said? There was a simple solution – she knew what it was, she just wasn't sure that she was ready to do it.

He'd told her that she needed to figure out if he was what she wanted. Of course he was – he was the only man she'd ever wanted. But she'd lived with that want – that need – for so long that she'd relegated it to the realm of what could never be. Could it really be so easy now?

In her mind it probably could be. Coming home and getting to be with Luke would be like a dream come true. But dreams didn't really come true, did they? Reality had this nasty habit of setting in and turning dreams into nightmares. She blew out a sigh and took a sip of her wine before going back to stand in front of the windows.

What was wrong with her? Why wasn't she over the moon? Why hadn't she called him the very next day, to tell him that yes, he was what she wanted. She shrugged and turned away from the windows. She hadn't done it because she was scared. That was the truth. People – including her – tended to think that Laney MacFarland wasn't afraid of anything. But she was. She was afraid that if she gave in to the way she felt about Luke a second time, things would only turn out the way they had the first time. And she didn't think she could survive that.

Movement at the edge of the property caught her attention, and she watched as a truck appeared through the trees that lined the driveway. She smiled when she recognized it as her sister's truck. She felt bad that she'd just walked out of the bakery that way this morning, but she just hadn't been able to stay. She probably should have called Janey to apologize. But then again, Janey probably wasn't even worried – she had her own life, and she was getting on with it.

She went out to wait on the front porch and smiled when Janey climbed out of her truck.

"Hey, sis."

Janey scowled at her as she ran up the steps to meet her. "Don't you, *hey sis* me, Laney-Lou. What was that about this morning? Why did you leave like that?"

Laney shrugged and turned to go inside. "Do you have time for a glass of wine with me?"

"Sure, but I can't stay for too long," Janey said as she followed her into the house. "Come on, talk to me. I was so happy when you showed up."

The look on her sister's face made Laney feel awful.

"I'm really, really sorry that I didn't think to invite you."

Laney went to her and wrapped her in a hug. "Don't, Janey. You don't need to apologize. You don't need to feel bad. Why should you invite me? And wait, I'm not saying that in a bad way. It really didn't bother me. I just…" She met Janey's gaze.

"If you want to know the truth, I'm feeling a little unsure of myself being back here. I wanted to talk to you and Frankie, but I wasn't going to talk to you in front of all those other people. And you know me, I don't do well with sitting around making polite conversation just for the hell of it."

Janey smiled and rubbed Laney's arm. "All those other people are friends – and family now, if you think about Sierra. Well, if you think about the rest of them, too. Frankie and Spider are going to be getting married soon. That'll make him …" She laughed. "I don't know how all that works. I know they don't call it a cousin-in-law. But that's what he'll be. And Candy, she and Deacon are talking about having a quick wedding soon, too."

"Yeah, I know what you mean. But you know what I mean as well. I don't know them. Not really. I'm hardly going to go pouring my heart out to them." She handed Janey a glass of wine with a smile. "I don't pour my heart out to anyone except you and Frankie."

"I know. And I wouldn't try to make you talk in front of them. That's mostly why I'm here now – to see if you want to talk?"

"Want to come sit outside to watch the sunset with me?"

Janey followed her out onto the deck, and they sat facing the mountains, which were already starting to glow as the sun dropped toward them.

"What do you need to pour your heart out about? Is it about why you came back?" Janey asked.

Laney shook her head slowly. "No. There's nothing much to talk about there. I got to the end of my contract. They offered me a new one. I wanted to come home instead."

Janey chuckled. "Yeah, I know all of that. But I also know there's more to it. Like, why now?"

Laney shrugged. "Why not? I needed a break. Tom said that he's happy to give me a couple of months to take a break. I could go back and start a new contract when my month's up here."

"I know. You told me that. What I'm asking is why did you rent this place for a month? Why come back here this time? You've had a month off between contracts before. You don't usually come home. In fact, didn't you go to Argentina last time?"

Laney smiled at the memory. "I did. It was awesome." Her smile faded. "But that was a vacation. That was about riding the pampas with gauchos, drinking amazing wine, and visiting a friend's ranch down there. This is different. This is about taking my life in a new direction … maybe."

Janey leaned forward in her seat. "A new direction? Or an old one?"

"Both. Maybe."

"And just so we're clear – I'm talking about a Wallis direction?"

She nodded. "Yeah."

"Well, that's a Mona Lisa smile if ever I saw one. I want to hang around for the rest of the evening and ply you with wine until you tell me what's going on." Janey looked out toward the road. "But I told Rocket that I'd be home for dinner. And by the looks of it, you'll have more to tell me tomorrow anyway."

"Why tomorrow?"

Janey jerked her chin toward the driveway, and Laney's heart started to race when she saw a truck coming up it.

"That's Luke," Janey said.

Laney nodded. She might not have recognized the truck, but her racing heart had somehow known that it was him.

Janey got to her feet.

"Where do you think you're going?" Laney asked.

Janey grinned at her as she took her glass back into the kitchen. "I told you; home to have dinner with my husband."

Luke slowed when he saw that there was already a truck parked outside the house. After his conversations with both Deacon and Wade, he'd made up his mind that he needed to come and talk to Laney tonight.

Deacon had made him realize that perhaps he hadn't been as clear and honest with her as he should have been after … after what they'd done. And with Wade telling him that all the MacFarlands were going to descend on his place on Friday night, he knew that he had to talk to Laney before that.

But he hadn't planned on there being anyone else here. He felt a bit better when he recognized that it was Janey's truck. Janey had always been in his corner, and he knew it, but still, he needed to talk to Laney alone.

He couldn't help smiling when he saw the two of them walking down the front steps. If you didn't know that they were twins, you would never guess it from the way they looked – or the way they acted, for that matter.

Janey turned and waved at him with a smile. He cut the engine and waved back before meeting Laney's gaze. Damn, she was beautiful. She didn't look as happy to see him as her sister did, but he wasn't going to let that put him off. One way or another, they needed to talk.

As he climbed out of his truck, Janey passed him on the way to get into hers.

"Hey, Luke. I hope you're okay with Wade's plans for Friday?"

"I am. I think it's a great idea."

Laney shot her sister a puzzled look. "What plans?"

Luke wanted to hug Janey when she winked at him before turning back to her sister. "I told you; I've got to get home. I'll let Luke explain."

He and Laney stood in silence as they watched Janey's truck disappear back down the driveway.

He'd been hoping for a warmer greeting, but he wasn't going to let her silence put him off. It was starting to dawn on him that that might have been a huge part of the problem all along. When they were younger, he'd been so caught up in not wanting to antagonize her brothers, that he hadn't paid as much attention as he should have to what Laney really wanted.

He turned to her with a smile. "I hope it's okay, me coming out here."

"Yeah. Sure. Do you want to sit out back and have a drink with me?"

He wanted to feel happy that she was asking him to, but she didn't look thrilled about it. He'd just have to start talking, and hope that she'd hear him out. His throat went dry at the thought that she might have already decided that he wasn't what she wanted.

"I'd love to, thanks."

She didn't say a thing as she fixed their drinks and led him out onto the back deck.

He wasn't used to a quiet Laney. She used to be so full of life, so full of chatter. There had always been so many things that she wanted to do, wanted to talk about, wanted to tell him about.

It struck him that perhaps there was more going on in her life than he knew. He was doing the same thing that he'd done back then. Fixating on himself, and on how things between them might affect his life. What about her? He should find out if she was okay before he launched into talking about the two of them and anything that might happen between them.

"So, how are you doing?"

She rolled her eyes at him. "Seriously? *How are you doing?* What are we, Luke, strangers?"

He had to laugh. "Sorry. I just … That came off wrong. I wasn't trying to start polite conversation with you. It just hit me that I don't know anything about your life anymore. I wanted to make sure that you're okay – that's all."

"Oh." She took a long drink of her wine and then sat there staring down into her glass before she said anything else. "That's sweet of you, thank you. I'm okay. Life in Kentucky was good. I'm not back here because of any major upheaval. I'm between contracts, that's all."

She finally looked up and met his gaze. "How about you? How are you doing these days?"

He gave her a rueful smile. "I'm fine. Always have been. Just fine. Nothing much changes in my world. Your hair got really long. I like it."

She sat back in her chair, looking surprised, and he couldn't blame her.

"Sorry. It seems like I can't hold onto a train of thought when I get around you."

That won him the first small smile he'd seen on her lips since he arrived.

He smiled back at her. "You were so pretty when you were a girl." He shook his head and let out a low whistle. "But damn, baby, as a woman …"

She narrowed her eyes at him. "Are you trying to feed me lines again?"

He had to laugh. "Nope. I'm telling you the truth – finally. I think it's about time, don't you? The other night, you said that we'd have to talk about it one of these days. What do you think, is today the day?"

Her eyes widened as they stared back into his. His heart pounded in his chest as he waited for her to answer.

"No," she said eventually. "Not today."

His heart sank, and it must have showed on his face because she wagged her finger at him.

"I'm not saying never, just not today, okay?"

"Okay." He didn't know where that left them, but it wasn't total rejection, so he'd take it. "I want to say you tell me when you're ready, but I don't want to put it all on you. What do you think, should I ask you again in a couple of days?"

She raised her eyebrows. "What's this? You mean, we're actually going to communicate – like adults?"

He gave her a wry smile. "Yeah, I think we should. Don't you? I mean, we are adults now, after all. And the whole communication thing? It's something new – something we've never tried before."

He loved the way she was smiling back at him as she said, "I like the sound of that."

"Okay. So, now we've got that out of the way. I'll ask you again in a few days if you want to talk about our past. But in the meantime, if *you* want to talk about it, don't feel you have to wait."

She chuckled. "Sounds good to me. Anything else?"

He hoped that she wasn't trying to say that he should leave now that they'd agreed on that. But whether she was or not, he was going to try to get her talking so that he could stick around for a while.

"Yeah, actually, there is. What Janey said before she left – about Wade's plans for tomorrow. The whole gang is coming over to my place tomorrow night." He smiled. "And I wanted to deliver your invitation personally. You know, to make sure that there's no miscommunication."

She laughed at that. "Okay. I'm glad you came. I didn't know about it, but then I haven't seen any of them today. And Janey was only here for a short while."

"Okay, then. So, can I put you down as a yes?"

"Yes."

"Awesome."

"Who else is coming?" she asked.

"Just your brothers, Janey and Rocket, and Frankie and Spider."

She frowned. "If it's all my clan, how come it's at your place?"

He pressed his lips together, wondering if he should tell her – but the answer was obvious. He had to tell her the truth – had to be up front with her about everything going forward if he wanted to stand a chance.

"So that it's not at the ranch."

She chewed on her bottom lip as she thought about his answer. "Thanks," she said eventually.

"I'd love to take the credit. But it was Wade's idea."

"Oh, okay."

He shouldn't be so happy that she looked a little disappointed.

He leaned toward her and tapped his finger on her knee. "If it had been my idea, I wouldn't have invited the rest of them – only you."

Her head snapped up, and when she met his gaze, her eyes seemed to shimmer in the last glow of the sunset.

"I'm scared, Luke."

Those words were like a dagger to his heart. They weren't words he'd ever heard her utter before. Laney MacFarland didn't do scared. Before he had time to consider his actions, he took hold of her hands and pulled her toward him until she was sitting on his lap in his chair.

He closed his arms around her and hugged her against his chest. "Tell me about it. What are you scared of? What can I do to help?"

She bit her bottom lip as she looked down into his eyes. "You, Luke. I'm scared of you, of this, of us. What if we try it and it doesn't work out? What if we somehow screw up like we did before?" She frowned. "And before we even think about it, we need to talk about it – about everything. The things you said to me the other night? I know you'd never lie to me, so I believe you, but I'm so confused."

"What are you confused about, baby? Tell me, and I'll try to explain."

"Everything. How can you say you want me now when you didn't want me then?"

"I *did* want you then. There's never been a time when I didn't."

They both looked up at the sound of a truck approaching. Laney leaped up from his lap, and Luke understood why when he recognized that it was her brother, Ford's, truck.

Great. Just when it looked like they were finally getting somewhere.

Laney shot him a wry smile. "Don't look like that. Did you want him to see us that way – with me sitting on your lap?"

He held her gaze for a long moment. "Maybe not today, no. But I'm telling you now, Laney, I want us to get to the point where he – and the rest of them – will see that all the time, and not give it a second thought."

He hated that she still looked uncertain – scared, like she'd said. But he didn't have the time to try to convince her. Ford's truck pulled up beside Luke's, and he climbed out.

"We're going to talk, soon, okay?" he said in a low voice, just as Ford waved before jogging up the steps.

"Hey, Luke. It's good to see you're on the welcoming committee."

Luke had to wonder how happy he would be if he knew what he and Laney had just been talking about. But he smiled and said, "I'm just as happy as you guys to have our Laney back." He shot her a meaningful look from behind Ford's back as he went to hug his sister.

"I doubt you're *that* happy to have her home," Ford said. "Has he told you about tomorrow night?" he asked Laney.

"He has."

Ford turned back to him. "Then I guess you're done here, right? It's good to see you, bud. What time do you want us tomorrow?"

"Seven," said Luke, knowing that he was being dismissed.

At least Laney made a face at him, letting him know that she wasn't thrilled about Ford's intrusion either.

He held her gaze for a moment. "I'll see you tomorrow, then?"

"You will." She smiled. "And thanks, Luke."

Chapter Six

"Talk to me!"

Laney had to laugh at Frankie. She was more like a sister than a cousin – she always had been.

"What do you want me to tell you?"

Frankie rolled her eyes and fell back on the bed. "What do you think? You know damn well what I'm talking about – Luke!"

Laney's chest felt as if it were full of champagne bubbles just at the mention of his name. "What about him?" she asked with a smile.

"Laney MacFarland! Do not act all coy with me. Talk to me, talk to me now! I want to know everything that's happened since you came home."

"What makes you think that anything happened?"

Frankie laughed. "Come on. You know me. I have eyes everywhere in this valley – and especially in town. I've been waiting for a call from you since the very first night you got back."

Laney frowned. "Why? What did you hear?"

"Oh, nothing much. Just that Nixon was all but climbing over the bar to get at you, and that he failed, but only because a certain deputy took your hand and dragged you out of there."

Laney shrugged. "Then what do you need me to tell you? That's what happened."

Frankie narrowed her eyes at her. "Quit holding out on me. Have you forgotten that I'm one of the few people on earth who you can't lie to? More than that, I'm one of only two people who you don't *need* to lie to – not when it comes to Luke. I know it all, remember? I was there with you, through everything. Are you really going to shut me out now?"

Laney blew out a sigh and flopped down on the bed beside her. Frankie had called earlier to inform her that she was on her way. Spider was going to head to Luke's straight from the bakery with Rocket, and Janey was still out on a call, and would meet them at Luke's place whenever she got off work.

"I'm not shutting you out, Frankie. I'm just … I don't know what to think myself, so how am I supposed to know what to tell you?"

Frankie grinned at her. "I'm not asking what you think – not yet anyway. I need you to start with what's happened. You've avoided him every time you've come home. And if you even thought that there was any chance of running into him, you always made sure you had some guy in tow. I never figured that out, by the way. Was that to make sure he stayed away, or to make him jealous? In fact, no, you don't need to answer that right now. We can come back to that. But you do need to tell me what happened the other night at The Mint."

Laney rested her head back against the pillow and stared up at the ceiling. "Not much happened at The Mint."

Frankie dug her in the ribs. "Quit stalling."

She laughed. "Okay! He walked me back to the hotel."

"Oh my God! Did he go back to your room with you?"

"He did, but he only walked me to the door."

"You didn't ask him in?"

Laney closed her eyes. "I was going to."

"So, why didn't you? What happened?"

"He told me not to."

"What?"

Laney nodded and wrapped her arms around her middle, as if she could hold on to the feeling inside her when she remembered the look on his face as they'd stood outside her hotel room.

She turned her head to look at Frankie. "He told me not to ask him to come inside, because if I asked him, he would."

Frankie's eyes widened in shock, and a big smile spread across her face, before fading rapidly. "But wait, I don't get it. Why...?"

"I didn't get it either. But then he said that I need to be sure I want him – because if I take him into my bed again, he won't let me go so easily this time."

"Laney!" Frankie squealed. "This is awesome! Finally! You're home, and you and Luke ... So, what's happened since then?"

"Not a lot." She smiled. "Well, not a lot other than he kissed me and told me that I need to decide if he's what I want."

Frankie jumped up from the bed and strode into the closet.

"What are you doing?" Laney asked.

Frankie stuck her head back out of the closet with a big grin on her face. "I'm picking your outfit for tonight; what do you think I'm doing? If I know you, you've got some sexy, sassy little dress in here and a pair of cowboy boots that when you put them together, will tell that man loud and clear, in no uncertain terms, that hell yes, he's what you want."

Laney pushed up from the bed and followed her into the closet. "But Frankie …"

Frankie spun back around to face her, letting the dress fall from her hand. "But what? Don't tell me you've changed your mind? Don't tell me that he's not …"

"I wasn't going to say that. I was going to say …" She sucked in a deep breath. She wasn't used to feeling this way. She didn't do scared – not normally. And she knew that Frankie didn't either. But she needed her cousin's support more than she needed to feel – or look – like a tough girl. "I was going to say that I'm scared."

Frankie took hold of both of her hands. "Well, of course you are. That's only natural."

Laney was so shocked that she took a step back. "It is?"

Frankie chuckled. "Yeah. I know we're not the kind of people who usually get scared. But this? This love shit? Yeah, even I don't mind admitting that it's scary as hell."

Laney didn't even want to pretend that they were talking about anything less than love. She just stared at her cousin. "You were scared, too? When it came to Spider?"

"Hell yeah! That man …" Laney loved the way Frankie smiled when she talked about her fiancé. "He's everything. And we just… We work, you know? I know it doesn't look that way from the outside. From the outside, you'd think we were worlds apart. But it's like we were made for each other. But yeah, in the beginning, I was scared stupid. I thought that we came from such different worlds that the way we felt about each other wouldn't be enough."

She smiled. "I was scared, but I was wrong. And I think that you're wrong to be scared, too. You and Luke? As far as I'm concerned, you were always meant to be together. I don't think you have anything to be afraid of – just a lot of lost time to make up for. And speaking of which, here –" she thrust the dress into Laney's hands "– You don't want to waste any time tonight. Get yourself dressed up, made up, and let's go over there so you can knock that man's socks off."

Laney looked down at the dress. "You know, normally, I'd agree with you. I'd be totally on board with your plan. But you're forgetting something."

"What's that? What's the problem?"

Laney rolled her eyes. "The same problem it's always been. My brothers. I can hardly go and knock his socks off – or anything else – in front of them."

"Why not? You're not a kid anymore."

Laney had to laugh. "Tell me you're not serious? You of all people should know what I mean. How did you feel about introducing Spider to Maverick for the first time?"

"Oh. Right. Shit."

"Yeah."

"Well, they're just going to have to get used to the idea. Do you really think they'd have a problem with it?"

"That's the million-dollar question, isn't it? When I was a kid, they threatened anyone who dared to come near me. It was even worse for Luke, because of the whole *you don't go after your friend's little sister* thing."

"Yeah, but you're not a kid anymore, you're all grown up. They're going to have to face that you're going to end up with someone. How could they not be thrilled if that someone is Luke? Someone they know and trust – someone they already love like a brother? I mean, come on, they might act like assholes some of the time, but it's only because they love you. Look at Janey and Rocket. They came around to him pretty quick when they figured out that he loved her, that he's good for her. Why wouldn't they do the same with Luke?"

"I know what you're saying. I guess I just have to decide if I'm brave enough to find out."

~ ~ ~

Luke stood next to Tyler, who had commandeered the grill as soon as he arrived, just as he usually did. He straightened up from sprinkling some chunks of mesquite over the coals and gave Luke a puzzled look.

"Are you okay? Are you sure you're all right with us invading your place like this?"

"Of course. I'm happy about it. I kept thinking that I should do a housewarming thing, I just never got around to it."

"Yeah, but this is more of a welcoming Laney home than a housewarming for you."

"I'm more than happy to welcome Laney home."

His breath caught in his chest when Tyler narrowed his eyes at him. His heart raced as he wondered if Laney's younger brother was onto him.

"What's up?" he asked when he couldn't take the drawn-out silence any longer.

"Nothing." Tyler shrugged. "I kind of had the impression that the two of you didn't get along all that well. You guys don't usually hang out whenever she's home."

"I just ..." Luke didn't know what to say. How was he supposed to explain that he and Laney did their best to avoid each other? Or more importantly, how was he supposed to explain why? He should perhaps be relieved that Tyler, apparently, had no clue about the history between them, but at this point, he would rather have everything out in the open. "There's some history there." It was more than he'd risked telling any of the brothers before.

Tyler nodded slowly. "I wondered."

Luke braced himself, waiting for Ty to ask for more details, but he didn't. He grinned and pointed his spatula toward the driveway. "Here's Rocket."

Luke nodded. He liked Rocket, and perhaps he should be relieved that his arrival had distracted Ty's attention. Then again, perhaps it hadn't distracted him as much as Luke had thought.

"It took Rocket a long time to win Janey over." Ty met Luke's gaze. "But he knew that she was the one he wanted from the first time he met her. She tried to brush him off. She did her whole Janey thing – not believing that he was really interested in her. But Rocket never gave up."

Luke nodded. He'd seen Janey and Rocket's relationship develop, and he was happy for the two of them.

"Seems to me that Rocket could teach the rest of us a thing or two."

Luke swung back to look at Ty again, to see if he meant what Luke thought he did, but he'd ducked his head down to fiddle with the grill again.

Then, little Mateo came running to them. He didn't stop until he'd wrapped his arms around Luke's leg. "Deputy Luke, Deputy Luke!"

Luke reached down and ruffled the kid's hair. "Hey, little buddy, how are you doing?"

Mateo looked up at him with his big brown eyes and nodded solemnly. "I am good." He turned to Tyler. "I'm going to be the sheriff one day."

Tyler laughed. "I believe you, kid. But you've got some growing up to do first, and you'll have to get in line behind Deacon, and then Luke."

Luke made a face at him. People kept saying that more and more lately – they expected him to follow in his brother's footsteps all the way to the sheriff's office. Luke had followed him into law enforcement, but he wasn't sure that he wanted to go any further.

Mateo tightened his arms around Luke's leg. "You will be sheriff, too?"

Luke shrugged. "Maybe, maybe not. We'll have to see."

"Luke!" Tanner called to him from the kitchen. "Come give me a hand in here, would you?"

He looked down at Mateo. "Are you going to be okay here helping Ty cook?"

Mateo grinned at him. "I am. I'm going to be a chef, too."

Luke chuckled to himself as he walked away from them. Mateo and his sister might have had a rough start in life, but it seemed that he was spoiled for choice among the decent male role models he now had.

He glanced up the driveway before letting himself into the kitchen – he was glad that everyone else was here, but he couldn't wait for Laney to arrive.

Laney leaned back against the fence and tipped the brim of her hat up as she watched everyone mill around Luke's back yard. This was good, she was enjoying herself, but it still felt like she was on the outside – even with her family. They were all chatting, and laughing, and catching up with each other, and here she was, standing apart from them, observing from a distance. She took a long drink of her beer, surprised to find that she'd emptied the bottle. It was a good thing that Frankie had brought her; she'd had a few drinks already and wouldn't be able to drive herself home.

She smiled at little Maya who'd kept sneaking glances at her all evening. The little girl was adorable, but Laney didn't know the first thing about kids. She'd had no experience with them and hadn't expected to. She loved that Wade and Sierra had taken in Maya and her brother, Mateo. But it was just one more thing that added to the feeling that life here in the valley had moved on so far that she might not be able to catch up.

The little girl glanced back over her shoulder at Sierra, but Sierra was chatting away with Janey and didn't notice. Maya seemed to make a decision and set out hesitantly toward Laney.

"Hi," Laney said when she reached her.

Maya looked up at her, wide-eyed. "Are you a cowgirl?" she asked in a voice so quiet that Laney had to strain to hear her.

"Kind of, I guess."

"You've got a cowboy hat, and cowboy boots," Maya said.

"That's right."

"But you're pretty and you're wearing a pretty dress, too." Maya looked back over her shoulder. "I didn't know that was allowed."

"Allowed? What do you mean, sweetie?" Laney asked.

Maya shrugged and came a little closer. "Cowboys wear the hats and boots. But they're not pretty."

Laney had to laugh at that. "No, they're not."

"And they're boys. I thought it was a boy's job. But you wear the boots and the hat. Do you do the job? Do you work with the horses?"

Laney smiled. "I do.

Maya's eyes grew wide, and she smiled big. "So, it's allowed?"

"Yeah, sweetie, it's allowed. Why? Do you want to be a cowgirl?"

Maya looked back over her shoulder again before nodding rapidly. "I do. I have a pony. I can ride." She frowned. "I can't throw the rope yet, though."

"You'll learn. It takes time. You just have to keep practicing."

"Will you teach me?"

Laney stared at her for a moment. She didn't know what to say. If the kid wanted to learn to throw a rope, Wade should be the one to teach her. And apart from that, Laney had the impression that Sierra didn't like her much; she didn't want to go causing any trouble.

"Have you asked your daddy to teach you?" It felt strange to call Wade her daddy, but she knew that was what the kids called him.

She was horrified when Maya's chin started to wobble. She had no clue what she'd said wrong, but she'd upset the kid somehow. She crouched down in front of her and cautiously reached out to touch her arm.

"Hey, sweetie, what's wrong?"

The little girl's eyes brimmed with tears. "You don't want to teach me?"

"I didn't say that. I just … I thought your daddy would want to."

"But I want *you* to. You're a cowgirl, and I'm not a boy. It's different for us."

Laney smiled through pursed lips. She knew exactly what the kid meant; it just hadn't occurred to her that Maya would already know the difference. Then again, perhaps she should have known. Laney had been fully aware of how much more difficult it was for girls when she was Maya's age.

"You're right. It is different. How about we talk to your daddy ..."

"Maya, what are you doing?"

Frankie hadn't noticed Sierra approach them. She shot her a smile, but Sierra was focused on Maya – she'd noticed that she'd been crying. She wrapped the little girl in a hug as she asked, "What's the matter? What's wrong, baby girl?"

Laney's heart sank when Sierra scowled at her over Maya's shoulder. She supposed it was a fair assumption to think that she was the one who'd made Maya cry.

Maya didn't help matters when she put her head down and clammed up. Sierra picked her up and hurried away with her back to where she'd been sitting with Janey.

Awesome! Laney had been thinking that at some point tonight she should make an effort to try to get to know Sierra and hopefully show her that she wasn't the wicked bitch of the West. Now, it looked as though she'd only reinforced the impression that she was.

She blew out a sigh and headed for the cooler on the porch to get herself another beer. She might have thought she'd had enough, but right now she needed another.

Luke reached the cooler at the same time she did. He took out a bottle and popped the top before handing it to her.

"How's it going?"

She rolled her eyes at him. "It's going."

He reached out and touched her arm. "Is it tough, being back with them all? I bet they're all bombarding you with a thousand questions, wanting to know what's been going on with you."

She let out a short laugh. "Not exactly. How many of them do you see talking to me?" She waved her arm in a gesture that took in the whole yard, where all her family sat chatting and laughing with each other.

Luke frowned. "Wow. I didn't realize. Is everything okay?"

"Yeah. Everything's fine. I know they're glad that I'm here, but I'm not the prodigal daughter or anything, I don't need them to roll out the red carpet."

"No. I guess it'll be different as you settle back in. I know they're all talking about stuff that's been going on around here. The longer you're here, the more you'll be a part of it."

"I suppose – if I stay."

His head snapped up at that. "If?"

She nodded slowly. "It was only ever an if." She looked over to where Sierra had now rejoined Wade, and Maya was sitting on his lap. That situation had left her feeling a little unsettled, and not sure that she even wanted to stay. She looked back at Luke – except for him.

The lines around his eyes deepened and he trailed his fingers up and down her arm before letting go. "I don't want you to go."

His words hit her right in the chest and knocked all the air out of her. She held his gaze for a long moment.

He smiled. "And we're going to talk about that, right?"

She nodded, not sure that it was such a great idea. Perhaps she'd do better to leave. She wasn't sure that she wanted to have to earn herself a place in her own family again. But more than that, perhaps it would be better to not even try with Luke.

His smile had faded. "We are still going to talk, aren't we? I was thinking I could give you a ride home."

That surprised her. She'd assumed that Frankie would drop her off, since she'd been the one to bring her.

Luke raised his eyebrows. "You'd have to stick around after everyone else leaves."

All her breath caught in her chest. She couldn't think of anything that she wanted more, but at the same time she was scared to go there.

Luke gave her a rueful smile. "Although, it might not be up to us. They will no doubt insist that they should take you."

She narrowed her eyes at him, not sure if he did it on purpose. "Are you just playing on my stubborn nature? You know damn well that when they try to make me do anything, I refuse."

He chuckled. "I'm hoping."

Chapter Seven

Wade was the first one to call it a night; that was hardly surprising since he and Sierra had to get the kids home. Luke made a big fuss over Mateo and Maya before they left. He loved those kids. He couldn't help noticing that while Sierra was her usual sweet self and had hugs and goodbyes for everyone, she didn't hug Laney. It made him wonder what was going on there.

He turned when a big hand came down on his shoulder, and grinned at Rocket.

"We're going to take off in a minute here, too. Janey's had a busy week and I want to get her home."

Luke had to laugh when Tyler spoke on his other side. "You know I love you, Rocky, but don't push it. You could have just left it at Janey's had a busy week."

Rocket shook his head at him. "I didn't say anything that should upset you. All I said was that I want to get her home – so that she can rest."

Ty rolled his eyes. "Whatever."

"You wouldn't believe the shit these guys still give me," Rocket told Luke. "You'd think they'd give up on it by now. She is my wife, after all."

Luke didn't comment. He didn't need to imagine the grief that the brothers gave Rocket. He was more concerned about what they were going to say to him. And they were going to have a lot to say, he was sure of it. Because this time, he wasn't going to let them and their opinions get in his way. The only thing that could stop him from being with Laney now was Laney herself.

"Are you heading off to Chico with the rest of them?" Rocket asked Luke.

Luke looked at Ty. "I didn't know you were going."

Ty shrugged. "Tan just suggested it a little while ago. Ford's up for it, and I thought I'd go along." He narrowed his eyes. "I thought I could drop Laney back at her place on my way."

Frankie bounced up to join them at that moment. "You don't need to give her a ride, Ty. I brought her, I'll take her back."

Luke was relieved that he wouldn't have to argue with Tyler about being the one to take her. He glanced at Frankie; she looked as though she was trying to hide a smile. Did she know? He'd always wondered if she knew about Laney and him.

Tyler just shrugged. "It sounds like you've got her covered either way. I'll leave you to it."

Tanner came and draped his arm around Luke's shoulders. "Are you ready, wingman?"

Frankie burst out laughing. "I think Ty's going to have to be your wingman tonight."

Tanner gave them a puzzled look. "What's so funny? What am I missing?"

"Nothing," Frankie said hurriedly. "It's just that I heard Luke saying earlier that he wasn't going out tonight. He needs to stay here and straighten things out."

Luke's gaze snapped up to meet hers. She wasn't about to land him in it, was she?

Rocket looked around. "I thought we picked up after ourselves pretty well."

"You did," said Luke, relieved.

Tanner looked at him. "So, you're not coming?"

"No."

Tanner shrugged and let go of him. "Do you want me to stay and help clean up?"

"No, thanks. There's really not that much to do."

"And nothing you could help with, anyway," said Frankie.

Either he was paranoid and reading more into her words than she meant, or Frankie knew damn well what was going on.

Luke watched her herd everyone back to their trucks. Laney went with them, hugging her brothers good night, and saying that she'd see them soon.

Spider came to stand beside Luke. "This was great, thanks for having us over."

"Thanks for coming. I enjoyed it."

"I don't know what's going on, but Frankie said we need to be the last to leave. Is everything okay?"

Luke chuckled. "Everything's fine, thanks."

Spider looked out to where Frankie and Laney were standing, waving as the last of the trucks disappeared down the driveway. "Mind if I ask you something?"

"Fire away."

"I've wondered for a while, but I've never wanted to ask – since it's none of my business – but is there something going on between you and Laney?"

Luke sighed. "The honest answer to that is, I don't know yet."

Spider nodded. "And the brothers don't, either?"

"Nope." He turned to look at Spider. "If there's something you want to say, go ahead and say it."

"Just that you know where I am if you need me."

"Thanks."

Spider chuckled. "I'm guessing that Frankie's insistence that we needed to be the last to leave – and that she had to be the one to give Laney a ride home – is because she knows, too?"

Luke laughed with him. "Yeah, I'm guessing the same thing."

~ ~ ~

Laney stood beside Luke, watching Frankie's truck disappear down the driveway.

When the taillights finally disappeared, Luke turned to her with a smile. "Alone at last."

She wrapped her arms around her middle. She couldn't count the number of times she'd hoped for this – to finally be alone with him again. But things were different now. When she was younger, all she'd wanted was to get him alone – and into bed. She hadn't really believed that there would be a chance for anything between them.

Now, they had a chance at everything; if she was brave enough to take it.

He stepped closer. "Are you okay? Do you want to be here?"

She looked up into his eyes. "Yeah, I want to be here."

He took another step, and then he was sliding his arms around her waist, pulling her toward him. She went willingly, until she was pressed up against his chest. He rested his cheek on the top of her head, and she closed her eyes, reveling in the feel of him.

"Damn, baby, this feels so right. This is all I've wanted since you left."

She closed her eyes, wishing he hadn't said it. But he had – and so they needed to talk about it.

She tipped her head back so that she could look up into his eyes, but she didn't loosen her arms around his waist.

"If you still wanted it – wanted me – why did you let me go?"

He pressed a kiss to her forehead. "I was a fool, and I'm sorry."

"I'm sorry, too, Luke."

"I'm not making excuses, I just … I fucked up, Laney, there's no other way to say it. I was a kid – and that's not an excuse, it's just the only explanation I can come up with for myself. It felt as though your brothers' disapproval was more important than … I don't want to say that it was more important than you, than us. But I let it be more important. I let my worries about what they would say and do stop me from coming after you."

She rested her forehead against his chin. "I know. But I figured that to you, they were more important. They've always been a huge part of your life. I couldn't even blame you for choosing them over me."

"No!" His voice cracked as he said it, but it was true.

She looked up at him again. "You did. I'm not saying it was wrong. I'm not saying that I blame you. What I'm saying is … I'm saying that you broke my heart."

His arms tightened around her, and he crushed her to his chest. "I'm sorry, Laney. So, so sorry. If it's any consolation, I broke mine, too."

She closed her eyes. "This is weird, this isn't like me. You know me. I jump in with both feet, and to hell with the consequences. But I don't feel like I can do that now. I meant what I said, Luke, I'm scared – scared that things will end up the same way they did before."

"They won't. I won't let them. If you give me a chance – in fact, no. I was going to say that if you give me a chance, then I'll just get them all together and tell them. But that's not fair, that's still me putting it all on you. Unless you say that you don't want me to, I'm going to do it anyway. I'm going to tell them that I have no idea if you'll give me a chance but that I'm going to try."

Laney's heart felt as though it melted in her chest. How many years had she wished that he would say something like that to her – that he might feel that way about her? Now, here he was saying it, and yet she was going to ...

"No."

"No?" It was hard to see the pain etched into the lines around his eyes.

She couldn't help reaching up to run her fingers over them. "I'm not saying no, I don't want you. I do. I won't lie to you about that. What I'm saying is that I don't think you should tell them anything – not yet."

He frowned. "Why not?"

She sucked in a deep breath. "Because I think we need to figure it out for ourselves first. You've been nothing more than a fantasy in my head for the last fifteen years. I've been nothing more than that to you. I don't know who you are now, not really. You don't know who I am. I don't think it's worth putting ourselves through the grief that they'll give us if this isn't going to work out."

"It's gonna work out, Laney. I'm not going to blow my second chance with you now that I've finally got it."

"I don't want to blow it either, but we don't know. We can't know, not for sure, until we give it a try." She smiled. "So, what do you say?"

His eyes bored into hers. "You're asking me if I want to give it a try? You and me?"

She nodded.

"But you're saying that *you* want to keep it a secret?"

She nodded again. "I do. You know it makes sense, Luke. If it all goes down the pan, and I leave and go back to Kentucky at the end of the month, you'll thank me. You know you will. If that happens, you'll be glad that you didn't blow up your life and your friendships."

His hand came up to close around the back of her head as he pressed a kiss into her hair. "That might have been true back then. But not now. I'll blow it all up for just a chance."

She loved hearing it, but she had to be realistic. "If that were true, tonight would have been very different. Wouldn't it?"

"No. It wouldn't. Not if I'd known ..."

She raised her eyebrows, and his shoulders sagged.

"Okay, I admit that up until right now, I was still being a pussy. But not anymore, Laney. I'll keep it secret if you want me to, but as soon as you're comfortable with it, I'll tell the whole damn world."

She smiled. She was trying to be sensible – which wasn't something she was used to – but she did love the idea of Luke finally wanting to tell the whole world about them.

~ ~ ~

Luke felt as though they had come a long way. He finally had it straight in his head that he was the reason things hadn't worked out for them in the past. He'd always felt as though Laney had walked away from him without a second glance, but he could admit now that he hadn't even tried to show her that they could have anything worth staying for.

"Do you want another drink?"

She smiled. "No. I've had enough already. And besides, you don't need to get me drunk before..."

He tightened his arms around her; they were still standing at the end of the driveway holding onto each other. "If I thought you were drunk, I wouldn't even try. After all this time, when we go there again, I don't want to doubt that it's what you want."

Her eyes glimmered as they looked up into his. "It's what I want. It's what I've always wanted."

He raised his eyebrows, needing to know but not wanting to ask if she wanted it right now.

She let out a short laugh. "You don't need to get me drunk, but I'm not quite ready to just jump your bones."

He gave her a rueful smile. "Want me to take you home?"

She shook her head rapidly. "No, I want you to show me around this place. I can't believe that Haley and Walt left. I always loved this place – always thought it would be perfect as a small training barn."

He stepped back and took hold of her hand. "Come on then, let's show you around. I think you'll be surprised what they did with the place over the last few years."

She fell in step beside him as they walked past the arena and out to the barn. Luke felt as though every step would be etched into his memory forever. He was finally starting to believe that there might be a chance for the two of them.

Laney looked around in wide-eyed wonder when they reached the barn. "Damn! They sure poured some money into this place. It surprises me even more that they'd leave after doing all of this."

Luke looked around at the new stalls, the wash bay, and the tack room. "Walt didn't want to leave but he did get a few good years use out of it before they went."

Laney nodded. "I forget just how long it's been. I remember coming out here to ride for him. This place was always nice, but it was old."

She looked around at the stalls again and shook her head. "At first, all I could see was that it's new – no longer what it used to be. Now, I can see that it's only new to me. How long ago did he upgrade it all?"

"I don't know. Four years? Maybe five."

She met his gaze. "Did you stay close with them?"

He nodded. "Not super close, but I did come and ride for Walt on and off over the years. He kept up with things after Maddie and Hunter left, but it got harder for him to ride any of the horses, let alone all of them."

Laney let go of his hand and wandered down the breezeway between the stalls. "Do you ever think about it? I mean, think about turning in your badge and doing something here?"

Luke watched her back as she walked away from him – okay, so he watched her ass. He couldn't help it; she'd always had a great ass. When she turned and looked back at him, he shrugged. "I think about it all the time, but ... I don't know. I was never as good as you or Tanner. I don't know that I could ..."

She frowned as she walked back to him. "Why do you do that? Why do you put yourself down?"

He chuckled. "I'm not putting myself down. I'm just saying how it is. I'm not saying I'm terrible – I know I have a way with horses. What I'm saying is that you and Tanner have something special – you just have the magic, whether it's breeding, or training, or whatever. You guys have natural ability, like some kind of sixth sense. All I ever had was a willingness to learn and to work hard."

Laney looked around the barn again before turning back to face him. "Maybe you should think about it now."

He held her gaze for a long moment, wondering if – hoping that – she might possibly mean that he should think about it with her.

She came all the way back to him and rested her hands on his hips. "You should at least get yourself a couple of horses – it's a crying shame to let this place stand empty."

"I know. It is. I've kept thinking about it, but with work... I just don't know."

She laughed. "Have you gone soft on me, Luke Wallis? Growing up, everyone we knew worked a full-time job and had a full-time barn, or ranch to take care of when they got home. Are you telling me you can't handle your deputy duties and a couple of horses?"

He smiled at her through pursed lips. "No. I just haven't had the motivation until now. What are you doing this weekend?"

She shrugged. "Depends."

"On what?"

She smiled. "On you. What do you want to do?"

Luke felt a rush of warmth spread through his chest. "Want to go to the sale barn with me?"

"Hell yeah, I do. You're serious? You're going to buy yourself a couple of horses just because I busted your balls?"

He laughed. "No. I'm going to do it because I've been thinking about it for a while and now, I have reason to do it. Although, I'm not going to buy myself a couple of horses."

"You're not? It's not fair to get just one."

He cupped his hands around her neck and smiled down at her. "I know. I'm going to get myself one, and one for you."

Her eyes widened. "You don't need to do that."

He dropped a kiss on her lips. "Yeah, baby, I do. I want us to be able to ride together."

She bit down on her bottom lip. "I told you, Luke. I'm not promising that I'm going to stay yet. I really think that we need to take our time – to see if this can be what we hope. It might not work ..."

He interrupted her by pressing another kiss to her lips. "I know. But Laney, I'm going all in this time. Even if you're only here for a month and you decide you don't want me after that, then I'll still have two horses and a whole new bunch of memories."

His throat tightened at the thought that a month might be all he got with her, but even if it was, he wasn't going to hang back this time. He was going to make the most of every moment just like Deacon had said. If it didn't work out, if she walked away and left him behind again, he'd just have to pick up the pieces and put his life back together after she'd gone.

Chapter Eight

Laney was nervous as they walked back up to the house. Luke had shown her around the place in the moonlight. Her damn imagination kept picturing what life could be like here – not just here in the valley, but here on this property. She could see herself working in the barn, riding in the arena, and of course, coming back to the house at the end of the day, coming home to eat dinner – and go to bed with Luke.

Was that what they were going to do now – go to bed? She hoped so. Then again, part of her wasn't so sure. That one night they'd shared, had been her first time. From what she'd heard, the first time wasn't great for most girls. That hadn't been the case for her.

She'd known that Luke made her feel a certain way before she'd even known what sex was. All through her teenage years, she'd known that she wanted him to be the one. Of course, he'd tried to keep her at arms-length. It wasn't just about her brothers, either. She knew that. He respected her. If she'd gotten her way, he would have slept with her when she was fifteen. It had taken her another three years to finally seduce him. And when he finally gave in to her, it had been … magical. The whole night had been amazing, they'd danced together, and laughed. She'd taken him out to a bar when they were up in Great Falls – where no one knew them. And afterward, she'd taken him back to her room and he'd finally given in to her.

It might have been her first time, but it had also been her best. Yes, it had hurt a little a first, but just the feel of him, the connection – he'd taken her to heights that she'd never reached again with anyone else.

"What do you want to do?" he asked, his words interrupting the memories. "I can take you home if you like."

She met his gaze. "Is that what you want?"

He shook his head slowly. "No. You know what I want. I want you. I always have."

She smiled. "You have no idea how many times I've dreamed of hearing you say those words to me again."

He drew her closer and wrapped his arms around her. "I'm just sorry that I didn't say them sooner. I should have said them again the next day – and every day since; they never stopped being true."

She rested her head against his shoulder and spoke into his neck. "I wish you had, too. But that's the past, and I think we should leave it where it belongs. It wasn't all your fault, Luke. I was so mean to you afterward because I was mad at you. I was hurt."

She shrugged and looked up at him. "I was a teenage girl in love; what do you expect? I couldn't see the big picture. All I knew was that I loved you. In my mind it was a quick and easy fairytale. In my mind, after you slept with me, we were going to live happily-ever-after. It was that simple."

She gave him a sad smile. "I didn't understand that life's more complicated than that. All I understood was that after you slept with me, it didn't … We didn't …" She blew out a sigh. "I didn't understand how it was for you. I was just mad at you. I was hurt and I was angry. So, I took it out on you. I couldn't stay around here and be near you but not with you. And after that, I just couldn't face you whenever I came home."

He ran his hand over her hair and pressed a kiss to her forehead. "I'm so sorry, baby. If I could go back, I'd do it all the way you saw it. It could have been as simple as you wanted it to be – it should have been. I should have manned up and told the guys."

She choked back a laugh. "Yeah, right! We both know damn well that if you told them what we'd done, we wouldn't have had a future. They would have killed you, then and there."

He gave her a rueful smile. "I should have found a way to tell them – I should have been able to make them understand." His smile faded. "I should have at least tried."

She couldn't argue with that. "Maybe. But we can't go back, Luke. All we can do is figure out if we want to go forward."

His arms tightened around her. "I want to go forward, Laney." He looked down into her eyes. "Do you?"

The intensity in his gaze sent a shiver down her spine. She wanted to throw all her caution to the wind and tell him that hell yes, she did. Instead, she said, "I think so."

He pressed his lips together as he nodded. "Then I should take you home. I don't think you should stay here if …"

She laughed. "Don't you dare tell me that I need to be sure before you take me to bed again." She winked at him. "How can I be sure when I don't know if you'll live up to what I remember?"

He smiled through pursed lips. "Good point. I like the way you think." He winked back at her. "And I'll do my best to live up to the memory."

He held her closer, and one hand slid down over her ass. She could feel his hard length pressing into her belly, and goosebumps broke out on her arms as she slid them up around his neck. "Take me to bed, Luke."

~ ~ ~

Luke's heart hammered in his chest as he led Laney up the stairs. It was finally happening; after all these years, he was finally getting a second chance with her.

She followed him into his room, and he closed the door behind her and locked it. She looked back over her shoulder at it and gave a nervous laugh. "Are you making sure that I can't escape if I change my mind?"

"No! I'm not … You're not locked in. It opens from this side…"

She came to him and rubbed her hand up his arm. "Joking, Luke. I'm joking."

He sucked in a deep breath and blew it out slowly, trying to relax. "Sorry. I guess I'm nervous."

"I am, too."

He took hold of her hand and led her to the bed, where he sat down and patted the space beside him. She sat and leaned her head against his shoulder.

"Maybe you should have gotten me drunk first," she said.

He chuckled. "Nah. We don't need that. I prefer this."

She looked up at him. "You do? This is awkward and … I dunno …"

He hooked his finger under her chin and made her look up at him. "Yes, it's awkward. It's not drunk and fumbling, wild passion. You know what that makes it?"

She shook her head slowly. "Other than awkward? No."

He smiled. "Real, Laney. This is real. You said that all we've had of each other for all these years is a fantasy. Now, we get the reality." He shrugged. "And yes, it's awkward. But it's also honest. I think we need that more than anything."

Her eyes shone as she looked up at him. "I don't know, I think I'd take blind passion over awkward honesty right now."

He had to laugh. "Okay then. If you insist." He moved up the bed until he was leaning back against the headboard, then he held his arms out to her. "Come here and ride me, cowgirl."

His eyes closed and his fingers dug into her hips when she straddled him and rested her hands on his shoulders.

He could see the laughter in her eyes as she looked down at him. "This doesn't feel so awkward," she said as she rocked her hips, torturing him through the two layers of denim that, sadly, still separated them. "I'm still waiting for wild and passionate, though."

He slid his hands down, holding onto her tight, round ass as he rocked her against him. "I'm working on it."

"Not fast enough," she said as she pulled her shirt off over her head.

He groaned when he found himself face to face with her breasts. His hands moved of their own accord, unfastening her bra, and throwing it to the floor. She'd filled out since he'd known her. Her breasts filled his hands as he leaned in. Her nipples pulled into taut peaks when he nipped and teased. She arched her back, offering him more of herself, and he took it hungrily. He wanted to spend longer worshipping her perfect breasts, licking, and sucking, and listening to her needy little moans, but the way her hips rocked so eagerly against him, had him pulling back.

As soon as he did, she pulled his shirt off and then she climbed down, and they held each other's gaze as they raced to get rid of the rest of their clothes. Then, they stood naked before each other.

He reached out and pushed a strand of her hair back off her shoulder. "You're beautiful."

She stepped closer, running her hands up over his chest. "Right back at ya, Deputy."

He tensed at that. *Deputy*? Sure, he'd called her *Cowgirl*. But that was who she was. It wasn't just a name; it was a part of what defined her. Did *Deputy* define him? He lost track of the thought when her hands slid back down until she was drawing circles on his upper thighs. Then she closed her fingers around him, and he closed his eyes.

"You've grown," she said in a breathy voice.

He opened his eyes and put his hands on her waist, lifting her up so that she had to wrap her legs around his waist.

"Ooh! I like it," she exclaimed.

He'd wanted to take his time, wanted to learn her body, and give her pleasure first. But now that her wet heat was open to him, pressing against him, inviting him inside, he didn't think he could wait.

He pressed her back against the wall, and she reached down between them, trying to guide him into her.

"Shit!" he groaned.

Her gaze flew up to meet his. "What is it? What's wrong?"

"Condom. I'm going to have to put you down."

She shook her head slowly. "I have an IUD. And you can trust me."

He swallowed.

Sadness clouded her eyes. "But it's okay if you don't. I can …"

"Jesus, Laney! I trust you. I was going to ask how *you* can trust *me*?"

Her smile returned, and he could see the answer in her eyes, even though she didn't say the words.

He couldn't have stopped himself then, even if he tried. "I love you, too," he breathed as he lifted her up until he was notched at her entrance. They both gasped when he thrust up at the same time that he let her weight come down on him.

He had to close his eyes and clench his jaw. She felt so damn good. Her arms tightened around his neck. He thought he might have died and gone to heaven when his face got lost between her breasts as she writhed against him, lowering, and lifting, taking him deeper and harder.

He drove into her over and over, losing himself inside her as she chanted his name. He didn't know if he could last long; the feel of her threatened to push him over the edge from the moment he entered her. But he didn't have to worry. With every thrust, Laney gasped louder, and clenched him tighter.

"Oh God, Luke! Yes. Yes. Yesss!" she cried in time with their movements. Then she was pulsating around him, her orgasm wracking her body, and demanding his surrender. He threw his head back as he let go, his whole body quivering as he emptied himself inside her. He came so hard that he saw stars behind his eyes before he finally came back to earth.

Laney held his gaze as their bodies stilled. Her eyes were big, her cheeks flushed; he'd never seen her look more beautiful. Not even that one time.

He pressed a kiss to her lips, then pulled back when he realized that her eyes had been filled with ... he looked up into them again ... fear?

"Hey. What is it?"

She wriggled to get down. "You're going to break your back standing there. Let me down."

He didn't want to. He wanted to stay like this – still connected. But Laney tried again to get off him, so he let her down, but he didn't let her go.

"Come here." He closed his arms around her and held her against his chest, not ready to lose the feel of her naked skin against his. "What is it, baby? What's wrong?"

He felt her sigh before she looked up at him. "Nothing. Sorry, I guess I freaked out. I kind of had it in my head that if we ever did this again … that … I don't know … that we'd be over again afterward."

He tightened his arms around her and walked her back to the bed where he lay down but wasted no time in arranging her against him again. "It's not over, Laney. It's just beginning."

She bit down on her bottom lip as she looked up at him. "You can tell me if you don't want me, you know."

"I want you, Laney." He smiled and rolled her onto her back. "And I think maybe we need to keep doing this until you believe me."

She smiled back at him. "Hmm. Maybe you have a point there. If we do it enough times, then maybe I'll replace the fear of losing you again with something new – make a new association."

He pressed a kiss to her lips. "That sounds better. And I think I know what kind of association I want you to make."

"What."

He leaned in and nipped her neck before soothing the sting with his tongue. "I think I need to make love to you so hard and so often, that every time we do it, you can only associate it with doing it again. And again," he added as he slid his hand between her legs.

She started to get up, but he shook his head with a smile.

"But we just …"

He nodded. "And now we will again. You don't have to be anywhere before morning, do you?"

She shook her head, and her eyes glazed with lust as his fingers teased her. "Good. Then I have work to do here."

Laney kept her eyes closed as she drifted up to the surface. She didn't want to wake up – didn't want to come back to reality. She tightened her arm around Luke's waist and pressed herself closer against him. She hadn't dared to believe that she would ever find herself in bed with him again. But here she was, and she didn't want it to end.

Last night had been amazing. He'd proved to her that things between them really were that good – she'd wondered sometimes over the years if she'd just managed to glorify the memory. But she hadn't. Sex was different with Luke – better. She'd had a few boyfriends over the years, had some good sex, but it had never been great, not Luke kind of great, anyway.

She looked up at his sleeping face. The hard lines of his jaw and cheeks weren't softened by sleep. She was so tempted to run her fingers over the dark stubble that shadowed his chin, but she didn't want to wake him. She wanted to lie here and enjoy this. She was less afraid this morning that things were going to go wrong between them again, but a little doubt still lingered.

She wondered if he'd still want to go to the sale barn today. Was he really serious about buying a couple of horses? Perhaps she'd be able to talk him into borrowing some from Tanner instead. That was a better idea – Tan could probably use the help, anyway. They could talk about it later.

She meant what she'd told him last night. She wasn't ready to have a showdown with her brothers yet. It wasn't even that she doubted Luke's intentions so much as she wanted to be sure that she and Luke were in this for each other. She knew damn well that if her brothers gave them a hard time, it would feel like the two of them were united in the face of adversity. She didn't want that. She wanted to know that whatever they shared now was something worth pursuing in its own right.

She already knew that it was, she just wanted to prove it to herself.

It was going to make things difficult – keeping what they were doing a secret from her brothers. But it would be worth it. If they decided that they wanted to be together for real, then she and Luke would face the brothers together. Until then, she was looking forward to enjoying his company without anyone else knowing.

It made it easier that she and Luke were neighbors. Okay, so the place she was renting was still a couple of miles down the road, but that was a lot closer than the ranch. She had to feel as though fate, or some other guiding power, had led her to rent a place at Mill Creek.

She frowned when she thought about it. Even if he was the reason that she wasn't staying at the ranch, her father was not a guiding power in her life. He had been while he'd been able to impose himself, but those days were far behind her. She looked up at Luke's sleeping face. Maybe things working out the way they had was all part of a bigger plan. It was bad enough thinking about what the brothers would have done to Luke if they'd known about them back then – she didn't even want to imagine what her father might have done to him.

An involuntary shudder shook her body, and Luke opened his eyes and smiled at her. His arms tightened around her, and he pressed a kiss to her forehead.

"Good morning," she said.

He smiled so big that the lines around his eyes crinkled. "It's not just a good morning, it's the best morning. The best morning ever – except one."

Laney's hand came up to cover her mouth and tears pricked behind her eyes. "Do you really mean that?"

His face sobered, and he nodded solemnly. "I do. Although, maybe this morning is even better than that one. The last time

I woke up with you in my arms, I didn't know what was going to happen – where we could take it. Now, I know where we can take this. I know where I want us to go."

She almost asked him where exactly, but she didn't. Not because she didn't want to know, but because she didn't want to hear it until she was ready to believe it might be possible.

Instead, she just looked back into his eyes and nodded.

He was leaning in to kiss her, and she was hoping that they were about to start the day in the right way when his phone rang.

He rolled his eyes at her and said, "Ignore it."

She tried, but she couldn't. She pressed a quick kiss to his lips and gave him a rueful smile. "Take care of it first, then we can get back to where we were."

She wished she'd kept her mouth shut when he answered, and she heard him say, "Hey, Tanner. What's up?"

As it turned out, she was grateful that she'd made him answer. From what she could gather from Luke's side of the conversation, Tanner was on his way here.

When Luke ended the call, he made a face at her. "He's coming over."

Laney was already rolling off the bed when he caught her arm. "I need to go."

"Stay."

She shook her head adamantly. "I already told you. I don't want…"

"I know. But I think he'd thank me for letting you stay over, considering that we'd both had too much to drink for me to drive you, right?"

Laney thought about it for a moment before she nodded. "Yeah. I guess. Just because I feel guilty doesn't mean that he'll suspect anything, does it?"

He gave her arm a squeeze. "We've got nothing to feel guilty about. I know it took me a long time, but now that I've finally seen sense, I'm looking forward to the day when I can come clean with them."

"Yeah."

"How long do you want to wait?"

She shrugged. She knew that it would probably be better to just get things out in the open now. But she wasn't ready yet.

Luke leaned in and pressed a kiss to her forehead. "I don't want to push you, baby." He smiled. "But we probably should push ourselves to get dressed before he arrives."

Chapter Nine

Luke pushed the brim of his hat up so that he could watch Laney as she rode around the arena. Today hadn't exactly gone the way he'd planned. He'd hoped that he and Laney would be able to spend the day together over at the sale barn, and then maybe stop to get dinner on the way home.

Tanner had thrown a wrench in the works with his phone call this morning, and then showing up like that, but Luke had still thought the day might be salvageable after he left. Laney had other plans, though.

Instead of trying to help him hurry Tanner out of there, she'd engaged him in a conversation about the horses he had at the moment. In a way, Luke could understand – and appreciate – that she didn't want him going out and buying horses on a whim, especially not on her account. But the last thing he'd expected was that she would suggest that they should come over here to the MacFarland ranch with an eye to loaning some of Tanner's horses instead.

Tanner nudged him with his elbow, and he nearly fell off the top rail of the fence where they were sitting.

Tanner laughed when Luke scowled at him. "What the hell, dude? What was that for?"

Tanner jerked his chin at Laney. "She's something else, isn't she?"

"She sure is."

Tanner turned his attention back to his sister, watching her put the horse she was riding through its paces. "I'm surprised as hell that she wanted to come over here."

Luke pursed his lips. Tanner probably wasn't as surprised as he was. But he needed to pull himself together. He didn't need to be selfish about her time. It would no doubt do her good to spend time here at the ranch. He didn't know all the details about the blow-up she'd had with her dad. He just knew that it had ended with her vowing not to set foot on the ranch again until the old man died. He was glad that she'd already broken that vow for Janey's wedding, but he knew that she still wasn't comfortable being here. He smiled to himself, liking the idea that maybe he was contributing in a roundabout way to getting her used to being here again.

"What's up with you, anyway?" Tanner asked.

Luke had to grab onto the fence again to keep his balance. "Why? What do you mean?"

Tanner chuckled. "I mean, I've been telling you ever since you moved into the Bennett place that you need a couple of horses in the barn, but you kept saying no. What changed?"

Luke glanced over at Laney again. He was so tempted to tell Tanner that *everything* had changed. That Laney had changed it all. But he had to respect what she'd said. If she wanted to keep it a secret for now, then he'd go along with it. He just hoped that she'd be ready to face her brothers at some point soon.

He shrugged. "I dunno. I just…"

Tanner grinned at him. "It's okay. You don't have to tell me. I think I know."

Luke's heart started to race. Did Tanner really know? He'd be relieved if he did. He glanced at Laney again, hoping that she wouldn't be mad if Tanner had figured it out.

"What do you think you know?" he hedged.

"It's Laney, isn't it?"

He hesitated, wondering what to say, but Tanner cut him off with a laugh and slapped his back.

"Thanks, bud. You've always been such a good friend. I should have thought of it myself."

Luke opened his mouth to explain himself, but Tanner continued.

"I mean, she's bound to want to ride while she's home, and we all know she's not comfortable here on the ranch. Having a couple of horses just around the corner at your place will be perfect for her. I appreciate it."

Luke closed his eyes. Damn. He'd really thought that Tanner had figured out the truth, and that he'd finally be able to be honest with him.

Tanner cocked an eyebrow at him. "You don't have to do it, though, you know. I know you might not want her out at your place all the time."

"No. It's fine. I like having her around." It hadn't been his intention when he suggested it, but having a couple of horses in his barn would provide a good cover story for Laney spending time at his place.

"You might regret saying that. I don't know for sure yet, but I think she might actually stick around." Tanner grinned. "Maybe it's wishful thinking on my part, but I get the impression that she's ready for a change."

Luke had to ask. "What makes you think that?"

Tanner shrugged. "I don't know. She seems more relaxed about being here this time. Usually, whenever she's home, you know what she's like – she's like a long-tailed cat in a room full of rocking chairs. She's always on edge, always seems like she's ready to take off at the drop of a hat. She hasn't said anything, but I'm not getting that vibe from her this time."

He shot Luke a puzzled look. "I'll tell you what's weird, too. I just said that you know what she's usually like when she's home, but you don't really, do you? Ty mentioned something last night. He said that the two of you seemed to be getting along well. I told him that you guys always had, but it was only when he said it that I realized – you two got along great when we were kids, but I don't remember you being around much whenever she's been home."

Luke shrugged, torn between wanting to make some excuse about his work schedule and wanting to just finally tell his friend the truth.

Laney saved him from having to comment at all when she trotted over to them with a big smile on her face.

"This guy's awesome, Tan. I'll be happy to work with him if you want me to."

"You'll be doing me a big favor if you do, sis. Want to try that gray mare? She's a bit greener, but I think you could work wonders with her."

"Sure," Laney replied. "And if you've got any more you want to send over, Luke can give me a hand with them."

Tanner laughed. "I've given up asking Deputy Wallis to spend any time in the saddle for me."

Luke turned to him. "You have? Why?"

Tanner made a face at him. "Because you're usually too busy working. And when you're not working, I may be guilty of putting your talents as a wingman ahead of your talents as a horseman."

Shit. Luke could only watch as Laney reined the gelding around and rode away.

"Sorry, dude." Tanner had no clue how his words had affected his sister. "I wouldn't have thought you even wanted to ride the last few years. Do you? You can have your pick if you do."

Luke couldn't do anything about Laney right now, though he knew that they would need to talk later. Part of him liked that she was apparently jealous of him acting as Tanner's wingman, but most of him was just worried by it.

"You're right, I haven't really had the time or the interest in a while. But if Laney's going to be around, I think it'd be good to join in with her."

Tanner gave him a weird smile. "In that case –" he gave Luke a shove "– quit riding the fence and follow me. I think I know a little mare you can help me with."

~ ~ ~

Laney had thought she was being clever this morning when she suggested that they should go to the ranch and see Tanner about horses instead of going to the sale barn. Now though, now she was regretting it. She wasn't regretting the horses that they'd trailered back to Luke's place – three of them: the buckskin gelding and gray mare that she'd been riding this morning, and another mare – a palomino – that Tanner was convinced was going to steal Luke's heart.

She had no regrets about the horses, but she wished that their visit to the ranch hadn't ended with them getting roped into going to Chico with everyone tonight. She had no one to blame but herself and she knew it. She was the one insisting that they shouldn't say anything to her brothers yet. Given that, it was hardly Luke's fault that Tanner was still rattling on about what a good wingman he was. Nor was it his fault that her brothers still expected him to go on the hunt with them when they were out.

She'd been mad about it – even though she knew that wasn't fair. Poor Luke had only been able to watch as she rode away in Tanner's truck with him after they dropped the horses off at Luke's place. It made sense; she needed to go back to her rental and get changed and ready if she was going out with them tonight. But she knew that Luke had been expecting her to stick around with him for a while. They even had the built-in excuse of her helping him to settle the horses in. But she needed a bit of time away from him – she needed to gather her thoughts and get her act together.

She wasn't a kid anymore. She prided herself on having grown into a strong, independent woman; and if that were really the case, she needed to start acting like one. She wasn't going to let history repeat itself. When they were younger, Luke had hurt her with the way he hadn't wanted her brothers to find out about them. The way things had gone wrong wasn't all his fault, though. She'd reacted in the way that came naturally to her – she'd gotten mad at him, and she'd left.

This time, if things didn't work out between them, she wanted it to be because they'd given it a fair shot. Not because either of them fell back into their old ways. They'd already said that they were going to communicate – like adults. And she could admit that her behavior this afternoon had been kind of childish.

Of course Luke had been with other women. She didn't hold that against him. She really didn't – she just didn't like hearing about it or having evidence of it thrust in her face.

She needed to apologize to him, and she wanted to do it as quickly as possible. She knew that he'd be busy settling the horses in, but she didn't want to wait until later to talk. It wasn't as though she'd be able to pull him aside tonight and have the kind of conversation they needed to – not while they were at Chico, and not with all her brothers watching.

She took her phone out with her onto the back porch and dialed his number, hoping that he wasn't mad at her for the way that she'd behaved.

"Hey, baby. Listen, I'm sorry about earlier …" he answered.

"Don't go saying sorry. We both know that I'm the one who owes you an apology. *I'm* sorry. I didn't mean to be a bitch. I just …" She gripped her phone tighter. "If you want to know the truth, and I think this is only going to work if we're honest with each other, I got jealous."

Luke was quiet for a few moments, and it hit her for the first time just how important this was. She didn't want him to be mad at her. She didn't want to hurt his feelings. She wanted this to work.

"I know, and I'm sorry." She heard him suck in a deep breath. "If we're being completely honest here, I don't hate that you're jealous."

She let out a short laugh. "Yeah, I wouldn't be jealous if I didn't care."

"And I like that. But you have to know that I would never intentionally do anything to make you jealous or to hurt you."

"I know. You're a better man than I am."

The silence drew out before Luke spoke again. "Every time, Laney. Every single time you brought a guy with you when you came to visit. Every time you hooked up with someone while you were here, I was more than jealous."

"I know it doesn't make it any better, but you should know that was the only reason I did it – any of it."

"It was?"

She closed her eyes and nodded. "Yeah. It was always you, Luke. I hated coming back here knowing that I couldn't be with you. I hated knowing that you didn't want me. So – it was childish, and I know it, but – I brought guys back with me, or at least tried to find one to latch onto whenever you were around."

Luke didn't say anything for a long few moments.

"Are you mad at me?" she asked when she couldn't take the silence any longer.

"No, hell no! I'm not mad. I'm surprised. I thought that you were just busy getting on with your life. I mean, it's hardly a surprise that there's no shortage of guys who want to be with you. I just figured that I'd blown my chance and part of my punishment was that I had to see you with other guys."

"Aww, Luke. I'm sorry."

"Don't be. It's like you said, it's the past. We can't change it, but we can learn from it."

"We can. And the first thing I need to learn is that I can't go getting jealous of your past. I'm not surprised that there were plenty of girls who wanted to be with you, either. I'll try to rein it in, okay?"

"Okay. And I promise you here and now that none of them meant anything. It's always been you for me, too, Laney."

"Aww."

He chuckled. "I just hope that you can be understanding about what will no doubt happen later. I give you my word that I'm not interested in anyone else. But if you insist that we can't tell them yet, I guarantee you that Tanner will keep talking the way he did this afternoon – and he'll expect me to be his hunting partner."

Laney made a face. "I don't like either option."

"I'd really like to tell them."

She had to smile. "I love that you're finally there. It makes me feel like this is real, knowing that you finally want to tell them. But Luke, I… I want to give it a bit of time."

"I know, and I'll wait until you're ready. But I think we'll have to be prepared for a few awkward moments in the meantime. Are you good with that?"

She sighed. "I wouldn't say that I'm good with it, no. It's more like it's the lesser of two evils, so I'm prepared to go along with it."

"Okay then. Do you want me to pick you up on my way out?"

"I'd love you to, but Frankie and Spider are coming, and she said they'd pick me up. Just don't go getting yourself caught up in anything with Tanner that means you have to take anyone else home." Her heart thundered at the thought. "I need you to be my ride."

His voice was deep and husky when he replied, "You can ride me anytime, baby."

A rush of heat coursed through her veins. "I think I'll keep you to that later."

"I'll look forward to it, and don't go thinking that I'm going to drop you off at your rental. You're coming back here with me. I mean, there's no reason why you shouldn't be at my place early tomorrow morning settling the horses in, is there? And there's no reason that I shouldn't take you out for breakfast as a thank you afterward."

"No reason at all," she said with a smile. "I'll see you at Chico."

"See you there."

Chapter Ten

Luke narrowed his eyes as he watched Nixon maneuver Laney around the dance floor. This was so not how he wanted tonight to go. He just wanted to be able to tell the guys what was going on. *He* wanted to be the one out there on the dance floor with her. After all these years of waiting and hoping for a second chance, he wanted to be able to make the most of it. He wanted to be able to spend time with her without looking over his shoulder. Most of all – he set his glass down, feeling as though he might break it, he was gripping it so tightly as Nixon dipped Laney back over his arm – he wanted to let her know how much she meant to him, and he wanted the whole world to know it.

He turned when Rocket spoke beside him. "You know, if you and Laney are supposed to be keeping secret what's going on between you, you might want to stop looking as though you're about to go out there and wring Nixon's neck."

Luke picked his glass back up and took a long swig of his beer. "You know? Is it that obvious?"

Rocket shrugged. "I can't say that I knew for sure until you just confirmed it. No one's told me, if that's what you're worried about. But damn, Luke, you are making it kind of obvious."

Luke closed his eyes and blew out a sigh. "Shit. I was trying not to."

"Why?"

"Because she doesn't want the guys to know."

"Why not?"

Luke shook his head. "It's a long and sorry tale. We have history ... History that the guys never knew about."

Rocket nodded slowly. "I figured there was history between the two of you."

"Why? What gave me away?"

"Just a few things here and there. I remember one time when you came in the bakery and just the mere mention of her name had you walking straight back out again. The look on your face said there was history there – unfinished history, right?"

Luke nodded. "Yeah. Although, at this point, I think we'd both be happy to leave the history behind and make a whole new start."

"And you don't think her brothers would be happy about that?"

Luke looked out at the dance floor. Tyler had been dancing with a tourist, but when the song ended, he let go of her and elbowed Nixon out of the way, spinning Laney away from him and two-stepping her to the other side of the dance floor.

Rocket followed his gaze. "I mean, I know they're protective of her. I had to win them over before Janey and I really stood a chance. But I would have thought it'd be different for you. I'm an outsider; I was an unknown quantity. You've been friends with them all your life, right?"

"Right. But you know the whole thing about not going after a friend's little sister, don't you?"

"I guess. Maybe. When you're younger. But at our age? Hell, we're all in our thirties, Luke. We're not kids anymore. Obviously, I don't have sisters. But if I did, I think I'd rather she ended up with a friend – with someone I knew and respected than with a stranger." Rocket chuckled. "Damn, I think I'm giving myself a little insight into how lucky I am that the guys accepted me."

"It's not luck, Rocket. You earned their trust and their respect."

"And you're going to tell me that you haven't?"

Luke shrugged. "It's not me that you need to convince. Laney's the one who doesn't want to say anything to them until we're sure that we know where this is going."

He was surprised when Janey edged her way between them. "Well, I wish you guys would hurry up about it."

Luke met her gaze.

She smiled. "I've always known, Luke. I thought you knew that. And in case you don't know, I'm in your corner – I always have been. I think you should tell the guys and just brave it out." She smiled up at Rocket. "Like we had to."

"As soon as Laney's comfortable with it, I plan to." He froze when Tanner's hand came down on his shoulder. Damn, he was letting far too many MacFarlands sneak up on him tonight; he'd have to watch his mouth.

"What are we waiting for Laney to be comfortable with?" Tanner asked.

Luke didn't know what to say and was relieved when Janey piped up. "I told him he should go and dance with her."

Tanner looked out at the dance floor and then back at Luke. "Yeah, you probably should. Ty's got his eye on that redhead again, and Nixon's still hovering. As soon as Ty lets her go, I bet he'll swoop back in. You should go and relieve Ty."

Luke didn't need telling twice. He elbowed his way through the sea of bodies until he reached Laney and Ty.

Her eyes grew wide when she saw him, but he just smiled as he tapped Ty on the shoulder and said, "My turn."

Ty narrowed his eyes at him, but Luke kept smiling. "Are you going to tell me that you'd rather keep dancing with your sister than go and give that redhead what she wants?"

Laney laughed. "You'll be doing us all a favor, Ty. That chick's been giving me daggers ever since you rescued me from Nix."

The redhead in question gave Ty a little wave, and he grinned. "Well, since it's for the highest good of all concerned …" He let go of Laney, and she slapped his shoulder. "Go get her, cowboy. You always did like your redheads."

"It's true," Ty said before shooting Luke a weird look. "And you always liked your blondes."

Luke's heart sank as Ty walked away from them, and Laney stood there frowning at him. He couldn't deny that he'd always gone after blondes. And he didn't think that Laney was in the mood to hear the reason why. How was he supposed to tell her that he'd been trying to recapture what they shared in the arms – and between the legs – of every woman he'd been with since?

He held his arms out to his sides. "Are you going to get mad at me, or are we going to dance?"

She pursed her lips, and he thought she was going to walk away, but after a moment she relaxed and stepped toward him. "Sorry. I really am trying to do better."

"Hey, I thought we weren't apologizing to each other for this stuff anymore." He brought his hand up to cup the back of her head and leaned in so that he could whisper in her ear. "Because if we are apologizing, then I need to say sorry for almost coming out here earlier to rip Nixon's head off."

Her arms tightened around his waist, and she looked up into his eyes. "Are you serious?"

He nodded as he held her closer and started to move her to the music. "Deadly serious."

He loved the little smile that tugged at her lips. "I have to tell you, I'm not mad about that."

"I'm glad. Now perhaps you understand what I meant earlier when I said that I don't hate that you're jealous."

She smiled up at him. "Yeah, I guess I do."

~ ~ ~

After dancing with Luke and not being able to get as close to him as she wanted to, Laney lost interest in the rest of the evening. Sure, it was good to hang out with her brothers and with Janey and Frankie and their men, but she was way more interested in getting to hang out with Luke – at home, in bed.

She was relieved when Tyler looked like he was ready to call it a night – and take his redhead up to her room. She was even happier when she saw that Tanner had cornered a leggy brunette and looked like he was talking his way into her pants, too.

She looked around the table where the rest of them were sitting. Janey and Rocket were deep in conversation. Frankie and Spider were pawing at each other and looking like they'd need to get a room because they wouldn't be able to wait until they got home. Next, her gaze landed on Luke, and he smiled.

Yeah, it was time to go home. And it looked like they had the perfect excuse for him to be the one to take her.

She got to her feet and jerked her head, indicating that he should join her. The girls gave her knowing smiles when she said, "I'm ready to head home."

Frankie looked around for Ty and Tanner and grinned when she spotted them. "And I'm sure those two will be grateful that Luke offered to give you a ride."

"If they even notice that we're leaving."

"Oh, they'll notice," said Luke.

He was right; as soon they left the table and started making their way to the exit, both Tan and Ty excused themselves from their girls and headed toward them.

"Laney's ready to call it a night," said Luke. "It looks like you guys are both busy. Frankie's not ready to leave yet, and I am. So, I'm giving her a ride."

Laney squeezed her thighs together. She didn't know if he chose those words purposely, but she doubted that he would have forgotten that she was expecting him to do just that once they got back to his place.

Tanner grinned and slapped Luke's shoulder. "Thanks, bud. It's bad enough that you struck out tonight. Now, you're taking my little sister home, too." He chuckled. "That's what you call a real friend."

Ty simply nodded. She had the feeling that he might be onto them, but he didn't say anything.

"Are you coming over to the ranch tomorrow for lunch, Laney?" Tanner asked.

She shook her head. She felt bad, knowing that they would assume it was because she still wasn't comfortable on the ranch. If it weren't for Luke, she probably would have gone. But as it was, she was grateful that she had a built-in excuse. She'd much rather spend the day with him.

Once they were out in the parking lot, Luke took hold of her hand as they made their way to his truck. It was such a simple gesture, but it sent a thrill through her. It felt so right.

"So," she said with a smile, "you still plan on giving me a ride, do you?"

He grinned at her. "Hell yeah, I do. We'll have to wait until we get home, though."

She laughed. "I suppose I can wait till then. But you know, you could always give me a ride in your truck."

His fingers tightened around hers. "I'd love to, but I think we should deal with one risk at a time."

She cocked an eyebrow at him. "What do you mean?"

He chuckled. "For now, there's still the risk of your brothers finding out. That's enough on my mind. I'd rather wait until they know that we're together before I run the risk of getting caught for public indecency."

She laughed. "Okay. I guess I can wait a while."

She leaned her forehead against the passenger window and watched the big, starry sky go by as Luke drove them home.

"Are you okay over there?" he asked.

She sat up and shifted in her seat until she was facing him. "I'm good. Great actually. I wasn't ignoring you, looking out the window like that. It's just … This feels so good, so… Normal. I was thinking that this is how it should have been all along. Us going out for a night, you driving me home. This is how it should have always been."

He reached across the console and took hold of her hand. "I wish it was the way things had been." He shot a glance at her before turning his attention back to the road. "And even more than that, I hope it's the way things will be for us going forward."

She nodded. "Me too. You know, at first I felt kind of out of place being back. Everyone's been getting on with their lives while I've been gone. I knew that, of course, but it still felt strange to experience it. I suppose it's selfish, but I felt kind of left out at first. I mean, Wade's got the kids and Sierra. Janey's got Rocket and they're married. Frankie's got Spider ... And I'm happy for them all, really I am. I just didn't know how to fit in."

"You'll fit in. They're your family. You're..."

She smiled. "That's kind of the point though. I figured it out. I don't need to fit in. I don't need to see how I can find my place in their lives. I just need to start living my life alongside them. Then, we'll all just overlap naturally, and it'll get to the point where I just am part of it all again."

Luke smiled back at her. "I like the sound of that. And I need you to know, Laney, that I plan to be a big part of your life."

When they got back to Luke's place, he came around to the passenger door and opened it for her. It made her smile – it made her realize how much they'd both changed – how much they'd both grown up. It wouldn't have occurred to him to open her door before, and she sure as hell wouldn't have been thrilled to let him.

He took her hand again as they walked up to the house. He hadn't been the hand holding kind before, either. But she loved the way he did it whenever he got the chance now.

"Do you want to check on the horses first?" he asked.

"Yeah." She was sure that they'd be fine, and she was more interested in getting him upstairs, but this was the horses' first night in a new place, so they really should go check on them.

Walking down the aisle between the stalls, hand-in-hand with Luke, made her feel as though she'd somehow jumped into the future. She couldn't help but hope that this was how their lives would turn out. That this could be it for them. If she was going to stay here, she'd been thinking about buying a place – a place that was set up for horses. Luke had told her that Walt and Haley had rented him this place so that they could make the move to Austin to be closer to their kids, but that they planned to sell it before too long.

Luke squeezed her hand. "Penny for them?"

She shook her head. She wasn't ready to tell him that she was wondering if they might buy this place and start their life together here. She didn't imagine that he'd be ready to hear it either. "Just getting ahead of myself. That's all."

She had to wonder what he was thinking when he chuckled and said, "That makes two of us."

The horses were fine, and after spending a few minutes with them, they made their way back up to the house. As she looked around, Laney realized that he had made it into a home. It was the kind of home that she could see herself sharing with him.

"Do you want a drink?"

She turned to him and put her hands on his shoulders. "No, thanks. I'm not here for a drink. I'm here for the ride, remember?"

His eyes turned a deeper blue as he bit down on his bottom lip. "I remember." He slid his arms around her waist and started backing her toward the stairs. When they reached them, she turned around and ran up ahead of him. He was close on her heels, smacking her ass as they went.

They were both laughing by the time they reached the bedroom, and he closed the door behind him. She watched him turn back to lock it.

"Does that bother you?" he asked, looking more serious as he came toward her.

"No. Not really. It's not that it bothers me so much as it surprises me."

He smiled through pursed lips. "I'm not locking it to make sure that you can't escape. I promise you that. It's just ..." He ran a hand through his hair. "I suppose it's a subconscious thing. I guess since no one knows what we're doing here, I lock the door to try to make sure that they won't find out."

She went to him and slid her arms up around his neck. "I don't want to drag it out forever. And I know you're not thrilled about keeping it secret. I just ..." She searched for an explanation, hoping that he'd say something to let her off the hook. But he didn't.

In the end, she shrugged. "Just give me a bit more time, okay?"

She could see the disappointment in his eyes, but he nodded. "I've told you; I'll wait until you're ready."

His hands slid down to close around her ass. "At least, I'll wait to tell the world about us. I can't wait much longer to ..."

She didn't let him finish the sentence. She closed her hands around the back of his head and pulled him down into a kiss – the kind of kiss that told him just how much of a hurry she was in, too.

When they broke away, they each peeled off their clothes – not taking their eyes off each other for a moment. Laney drank in the sight of his hard, muscular body. He'd grown up and filled out in all the best possible ways.

He climbed onto the bed and sat back against the headboard. "You ready to ride, cowgirl?"

She nodded eagerly and climbed up to join him, straddling his hips as she claimed his mouth in another deep, hungry kiss.

She moaned into his mouth when his hands closed around her breasts. Then they slid down to cup her ass, and his mouth took over where his hands had left off. Laney let her head fall back as he teased her sensitive nipples with his lips and tongue. He lifted her, positioning her over him. She reached between them and curled her fingers around his hard length, stroking herself with him — tormenting them both until he let out a low growl. "Take me, Laney."

She notched his head at her entrance and they both gasped when he thrust deep and hard, stretching her, filling her, as he held her close. They stayed that way for a few long moments; she could feel him pulsating inside her. The look in his eyes when she met his gaze almost took her over the edge.

"There's something I've been wanting to say to you."

"Yeah?" She smiled as she rocked her hips. "Do you really want to stop for a chat right now, or are you going to give me that ride?"

He thrust deep and hard, sending her mind spinning away, but then he held still again until she came back to her senses and looked into his eyes. "I'll give you the ride of your life, baby, but I need to say this first."

She held his gaze and waited.

"I love you. I loved you back then. I love you now, and no matter what happens, I always will."

Laney's heart felt as though it melted in her chest. She leaned in and claimed his mouth in a kiss as they started to move together. His words were so sweet, but she rode him hard. She'd waited all her life to hear him say those three words to her. Now that he had, she needed him to prove them. He picked up on her urgency – and her need. His fingers bit into her hips as he moved her over him. He was so deep and so hard, she felt as though they were melding into one. Every thrust carried her higher and she clung to his shoulders, wanting to take him with her. He slipped a hand between them and strummed her clit with his thumb.

"Luke!" she gasped.

"Come for me, baby."

Her orgasm hit hard, her whole body quivering as he carried her higher. "I love you," she gasped with her last coherent thought before her mind spun away.

As if her words triggered his release, he clamped her to him and let go. All she could do was cling to him as he filled her, giving her everything he had. She took it willingly, trying to make him a part of her – a part that this time, she never planned to let go again.

When they finally slumped together, breathing hard, he rested his head on her shoulder. His breath sent shivers down her spine.

"Say it again." His deep, husky growl that sent aftershocks racing through her.

"I love you, Luke. I always have, I always will."

He looked up into her eyes. "Nothing can stop us this time. Not even us."

She pressed a kiss to his lips. "Nothing. I won't let it."

His arms tightened around her, and as he held her to him, she forced herself to focus on the future they could have – and not on all the years that they'd missed out on.

Chapter Eleven

"Luke," Deacon called after him just as he was on his way out of the station at the end of the day on Tuesday. Luke's shoulders sagged. He was ready to get out of here, ready to go home – home to Laney. But he swung back around and popped his head in through the doorway to Deacon's office.

"What's up?"

Deacon jerked his head, gesturing for Luke to come inside.

"Close the door behind you, would you?"

Luke did as he asked and then took a seat in the chair across the desk from him. "It's never good when you want me to close the door."

Deacon chuckled. "It's not bad this time. It's just … Private. Or at least, I'm assuming that it's still private since I haven't seen you sporting a black eye yet, and the grapevine isn't buzzing with any gossip about you and Laney."

Luke met his gaze and waited.

"I know it's none of my damn business, but I can't help it, I want to know. My guess is that having the horses at your place is just a way to explain the fact that Laney's there all the time."

Luke gave him a rueful smile. "That wasn't actually the intention – but I can't deny that it's worked out pretty well."

"And things are going well?" Deacon smirked. "Okay, you don't need to answer that – your goofy smile just answered it for you. But if things are going well, I'm sure you can guess what my next question is going to be."

Luke sighed. "Why haven't I told the guys yet?"

Deacon nodded. "I would've thought you'd want to get it out in the open as soon as possible."

"I do,"

"Laney doesn't?"

He shook his head sadly. "No. She wants to wait."

"Wait for what?"

"Wait until she's sure that this is going somewhere. She says she doesn't want me to blow up my life – to incur the wrath of her brothers – if it's not going to work out."

Deacon frowned. "She thinks it's not going to work?"

Luke had to smile. "I think we're both feeling more confident every day, but she doesn't want to rush it – rush the telling them part."

Deacon shook his head. "I know I don't get a say, but if I did, I'd tell you to hurry up about it. The last thing you want is them finding out from someone else."

"I know. I want to tell them. If it were up to me, I'd do it right now, but she wants to wait."

Deacon shrugged and gave him a smile. "Well, after all this time, I can understand that you have to give her what she wants. I just hope it doesn't come back around to bite you in the ass."

"Yeah. Me too. I don't like it. I don't like lying to the guys — even though I'm not exactly lying, I'm lying by omission and deceiving them."

"If I were you, I'd work on convincing her that it's time to go public."

"I'm going to try. What's going on with you, anyway? Are you and Candy doing okay?"

He loved the way his brother smiled whenever Candy's name came up. "Great. Everything's great. In fact, there's something I've been meaning to talk to you about."

"What's that?"

"I want to marry her."

Luke laughed. "Yeah, I kind of knew that. I figured that's what that big ass diamond on her finger was all about."

Deacon smiled through pursed lips. "The ring was just a declaration of intent. You know I don't like to waste too much time between saying something and doing it. I've finally got her talking about what kind of wedding she wants. She kept saying that she was fine with whatever, but I know that she's not. She was married to that asshole for most of her life, and he just dragged her off to the courthouse one day. She wants a wedding — something big and fancy — and I have no freaking clue how to go about any of that."

Luke had to laugh. "And what, you want me to help organize it? I'd do anything for you, and anything for Candy, but I don't think I'm your man when it comes to wedding planning."

Deacon waved a hand at him. "I know that. I just want you to help me brainstorm." He looked more serious as he continued. "I'm going to need your help — that's what the best man usually does."

Luke sat back in his seat. "Wow! You mean...?"

"Yeah. I want you to be my best man."

Luke couldn't help the grin that spread across his face. "Wow!" he said again. "That's awesome. I'm honored. I… Yes. I'd love to do it. If I'm honest, I kind of assumed that you'd ask one of the guys. Maybe Cash or Trip. Then again, no, you'd be more likely to ask Ace, wouldn't you?"

Deacon chuckled. "That's the thing, if I were to ask one of them, I wouldn't know which one to ask. And although they're all supposed to be such tough guys, I have no doubt whatsoever that they'd bicker like little girls over who got to do it."

Luke laughed. "You've got a point there. I didn't think about that. In that case, I am truly honored that you asked me, and yes, I'd love to do it."

Deacon's eyebrows drew together. "I'm not asking you because I don't know which of them to choose. You were always my first choice."

Luke cleared his throat and had to blink a few times.

"You might be my *little* brother, but you're my brother. We've seen each other through everything in this life. I want to say the good and the bad – but we both know that it was mainly bad for a long time. Things have been getting better and better for the last few years, and there's no one I'd rather have standing beside me when I embark on the best part of my life."

Luke just nodded; he didn't dare to speak because he was afraid that he'd make a fool of himself and start bawling.

Deacon shifted in his seat. "Yeah, we don't need to get into all the emotional shit, do we?"

Luke laughed. "No, sir. All I'm going to say is yes. Hell yes."

"Thank you." Deacon's eyes shone as he smiled and nodded. "Now, what are you still doing sitting there? Get the hell out of here and go see Laney. In fact, tell her I said hi, would you? And tell her that I'm bitching that I've hardly seen her."

"I will. And once I do, you know damn well you can expect a visit from her."

"That's why I said it."

Laney was leading the little gray mare back to the barn from the round pen when she spotted Luke's truck coming up the driveway.

He'd said that she could hang out here as much as she liked while he was at work, and she'd taken him at his word. In fact, since Sunday, she'd only been back to her rental a couple of times to pick up more clothes. She'd been a bit nervous at first that someone – especially her brothers – might stop by and find it strange that she was here, but she'd gotten over that. The horses were the best cover story, and she'd managed to relax this afternoon and work with them without constantly looking over her shoulder.

She brought the mare to a halt and waited while Luke parked the truck and climbed out. His smile lit up his face as he stalked toward her, and she knew that she was wearing a matching one.

"Hey honey, I'm home," he said with a laugh.

She had to laugh with him. "How was your day, dear?"

"It was okay. How about you?" He rubbed the mare's nose. "Is this little lady behaving herself?"

"She is. And the other two. They're coming along well." She put her hand on his shoulder and rolled up on her tiptoes to press a kiss to his cheek. "I just wish you were here to help out. It'd be so much more fun that way."

Luke met her gaze and held it. "Don't tempt me. If you go saying stuff like that, I might just turn in my badge and apply for a job as your assistant."

Laney's heart thudded to a stop. "Seriously? I was only joking ..."

He rolled his eyes. "I know. Sorry. I just..."

"Don't you dare apologize! Are you serious? I thought law enforcement was your gig. I mean, that's a lifetime career, isn't it? Especially for you. Aren't you supposed to follow Deacon's footsteps all the way to the sheriff's office?"

He shrugged and dropped his gaze. "It seems like that's what people have always assumed."

She tucked her finger under his chin and made him look up at her. "Screw people! What about you? What do you want? I thought that *was* what you wanted."

He shrugged again. "I think I thought it's what I wanted too. But I never really questioned it, I just went along with it being the natural thing to do." He patted the mare's neck absently. "There are so many times, though, when I'm sitting there in my patrol car, that I envy the hell out of Tanner. Knowing that he's out in the barn, working with the horses... I envy him. I can admit that."

Laney shook her head. "Then you should do something about it."

He let out a short laugh. "Maybe I should. Are you hiring?"

She held his gaze for a long moment. "Maybe."

All the laughter left his face. "I'm joking."

"I'm not."

The mare butted his shoulder. "Yeah, well. We should probably get this lady put away, and then figure out what we're going to do for dinner."

Laney started leading the mare toward the barn. "We can do that, but we need to talk, too. I'm serious, Luke. If you're not happy…"

He wrapped his arm around her shoulders as they walked. "I didn't say I'm not happy."

She looked up at him. "You know what I mean. You know that whole *you only get one life* thing? Well, it's as true about your career as it is about relationships."

"I know."

"Then we need to talk about it."

He dropped a kiss on her lips before letting her go when they reached the mare's stall. "We can talk about it. But in my mind at least, it's a little way down the priority list. The first thing I want us to get figured out is whether we're going to be together for real. If we are, the second thing I want to get to is telling your family. You have to remember that you haven't even decided for sure if you're going to stay here yet."

She held his gaze. He was right that she hadn't come out and said that she'd made her decision yet, but she didn't know why. In her mind, she was ninety-nine percent sure that this move was permanent. She didn't want to leap in feet first to full-on commitment, but only because that would seem foolish – to others, not to her.

"Okay, we can work our way down your priority list. But when we get to the part about you deciding what career you really want to be in, I need you to promise that you will be honest with me, okay?"

He leaned in and pressed a kiss to her lips. "I promise you. I promise I'll be honest about that and about everything else, too. We owe each other that, Laney. Honesty all the way from here on out – deal?"

"Deal."

"Have you thought any more about when you want to tell the guys?"

She bit down on her bottom lip. "I've thought about it a lot, but…"

She hated the disappointment that she could see in his eyes. "What?"

She shrugged. "I just want a bit more time."

"I know you do, baby. I don't want to push, but your time – the month that you said you were going to be here – is fast running out." He sucked in a deep breath before he continued, and she wondered what he was about to say. "If you're going to stay on after this month is up – and I hope like hell that you are – I've been thinking that it'd be crazy for you to rent that house that you never sleep in for another month."

She finally turned the mare into her stall just to give herself a minute while she processed what Luke might mean. "It's not a problem, you know. That's something else we'll need to talk about at some point. But I've done well for myself in the years I've been gone. I've made good money and I've saved most of it so…"

Luke frowned at her. "I'm not talking about money, Laney. I'm saying that I'd like you to move in with me as soon as possible. You can't do that until we've talked to your brothers."

"Yeah."

He backed away when she came out of the stall. "I'm not trying to push you. If it's not what you want, just tell me."

"It's what I want. You're what I want. I just… Oh, what the hell! Let's tell them this weekend."

Luke's eyes grew wide. "Seriously, you want to? You're ready?"

She had to laugh. "What's up? Are you about to chicken out now that it's getting real?"

His smile faded and his expression grew serious. "No. I'm never going to chicken out again. No matter what happens, when it comes to you, whatever goes down, I'm jumping in with both feet first. I learned my lesson all those years ago, and I've paid the price for far too long. I'm not scared, Laney. I just want to be sure that you're ready."

She put her hand on his arm, feeling bad. She'd only been joking but she should have known better; she'd obviously hit a nerve. "I'm ready. I don't even know why I've put it off this long. I want to get it out in the open. I want my brothers to know – I want the world to know, that I love you."

His arms closed around her, and his eyes shone bright blue as he smiled. "I love you, too, baby." He lowered his lips to hers and kissed her fast and hard.

~ ~ ~

Luke put a frozen pizza in the oven and threw together a salad while Laney was in the shower. He usually took a shower himself as soon as he got home from work, but after spending the day with the horses, her need was greater than his. He would have joined her in there, but she'd said that she was hungry. He'd feed her first, and then see what they could get up to with the rest of the evening.

He scowled at his phone when it beeped with a text. He didn't want to talk to anyone else, he wanted to close the rest of the world out and just enjoy time with Laney. He'd waited so long to have this chance; he didn't want any intrusions.

He picked the phone up reluctantly and made a face when he saw Tanner's name on the screen.

Tanner: You up for a drink? I'm almost to your place.

Luke blew out a sigh. He'd love to reply with a short and simple *not tonight*, but he couldn't do that. He felt bad enough that he was keeping secrets from Tanner. He'd feel even worse if he just blew him off without any kind of explanation.

As he looked down at his phone, wondering what he should say, the screen lit up again.

Tanner: Never mind. I'm here.

Luke scrambled to the window and saw that Tanner had just pulled up outside. Shit! He wouldn't know that Laney was here because her Jeep was still parked at her rental. He'd offered to take her back over there to collect it before he left for work this morning, but she'd smiled and said she didn't need it. That had made him so happy this morning, knowing that she was content just to be here in his space. It was going to be a bit more difficult to explain now, though. Especially since she would be coming down the stairs at any moment fresh from the shower.

He went to the bottom of the stairs and shouted up, knowing that he wouldn't have the time to run up and back down again – and that if they came down the stairs together, that would look even worse.

"Laney!"

She didn't answer, and he hurried to the kitchen when he heard the back door open.

Tanner stood there grinning at him, holding up a six pack. "I haven't heard anything from you since Saturday night. Thought I'd stop by and see how you're doing."

He frowned when he saw that the kitchen table was set with two places, the salad bowl sitting between them. "Oh. You're expecting someone? And it's not me."

Luke decided to dive right in. "Not expecting someone – she's already here."

Tanner's eyes grew wide. "Shit. Sorry, man. I didn't even think. This isn't like you."

Luke shook his head rapidly. He didn't want Tanner to go making the connection that he had a woman upstairs for the usual reasons and then figure out that the woman in question was Laney.

"No! It isn't like that. It's Laney. She spent the day here working with the horses. I asked if she wanted to stay for dinner, but she needed to take a shower first."

"Oh." Tanner looked at the table again and then back at Luke.

Luke's heart pounded in his chest. He wasn't sure if he was hoping that Tanner would figure out what was really going on or whether he wouldn't.

Tanner gave him a pained look, and Luke thought that he was on to them, until he said, "Shit, Luke, I'm sorry. I thought it was a great idea her being able to work with the horses here. I didn't expect that it would take over your whole life."

Luke felt so bad. He held his friend's gaze, tempted to just come out and tell him. But he couldn't, not until Laney was ready. Granted, she had said that they should come clean this weekend – but it wasn't the weekend yet.

"I don't mind. I really don't." He kind of hoped that Tanner might understand what he meant. "To tell you the truth, I like having her around." If that wasn't enough to give him a hint, Luke didn't know what would be.

It didn't work. Tanner grinned at him. "She's awesome, isn't she? I'm keeping my fingers crossed that this is going to be a permanent move for her."

"Yeah, me too."

Laney appeared in the doorway from the hall. She looked a little panicked to see Tanner there, but Luke shot her what he hoped was a reassuring look.

"I was just telling Tan that I managed to persuade you to stay and have dinner with me. And now he gets to join us, too."

He had to wonder if Tanner could tell how fake her smile was – it was obvious to him. "Awesome! It's good to see you, Tan. Luke didn't say that he had plans with you tonight. I would have made myself scarce if he had."

"He didn't know I was coming till I arrived. And this works out great. How long has it been since the three of us sat down to a meal together?"

Laney let out a short laugh. "I don't know. This might be the first. You always used to chase me away whenever Luke came around."

Tanner rolled his eyes at Luke. "I never wanted to embarrass her by saying it when she was a kid, but she always had a crush on you, you know."

Laney's cheeks flushed red, and Luke didn't know what to say. He was sure that Tanner was onto them when he looked from Laney to him and back again. But he just laughed and said, "Jesus, guys, I didn't think it would still embarrass you now. Aren't we all grown-ups here?"

Luke let out a short laugh. "We're supposed to be."

Laney shot him a look from behind Tanner's back. He so couldn't wait for them to start acting like adults – and come clean with her family about their relationship.

Chapter Twelve

By the time Saturday rolled around, Laney had come to terms with the fact that it was finally time to tell her brothers. She still wasn't looking forward to the telling them part, but she was looking forward to having it over and done and behind them.

This week with Luke had been the best week she could remember. They worked so well together, they just fit. While he went to work during the day, she worked with the horses. She was loving every minute of that, too.

It was nothing like the work that she'd been doing for the last decade, but she was enjoying it more. Working in a racing stable was a high-pressure job. She'd worked her way up through the ranks and made a name for herself in Kentucky. She'd been with Tom for the last four years – he kept renewing her contract as long as she kept putting him in the winners' circle. But she felt as though she'd achieved everything she set out to.

Bringing on green youngsters in her own backyard – well, in Luke's backyard – was much more enjoyable to her now. She didn't know how much money she'd be able to make doing it –

at the moment she was just doing Tanner a favor, and she didn't know if he'd have the budget to set up a more formal arrangement. But she was in a very fortunate position that she didn't need to worry about the money.

Alongside her training, she'd made a few lucrative deals of her own during her time in Kentucky. She'd bought, trained, and sold a few horses, and the proceeds of those sales were enough to set her up for life. She hadn't told anyone back here that yet – she wasn't sure when or how she would.

She looked up from the stall she'd been cleaning when she heard Luke enter the barn. He'd still been sleeping when she woke, so she'd slipped out here to take care of the chores and to let him rest. She figured that he would need all the rest he could get before they faced her brothers.

She went out into the breezeway, and he greeted her with a kiss as he handed her a mug of coffee.

"You should have woken me up. I could have come to help."

She smiled. "That's okay, you've been working hard doing deputy things all week. And I'm more than capable of taking care of things out here."

He ran his hand over her hair, and his eyes twinkled as he smiled. "You're more than capable of doing whatever you choose to. I love that about you."

Her heart swelled in her chest. There had been plenty of times over the years when men had tried to put her down – to imply that she wasn't as capable as them. Luke had never been that way. She loved that he was a tough guy – physically and emotionally – but he wasn't hard, in either sense. There was a gentleness about him, something that made him soft in a way. Not a bad way – just...

He cocked an eyebrow at her. "What's up? Did I say something wrong?"

She laughed and pressed a kiss to his lips. "No, you said something very right, and I was just taking a moment to appreciate how awesome you are."

A big smile spread across his face.

"I feel like I want to capture this moment – you smiling like that? Us being relaxed and happy out here in the barn? I hate to say it, but this might be as good as this weekend gets. I have a feeling that it's all going to be downhill from here."

Luke's smile faded. "Yeah, but we need to do it – we need to tell them. I can't keep sneaking around anymore. I need to come clean with my friends. I hate lying to them."

She nodded. "I know and I'm sorry that I asked you to, but I appreciate it. Having had time together like this, it just being us without any outside pressure, has done me good. I needed to know that we worked – that we weren't just some fantasy that I'd clung onto that could never become a reality."

He closed his arms around her waist and smiled down at her. "I'll give you a fantasy you can cling onto if you like."

She laughed and slapped his arm. "You know what I mean!" She pressed herself against him. "Although I might take you up on that later."

"I'll hold you to that."

She looked down at the way their bodies were pressed up against each other. "I think you're holding me to it now."

He chuckled and let her go. "You're right, you know. I think we should enjoy this morning because the rest of the weekend could get rough."

She made a face at him. "Maybe they'll be okay with it?"

"Maybe. I have a feeling that it might be a long road to win them over to the idea." He blew out a sigh. "And even if they're okay with the idea of us being together, I can only imagine that they're going to be mad at me for hiding it from them."

Laney felt bad. "Let me explain to them that I wouldn't let you tell them."

He shook his head. "No. I had a choice, Laney. I had a choice, and I chose to go with what you wanted." He pressed a kiss to her forehead. "I need you to know that's the choice I'll always make going forward. I hope the guys will understand, but even if they don't, I can't regret choosing you over them."

A heavy weight settled in Laney's stomach. "I hate that, though. I mean, don't get me wrong, I love that you're putting me first. But I hate that you have to choose. I just hope that they can get used to the idea, and you won't ever have to choose again." She looked up into his eyes. "I know they're important to you, too. Especially Tanner."

"They are." He let go of her and smiled. "I just want to get on with it now, get it over with."

"I was thinking that we should ask them all to go to Chico tonight. We can tell them there."

Luke raised his eyebrows. "Yeah? I was thinking that we should go over to the ranch. You know there are probably going to be fists involved, right?"

Laney rolled her eyes. "You're not kids anymore. You don't need to solve everything with your fists."

Luke chuckled. "Believe me, I know. But old habits die hard. We grew up together, punching it out when we needed to. I fully expect that's the way this will go."

"Then is Chico a bad idea? I don't want you getting arrested for brawling in public."

Luke smiled through pursed lips. "Like I said, I think it'd be better at the ranch."

"I guess I should give them a call and see if we can go over there, then."

Luke looked resigned as he nodded.

She closed the stall and wheeled the barrow back outside before taking hold of his hand. "You look like a man ready to go to the gallows. I think it'd probably be best if we take a shower before I call them."

A small smile played on his lips. "I like that idea. If I was going to the gallows, you would be my last request."

"You say the sweetest things," she said with a laugh as she took his hand and led him back up to the house.

~ ~ ~

It was early afternoon by the time they made it back downstairs. Luke checked his watch and gave Laney a rueful smile.

"What do you think, shall we get this over with? Should I call Tanner and ask if we can come over?"

She nodded slowly. "You can call, but I don't know if we'll catch them all together yet. We might have to wait until this evening."

"Probably, but I'd rather call and set it up now. If they're around, I'd rather get it over with. But even if we have to wait until later, I'd rather talk to them before they decide that they're going out."

"Yeah, you're right. Although I'm still not sure that it wouldn't be better to just meet up with them at Chico."

Luke shook his head – he really didn't like that idea. "Let's give them a call and see."

Laney pulled her phone out. "Do you want me to do it?"

"No. I know they're your brothers, but I feel like I need to be the one to do this. Is that okay with you?"

"Yeah." She made a face at him. "I'm trying to be respectful of the whole man-to-man thing, but can you put it on speaker?"

He nodded reluctantly. He knew damn well how angry she could get at her brothers when she thought they weren't being reasonable. He was hoping this wouldn't get out of hand.

She gave him a shamefaced smile. "I'll be good – I promise. And besides, it's not as though we're going to tell them about us on the phone right now, is it? We're just setting up going to see them, right? We're going to tell them that we have something we want to talk to them about, aren't we?"

She was right. Luke knew that he would have to look his friends – her brothers – in the eye to tell them this. It wasn't something he wanted to do over the phone.

He hit Tanner's number and then pressed the speaker before setting his phone down on the kitchen table.

Tanner answered on the third ring. "Hey, bud, what's up? Are we on for tonight? I'm not working behind the bar this weekend."

"Yeah, I did want to talk to you about tonight – but not about going out."

"What then?" Tanner asked. "What's up?"

"Laney and I were wondering if we could come over there this evening. We want to talk to you." His throat was dry. Tanner had been his best friend since they were in grade school. He could only hope that this would work out okay.

He could hear voices in the background when Tanner spoke again. "Sure, we can all hang out here if you want. In fact, that might be better. That way, Wade and Sierra can come and bring the kids, too." He chuckled. "I'm surprised that Laney wants to come here, though. How's she doing?"

"Hey, Tan. I'm here," she said. "We're on speaker."

Tanner laughed. "Damn, Luke, you could have told me. I might have gone and put my foot in it."

Laney narrowed her eyes at Luke. "Put your foot in it how?"

Tanner laughed again. "You know what I mean, Laney-Lou. I might have gone talking about our plans for this evening. The kind of plans that won't be possible if we hang out here at home."

"Well, I'm sorry to spoil your fun, but the ladies will have to do without you for once. Is everyone around? Will they all be there?"

"Janey's out of town. She and Rocket have gone away for the weekend. Other than that, everyone's here. Ty was planning on coming out with us. Ford even said that he might, too. I don't know what Wade and Sierra are up to, but they never venture far at the weekends – not with the kids."

"Okay, what time should we come?" asked Laney.

"Damn, girl. I don't know. You don't need an invitation, do you?"

Laney rolled her eyes at Luke. "No, I don't suppose I do."

Luke wasn't surprised when Tanner finally asked, "What do you guys want to talk about, anyway?"

He swallowed. "We've got something we want to run by you."

"Something to do with the horses? If you've ironed out the kinks in the three you have, I'll happily trade them out for three more."

"No, it's not about the horses."

Tanner laughed. "So, tell me already! It's not like you to play guessing games, Luke. Although, then again, it is like *you*, Laney. What's up, bud? Did she put you up to something?"

Luke covered his eyes with his hand. "I guess you could say that."

Laney smiled at him and shook her head.

"Hang on a minute."

He heard Tanner cover the phone with his hand and they waited while he had a muffled conversation – Luke assumed it was with Ty and Ford.

"I'll have to talk to Wade, but the three of us will be here and ready to hang out any time after about six thirty. Just come on over whenever you guys are ready."

"Okay," said Luke. "We'll see you around seven then?"

"Sure, see you then. And, Laney?"

"Yeah?"

Tanner laughed. "Don't you go getting this guy in trouble, will you?"

Luke's breath caught in his chest, but Laney just laughed. "Why am I always the one who gets blamed for the trouble?"

"Because you're usually the one who causes it – and don't deny it. I'll see you later."

Tanner ended the call, and the two of them stood there staring at each other.

"Step one accomplished," said Laney.

Luke nodded. "Yeah, now I just wish that we had a fast-forward button to get through steps two, three, four, and five."

"Do you really think there are that many more steps to go?"

Luke shrugged. He didn't know how many steps remained, but he wasn't looking forward to any of them.

~ ~ ~

Laney looked over at Luke as she pulled the Jeep out onto East River Rd. "It'll be okay you know."

He nodded and smiled and squeezed her hand, but he didn't say anything, and the look on his face told her that he wasn't so sure.

She was nervous herself now that the time was finally here. She was grateful that Luke was as easy-going as he was. She'd told him that she wanted to drive, and he hadn't argued. He'd always been like that – he'd never minded letting her take charge, or take the lead, when she felt like she needed to be in control. Even when they were younger, her brothers, and pretty much every other guy she'd ever known, had all felt like they should be the one to drive – just because they were guys. She liked to think that Luke was so sure of himself that he didn't need to assert his manhood in such petty ways.

"We could tell them that this has just happened since I've been back. You know, that since we've been spending so much time together this has just developed out of the blue."

He squeezed her hand again, but this time he shook his head. "No."

She had to laugh. "That's it? Just, no?"

He gave her a rueful smile. "Sorry. I didn't mean to bite your head off. But I can't do that. This has laid heavy on me all these years. Now that I finally get to come clean, I have to be completely honest with them."

She sucked in a deep breath. "Are you sure? I understand why, but is it worth it? What if they can't get over it?"

She hated to ask and hated to see the pain etched into the lines around his eyes.

He shrugged. "That's a chance I'll have to take."

"They will – they'll come around." She gave him the brightest smile she could muster. "Who knows, they could be thrilled for us."

"We can hope. I just …"

The sound of Laney's phone ringing cut him off. "Could you grab that for me? It's in my purse."

Luke found the phone in her purse and handed it over, but it stopped ringing. She gave it back to him.

"Could you check to see who it was?"

"Tom." He ground out that one syllable in an icy tone.

She glanced over at him. "That's my boss," she explained. "My old boss. The guy I worked for in Kentucky for the last few years."

Luke nodded. "Sorry. I didn't mean to be an asshole. It was just seeing a guy's name on your phone like that when we're about to face your brothers…"

"It's okay. I get it. But you've got nothing to worry about there." The phone started ringing again, and he held it out to her. "No, thanks. I'll let it go to voicemail. Whatever he wants, I can talk to him tomorrow."

Luke looked at the screen. "It's not him again, it's Frankie."

"Oh. In that case, can you put her on speaker? Hey, Frankie. What's up?"

"Where are you?"

"On our way to the ranch, why?"

"Is Luke with you?"

"Yes. Why? What's up?"

"Holy crap! Are you going to finally tell them?"

Laney glanced over at Luke and smiled. "Yes, we are."

"Under any other circumstances I'd say good for you, but you might want to change your mind when you hear what I have to say."

"Why?"

"I'm calling you because Mav just turned up unannounced at our place. You know how they do that sometimes?"

Laney's heart started to race, and her knuckles turned white as she gripped the steering wheel. "*They?*"

"Yeah, girlfriend, *they* are both here. When Mav showed up here, the first thing I asked was if Cash is with him. He is; Mav said that Cash headed straight to the ranch to surprise the guys. I don't even know if he knows that you're here. But I figured if he turned up at Luke's place looking for you, he might be the one who was in for a surprise."

Laney pulled the Jeep over to the side of the road. "Shit!"

Frankie chuckled. "You're welcome."

Luke frowned at Laney as she set out again pulling a U-turn away from the ranch.

"Thanks, Frankie. I'll call you."

"Make sure you do. Let me know if I can help."

Laney ended the call and looked over at Luke. "There's no way we can go to the ranch if Cash is there. It's one thing to tell the rest of them, I was thinking that we'd have time to work our way up to telling him."

"I think we should still go, baby. We might as well get it over with."

She shook her head rapidly. "No way. I haven't talked to him in a while; he's mad at me anyway. I can't, Luke. We'll have to do something else instead."

"Like what?"

She shrugged. "Like live to see tomorrow for starters."

Luke let out a short laugh. "Come on, Laney. It's probably better this way. This way we tell them all together in one go, then we can start moving forward – and dealing with their reactions."

Laney drove all the way to Chico before she stopped. She found a space in the parking lot, and after she cut the engine, she rested her arms on the steering wheel. "If you still want to do it, then we can do it tomorrow. Let's have tonight to just enjoy ourselves?"

He held her gaze for a long moment before shaking his head. "You really think we're going to be able to enjoy ourselves here while your whole family is sitting at the ranch waiting for us to show up?"

He had a point. "We can call them – tell them that I changed my mind about going to the ranch. They'll believe that – and it's not a lie anyway, it's just not for the reason that they think. If they want to come and meet us here, they can. And Cash is less likely to kill you here in a public place than he is on the ranch."

Luke blew out a sigh. "Is this really how you want to play it?"

She reached across and rested her hand on his arm. "No. At this point, I think I'd rather we run away to Siberia or somewhere, but out of all the options available to us right now – and by that, I mean us going to the ranch, Cash and the rest of them coming out to your place looking for us, or hoping to survive the night here on neutral ground, I choose here."

"Okay then." He took his phone out of his pocket, but she stopped him.

"I'll make the call. I'll tell them. This one's on me."

Chapter Thirteen

Luke grasped his beer as he stood, leaning back against the bar. He was pissed. He wasn't pissed at Laney, but at the way this whole evening had worked out. He wouldn't claim that he'd been looking forward to facing the guys, but he had been looking forward to finally getting things out in the open.

Granted, he'd half expected to be getting pummeled by now – most likely by Tyler, probably by Ford, and possibly worst of all by Tanner. Hanging out here at Chico was an easier option, but it was only easier in the short term, physical sense. He'd still have to face their anger, and there was no way this was easier emotionally.

He glared out at the dance floor where Laney was dancing with Frankie and a couple of her friends. He narrowed his eyes when he saw Nixon standing close by, watching her. Luke was going to have to be careful not to take his frustration out on that guy tonight. It'd be all too easy to go over there and land his fist in the middle of Nixon's face.

He sucked in a deep breath in an attempt to calm himself, but it didn't work, not when he recognized Nixon's older brother Buck, standing with him. Luke might not want to admit it, but Nix was a good guy. However, the same couldn't be said for Buck. The guy was an asshole of the first degree. If he so much as looked at Laney in the wrong way, Luke was going to...

He jumped and almost dropped his beer when a hand came down on his shoulder. His heart started to pound when he turned and saw Laney's eldest brother, Cash, frowning at him.

"Luke."

"Cash."

Luke couldn't think of a damned thing to say to him. All he wanted to do was blurt out the truth. He didn't know how much more of this he could take. Tanner and Tyler had been easy enough to handle when they arrived – they'd just joked with him that he was letting Laney jerk him and them around, and mess with everyone's plans. But they'd been happy enough to be here since this had been their original plan for the evening anyway. Ford hadn't come out with them, and Luke knew that he would still have to face him at some point. But for now, the rest of them paled into insignificance compared with having to face Cash.

Cash cocked an eyebrow at him. "I heard that you and Laney were supposed to be coming to the ranch tonight."

Luke nodded.

"So, how come we're here?"

"She changed her mind." It wasn't a lie.

Cash narrowed his eyes, and his grip on Luke's shoulder tightened. "Were you planning on telling them?"

Luke's heart thudded to a halt. "Telling who what?"

Cash threw back his head and laughed. "What do you think?"

Luke's mind was scrambling, trying to catch up. Did Cash know? Or was there a catch? Was he trying to catch him out?

"I think you should tell me what you mean."

Cash shook his head and then jerked his chin toward the dance floor. "I mean Laney. You don't need me to explain. I know. I've always known. Right now, that's not the most important thing." He jerked his chin toward the dance floor again, and this time Luke followed his gaze.

Shit! Buck was dancing behind Laney, and as they watched, he put his hands on her hips and started to grind against her.

Cash pushed away from the bar at the same moment that Luke set his beer down and took a step forward.

Cash laughed. "If you don't get your ass over there and punch him, I will. And if I do it, she'll be mad at both of us."

Luke only hesitated for a second. Cash nodded at him. "I've known about the two of you since the night you spent in Great Falls when you were kids. I've waited a long time for this. But go on, I'll help you with the rest of them later – after you've dealt with that asshole."

Luke's gaze was locked on Laney and Buck. He didn't even have time to fully process what Cash had said as he elbowed his way across the dance floor. Laney was trying to push Buck away, but he was still pawing at her. Luke got in between the two of them and wrapped his hand around Buck's throat.

"What the fuck? What's your problem? I'm not doing anything wrong. She's single."

Luke's fist landed in the middle of his face as he growled out, "No, she's not. She's mine. Don't you dare ever touch her again."

As Buck tried to scramble back to his feet, Nixon grabbed his arms and dragged him away.

A fistfight was nothing unusual for Chico on a Saturday night, and Luke had only thrown a single punch – the whole scene barely registered as a disturbance, and people continued to dance around them.

Not everyone was still dancing, though. Laney and Frankie were standing there staring at him, as were a couple of their friends. Laney stepped toward him, and he couldn't help it, he wrapped his arm around her.

"Are you okay?"

She smiled up at him. "I'm fine, thanks. I could've handled him."

He didn't even stop to think what he was doing; he lowered his head, and she rolled up on her tiptoes to meet him in a kiss.

"Oh my God!" squealed Millie Jennings, one of Laney's old school friends. "You guys are together? That's awesome! Did you see that?" she shouted to Kelsey, another friend who was standing beside her.

Kelsey grinned at her. "See it? I'm going to be telling everyone about it for weeks."

She grinned at Laney. "You lucky bitch! We've all tried to land Luke Wallis over the years. Seeing him punch that guy and then be all growly like that, saying, *she's mine?*" She fanned herself with her hand. "Damn! Is all I can say."

"It's all I can say, too," said a deep voice from behind Luke.

He spun around and found himself face-to-face with Tanner and Tyler. Shit!

He met Tyler's gaze first and nodded. Then, he turned to his oldest, dearest friend, Tanner.

Laney leaned closer into his side and wrapped her arm around his waist. He kept his arm around her shoulders as he faced them.

Under other circumstances, Tanner's shocked expression would have been comical. But Luke didn't feel like laughing, he felt like an asshole.

"What the fuck, dude?"

"I fucking knew it," Tyler spat out.

"Hey, now!" Laney held her hand up and started to take a step forward, but Luke held her back. Yes, she had her own deal with them – they were her brothers. But right now, he hoped that she would understand that he really didn't want her defending him.

"I can't say I'm sorry." He looked down at Laney, and she smiled back up at him. "We've been wanting to tell you for a while."

Laney let out a short laugh beside him. "That's not completely true. Luke's been wanting to tell you for a long time. I wouldn't let him."

Tyler shook his head and glared at Luke. "So, what? You're going to hide behind her and blame her?"

"No. I'm not. I'll take all the blame. I should have told you guys years ago."

Tanner's eyes grew even wider – he was evidently struggling to take it all in. "Years ago? How many years ago?"

Luke swallowed. "A lot of years ago. Before Laney left."

Tyler stepped forward and landed a punch on his jaw. Laney tried to lunge at him, but Luke managed to hold onto her as he staggered backward.

When he recovered, he nodded. "I deserve that, and I know it."

"Too damn right you do," said Tyler.

Tanner's punch landed in the middle of Luke's face without warning. "You deserve that, too."

Luke squeezed his eyes shut and somehow managed to remain upright. This was the least he'd expected. He was going to stand and take it like a man.

Laney screamed and launched herself at Tanner. This time Luke couldn't manage to hang onto her, but Cash appeared out of nowhere and wrapped his arm around her middle, swinging her away so that she couldn't inflict any damage.

"Are you guys done?" Cash scowled at his brothers.

"Done?" Tyler scoffed. "We haven't even started. And you'll join right in with us when you hear this shit."

Tanner was shaking his head as he held Luke's gaze. "I can't believe it." He swung again out of nowhere and landed another punch – Luke heard his nose crunch, and his hands came up to cover his face.

"You and Laney?" Tanner asked in an incredulous voice. "You're *screwing* my sister?"

Luke did his best to stanch the flow of blood from his nose as he met his friend's gaze. "I love your sister. I always have."

Even as the music played, and people danced all around them, the silence that fell on the small group of them standing there was almost tangible.

Tanner's eyes grew wider still. "Say what?"

"You heard him, dumbass!" said Cash. "How the hell you never figured it out before now is beyond me. He loves her. He's always loved her. It's been plain as day since you were all kids."

He still had one arm wrapped around Laney, although she'd stopped struggling against him now. She looked up at him, her mouth hanging open before she pulled herself together and asked, "You knew?"

Cash laughed. "Yes, I damn well knew. I never wanted to interfere, but damn, baby girl. I can't tell you the number of times I've wanted to give you a shake or kick your ass and tell you to get your act together and get over yourself. I was starting to worry that you might let this guy get away."

Luke swallowed, wondering whether he was hearing right or if the blows to the head had him hallucinating and hearing what he wanted to hear.

"You love her?" Tanner asked into the silence that had fallen again.

Luke gave his friend a grim smile. "I do. I love you, too, brother. But Laney …"

She broke free of Cash and went back to his side. Standing there with their arms around each other, Luke finally started to relax.

He tensed when Tanner lunged toward him again, but this time instead of throwing a punch, he wrapped him in a hug.

"Why the fuck didn't you tell me?"

Luke rubbed his jaw and then dabbed at the blood streaming from his nose with his sleeve and let out a short laugh. "Err, I dunno, Tan. Why do you think?"

Tanner shoved at his arm. "It would have been different if I'd known … If I'd known that …" He grinned at Luke and then turned to Laney and shook his head in wonder. "And you love him too?" he asked. "You'd better be good to him, Laney-Lou. He's my best friend."

Laney laughed and pulled Luke against her. "Don't worry, I plan to."

Luke looked around. He couldn't believe how well this was working out. Cash, it seemed, had known all along – and was good with it. Tanner had come around faster than he could have hoped possible. And Ty … He frowned. Ty had disappeared.

Cash grasped his shoulder. "Come on, big fella. Let's get you cleaned up."

Laney kept her arm around his waist as Cash went ahead, clearing them a path across the dance floor – people tended to get out of his way to let him pass.

They were almost back to the bar when Luke spotted Ty again. He stalked toward them, and Luke braced himself when he raised his hand.

Tyler chuckled. "Ice." He held out a bag of it, wrapped in a bar towel. "I reckon you're going to need it."

"Thanks. Are we good?"

Tyler smiled through pursed lips. "We'll see. I think I made my opinion clear, but that was about how you handled things so far. I reckon we've got a clean slate going forward, so it's up to you now."

He held his hand out, and as Luke shook it, Tyler pulled him in for a one-armed hug and slapped his back. "I reckon I might like this idea once I get used to it."

Cash reached out and slapped the back of Tyler's head. "Get over yourself, squirt. Let the man get himself cleaned up."

~ ~ ~

Later that night, Laney snuggled into Luke's side as he lay on his back in bed.

"I know it's easy for me to say, but I think it went well."

She had to smile at the snort he let out. "I can't disagree."

"I'll still love you tomorrow, even though your face is all messed up."

He tightened his arm around her. "Good to know. It'd be a bummer if you left me now because they ruined my good looks."

She laughed and pushed at his shoulder. "Modest, huh?"

He laughed with her. "Yes, ma'am. That'd be me. Just a modest, unassuming kind of guy."

She propped herself up on her elbow so that she could look down into his eyes. "You're an amazing guy, Luke. The best guy I've ever known, and I love you."

He reached up and tucked a strand of hair behind her ear. "I love you, too, baby."

"Are you sure you want to go over there tomorrow? Maybe you need to rest up after my brothers treated you as their own personal punching bag."

"No. I'm sure. I want to go. Cash is there – how often do we get to see him home?"

"True, and Frankie said that she and Spider are going to bring Mav over, too. I just hope the rest of them aren't going to have a problem. I can't help feeling relieved right now, but we've only won half the battle, haven't we? We still have to face Ford and Wade – oh shit! And Kolby."

Luke nodded but then put his hand up to his head. "Shit. I shouldn't have done that."

She soothed her hand over his hair. "Aww, poor baby. I'll take care of you."

"I'm good. It's all okay. I have to be honest with you; this hurts a whole lot less than the stress I've been carrying around for the last few weeks."

She pressed a gentle kiss to his forehead. "I'm sorry. I'm sorry I put you through that. I just wanted to be sure."

He caught her hand and brought it down to rest against his heart, covering it with his own. "Are you sure now? Is this what you want – am I what you want?"

She wanted to joke and pretend that she wasn't sure, but she couldn't do it; her eyes filled with tears as she nodded at him. "I've never been more sure of anything in my life. You're all I've ever wanted, Luke."

He curled his arm around her and hugged her to his chest. She tried to be careful, but he chuckled. "It's only my face that hurts. The rest of me's fine. I didn't take any body blows – which surprises me with those two."

"That's true." She swung her leg over him and sat up to straddle him. "So, I won't do any damage if I want to go for a ride, will I?"

His fingers dug into her hips as he rocked her against him. "Nope. You won't do any damage. In fact, I think it might be part of the healing process – you might need to do it regularly."

She laughed and rested her hands on his shoulders as she leaned down to kiss him. "Do you think this is going to be a very lengthy healing process?" she asked when she finally lifted her head.

"I do. I think it'll last for years and years – probably the rest of my life. Are you signing up for that?"

Her heart felt as though it exploded in her chest. He was asking her to spend the rest of her life with him? Of course, that was where she hoped this was going. In her mind, it was the unspoken aim that they'd shared ever since she came back – but to hear him say it out loud?

She pressed a quick kiss to his lips when she saw the concern on his face. She'd taken too long to answer. "I'm signing up.

I'm signing up to heal you through this life and through the next one if we get the chance."

His expression gentled, and he nodded. "The rest of our lives, baby. That's what I want. To spend them together."

She nodded as his hands tightened around her hips and he lifted her. She curled her fingers around him, guiding him into her.

"I love you, Laney," he breathed as she impaled herself on him.

"Forever," she gasped as they began to move together.

Chapter Fourteen

Luke had been to plenty of Sunday lunches at the MacFarland ranch over the years, but today was different. Today was a day that he'd feared would never come – even though he'd also feared what would happen if it did. He was here with Laney. Tanner and Tyler were already over their shock at the news and had teased him from the moment he arrived. Cash had welcomed him in a way that surprised him – it seemed that *he* had been rooting for them all along.

Luke started toward the door when he saw Ford's truck pull up outside. Ford was the last brother he'd have to face today. Wade and Sierra had taken the kids up to some event in town – and Wade already knew anyway. Kolby was a different matter – he and Laney had been super close when they were kids, but he hadn't been home for more than a day or two at a time in years. Luke couldn't claim that he knew him all that well, but he wasn't too worried.

Laney caught hold of his hand as he passed the kitchen where she was talking to Ty. "Where are you going?" she asked with a laugh. "Have you decided that you can't handle it after all?"

He smiled at her. "You know better than that. Ford just arrived; I figured I'd catch him before he comes in."

She took a step to join him, but he shook his head. "Do you mind if I do this alone? I'd like to give him the chance to speak freely, and knowing Ford, he may not do that if you're there."

Laney made a face. "That's exactly why I was planning on coming with you."

"I've got this. It'll be okay."

She reached up and pressed a gentle kiss to his cheek. "Okay, but I'll be watching, and if he starts, I'll be right out there."

Cash laughed behind her and wrapped his arm around her middle, dragging her away. "No, you won't, honey. You stay here."

"But Cash …"

Cash winked at Luke over the top of her head. "Go, while you can."

Luke hurried out and met Ford on the front porch just as he was coming up the steps. Ford frowned when he saw him.

"The guys told me," he said without preamble.

Luke nodded. "I expected that they would. I want to apologize for hiding it from you guys, but I won't apologize that …" He shrugged and looked Ford in the eye. "I love her."

Ford held his gaze for a long moment, and Luke braced himself, not knowing what to expect but wanting to be prepared. He was already bruised up from last night, but if he had to take another hit, he'd take it.

Ford chuckled. "Do you really think I'd punch you? Have you seen your face?"

Luke gave him a rueful smile. "I've tried not to look."

Ford nodded. "Wise move. Listen, Luke. I'm too old to go punching you in the mouth. I wouldn't want to anyway – if you want to know the truth, I like the idea of you and Laney together. I won't lie; it took me by surprise. But perhaps it shouldn't have. I'm not going to give you a hard time; it's not like we're kids. All I'll say is, be good to her. Life's too short and love is too hard. If the two of you have a shot at building something good, then good luck to you. If I can help, let me know. And if it doesn't work out ... Like I said, just don't hurt her."

"Thanks. I've hated keeping it a secret from you guys. But I'm not blaming Laney," he added hurriedly. "She wanted to take our time before we said anything, and I can't blame her for that." He swallowed. He could just leave it at that, but he wasn't a coward. "I was the one who didn't want to say anything when we were younger. I was scared of how you guys would react." He rubbed his hand over his swollen jaw. "Of what you would do to me."

"Well, it seems to me as though you've already suffered enough for the choices you made back then."

Luke met his gaze and nodded. "I've regretted letting her go since the day she left."

Ford smiled. "Well, it seems to me that you've got a second chance that not many people get. Don't screw it up."

"I don't intend to."

Ford's smile faded. "I'm not sure anyone ever does, but it happens." He jerked his chin toward the house. "I know they all think that I'm the silent, broody, antisocial one of the bunch, but if you ever feel like there's something you need to say but you can't tell anyone, you come tell me, okay?"

Luke nodded.

Ford laughed and slapped his shoulder. "Don't look so skeptical. I'm not saying that I won't be as pissed at you as the rest of them if something goes wrong – I'm just saying that I won't punch you."

Luke laughed with him. "I appreciate that." He'd always liked Ford, but he didn't feel as though he knew him as well as the others. He was a bit older, and the way he'd just described himself – as silent, broody, and antisocial, compared to the others – was pretty accurate in Luke's experience. And that just made his offer even more meaningful.

They went inside, and when they reached the kitchen, Ty raised an eyebrow at Ford. "You're not going to give him a hard time?"

Ford shook his head. "Why would I?" He shot a smile at Laney. "If he's fool enough – or brave enough, I'm not sure which it is – to want to be with Laney, then I reckon he's in for enough hard times."

"Hey!" Laney lunged at him and slapped his arm. "That's not nice!"

Ford caught her and swung her around as he laughed. "Prove my point, why don't you?"

She smiled up at him. "You know you love me, really."

"Yeah. I do. And I'll tell you the same thing that I just told Luke. Don't screw it up."

Laney shot a glance at Luke as she said, "I don't plan to."

Luke leaned back against the counter, watching as Laney and the guys finished getting lunch ready and setting the table.

After a while, Cash came to stand beside him. He folded his arms across his chest, and Luke waited for him to speak, but he didn't.

When he couldn't take it anymore, Luke turned to look at him. "Go on, say it, whatever it is."

Cash's light green eyes twinkled as he smiled at him. "I've got nothing to say. I just wanted to make you squirm."

Luke had to laugh. "Mission accomplished."

Cash slapped his shoulder. "You've got no worries with me. I've been looking forward to this day."

"Thanks."

Cash jerked his chin toward Laney. "There's no need to thank me. We both know you've got your work cut out for you with her."

Luke had to smile; he knew what Cash meant, but he didn't agree. "I don't see it that way."

"She's not exactly easy."

Luke laughed. "I wouldn't want her to be. She's Laney – she strong, she's smart, and she knows her own mind."

Cash chuckled. "It's good to know you've mastered diplomacy ahead of time. Most people would say that she's stubborn and strong-willed."

"Perhaps. But then, most people don't know her the way I do."

Cash's expression sobered as he met Luke's gaze. "That's what I wanted to hear. I figured that you must really know her. You know who she is underneath the façade, right?"

Luke nodded slowly. "I wouldn't say that. I've never thought of it that way before – I don't think of it as a façade. But yeah, I know what you mean. With the rest of the world, she's smart, strong – the feisty, capable cowgirl. And sure, I love that side of her. But when it's just us, she's … I don't know how to describe it. It's like she knows she doesn't need to be the strong one."

Cash watched Laney across the room as she joked with Tanner and slapped the back of Ty's head. "Exactly. She trusts you to be strong for her. She doesn't need to be when you're around. That's why I've always held out hope for the two of you. I've never seen her that way with anyone else. You're what she needs."

Luke had to swallow and clear his throat before he could speak again. "I don't think I realized that until you just told me. But now that I do, I promise you I'll always do my best to be strong for her – to be her safe place."

~ ~ ~

Laney sat back in her chair and folded her hands over her stomach. "That was amazing, thanks, Ty. I'm stuffed."

"Well, don't get too comfortable just because you've eaten too much," said Tanner. "You're helping with dishes. You're not getting out of it."

Laney rolled her eyes at him. "I will. Just give me a minute."

Tyler grinned at Luke. "I hope you know what you're in for. She gets real lazy about helping out around the house."

Laney threw her napkin at him, but Ty just laughed. "What? You can't say it isn't true. You know, I wasn't sure how I felt about the two of you being together. But I'm starting to think it could be fun." He shot Laney an evil grin. "I can blackmail you by threatening to tell Luke all your dirty secrets and annoying little habits."

Laney just rolled her eyes at him. "He knows all my secrets, and I'm not annoying, am I?" She directed the question at Luke but looked around when laughter erupted all around the table. "What?"

Cash shook his head at her but didn't stop smirking. "You can't go doing that to him, honey. You might not annoy him – yet. But you're setting him up to lose either way. If he agrees with you, these guys will give him hell. And if he doesn't agree with you…" He winked at Luke. "I know which option I'd choose, buddy."

Laney pushed away from the table and stuck her tongue out at all of them. "I can't win with you guys, can I? I might as well just go and do the dishes."

She took her plate and Luke's through to the kitchen and started to rinse them. She had to dry her hands and run to get her phone from her purse when she heard it ringing.

She felt guilty when she saw Tom's name on the screen. She'd meant to call him back this morning, but with everything that had happened, she hadn't even bothered to check the voicemail that he'd left last night.

"Hey, Tom. How are things?"

"Didn't you get my message?"

"No. Sorry. I saw that you left one, but things have been a little crazy around here. What's up?"

Tom blew out a sigh. "I need you back. I know you said that you'd let me know what your plans were at the end of the month. I know you were thinking about maybe not coming back. But Tony was in a car wreck yesterday."

"Oh my God! Is he okay?"

"He will be. But not for a while. It sounds like he's got a long stretch in the hospital ahead of him. I can't function with you both gone. The place will fall apart, the program needs one or the other of you to be here. It can't be Tony, so it has to be you. Please," he added as if it were an afterthought.

Laney's heart pounded. Tom had been so good to her over the years. He'd given her a chance when no one else in town had been prepared to. It was hard to break your way into the racing world as a woman. And she knew that it had been almost as hard on Tom as it had been on her. Plenty of people had told him that he was a fool, but he'd believed in her, and ignored them.

"Are you still there?"

"Yeah. I just… When do you need me?" This couldn't be worse timing. She and Luke finally had everything together, they even had her family in their corner. They should be free and clear to make a start on building a life together, but she couldn't let Tom down. Not after everything he'd done for her.

"Yesterday," was Tom's short reply.

"Oh."

Tom blew out a sigh. "I wouldn't ask if I had any other choice, Laney. I've been expecting your call any day to tell me that you don't want a new contract. But you know how things are here; with Tony out, I need you."

Luke came into the kitchen and stopped in his tracks when he saw the expression on her face. "Is everything okay?" he asked in a low voice as he came to her.

She shook her head slowly. This so could not be happening – but it was.

Luke started to look concerned, and one by one, her brothers joined him, until all of them were standing there looking at her, wearing matching concerned expressions.

Her heart pounded in her chest, but there was nothing for it. "I'll be there," she told Tom.

She could hear the relief in his voice when he said, "Thanks, Laney. Let me know when you've booked your flight. I'll make sure the apartment over the tack room's ready for you. You gave up your apartment, right?"

"Yeah. I'll let you know when I'll be arriving." She ended the call and stood there staring back at them.

Luke stepped forward and put a hand on her arm. "What is it, Laney? What's wrong?"

"I have to go back to Kentucky."

"What the fuck, Laney?" Tanner asked. "You can't do this – not to Luke, and not to us. You can't go around telling us all that you're in love with him, and then go running back to Kentucky. No. Just no. That's all wrong."

"Button it, Tanner," said Cash.

Laney ignored them as she looked up into Luke's eyes. The hurt and confusion that she saw there killed her. "I need to explain."

"Too damn right, you do," said Ty.

"Jesus, guys! Grow the fuck up, would you?" Cash growled. Laney was vaguely aware of him steering the others out of the kitchen, leaving her and Luke alone.

"What's going on, Laney?" he asked when they'd gone.

"That was Tom on the phone. Remember, he left me a message last night? I didn't check to see what he wanted. He needs me to go back. Tony, his other trainer, was in a car wreck yesterday. Tom needs someone there to run the program – and right now, I'm his only option."

"What? When?" Luke shook his head as if to clear it. "How long …"

She slipped her arms around his waist and looked up into his eyes. "Not long. I promise. I wouldn't go but Tom has done so much for me, I can't let him down when he needs me. I… Do you understand? Can it… Will you? Dammit! I want to ask if you'll wait for me, but I don't know…" She shook her head. "I can't believe that I put you through all that with my brothers for nothing."

Luke's eyebrows drew together. "It wasn't for nothing, Laney. I told you that I wanted them to know. I told you I'd put up with anything they wanted to say or do just for even a tiny chance with you. And unless you're telling me it is, then this isn't goodbye. I haven't waited all these years just to let you go again now."

"But I don't know how long I need to be there for."

"It doesn't matter."

She felt as though her heart might break in two. Tears welled up in her eyes as she asked, "It doesn't matter?"

His expression gentled as he ran his hand over her hair. "No. It doesn't matter, because I'll wait as long as it takes. We can do the long-distance thing. And if it turns out that you need to stay there, then I'll move there to be with you. I'm not giving you up this time."

Laney sagged against him, all the tension leaving her when she understood what he was saying. "It won't be forever, hopefully not for long. I just... I'm sorry, but I can't let him down."

Luke pressed a kiss to her forehead. "You don't need to say you're sorry. You do what's right, and you're loyal, those are just some of the many things I love about you. It might not be working out in my favor right now. But baby, don't ever apologize for being you."

They both looked up when Cash popped his head back around the kitchen door. "Everything okay in here?"

Laney leaned into Luke's side, and he tightened his arm around her. "It will be," she said.

Cash took a step into the room, and Laney wasn't surprised to see the others close on his heels.

"Anything I can do to help?"

She shrugged. "I don't think so."

After she'd explained to them what was going on, she wasn't surprised that they all understood. She hated the thought of being away from Luke now that they were finally together, but he was right; she had to do the right thing – even when it didn't suit her – it was in her nature. As she looked around at her brothers, she realized that it was a family trait.

~ ~ ~

Luke couldn't believe that less than twenty-four hours after finally coming clean with her family – and thinking that they finally had a clear road ahead of them – he was now standing beside Laney at the airport, getting ready to say goodbye.

It had all happened so fast, he felt like he still needed to catch up. Cash had pulled him aside after Laney had broken her news and told him that he was flying back to his home base this evening. Cash and Mav had a company jet that they used when they came to visit. He'd told Luke that they could drop Laney off in Kentucky if she wanted to go with them tonight – if Luke was good with that.

Luke appreciated that Cash wanted to forewarn him, but it wasn't his decision to make. If she felt she needed to leave today, then he'd live with it. No way would he ask Cash to leave her behind, just so that he could have her for one more night.

As they stood there waiting in the general aviation building, Luke tightened his arm around her. He couldn't believe that he had to let her go again already.

There were tears in her eyes when she looked up at him. "God, I hate this! I'm so sorry."

He made himself smile and dropped a kiss on her lips. "It's okay, baby. It's not your fault, is it? You're doing what you need to do. I understand that. Hopefully, it won't be for too long. And no matter how long it is, I'll wait for you." He pecked her lips again. "I'll come visit you."

She wrapped her arms tightly around him. "I hope it won't be for long. I'll come back to you as soon as I can. I promise."

Luke could see Cash lurking by the doors that led out to the tarmac. It was time. His heart felt as though it might beat out of his chest. He wanted to scoop her up in his arms and carry her out of here, run away with her back to his place, back to the horses, and to the life that he'd hoped that they were starting to build.

Instead, he wrapped her up in one last hug and pressed a kiss to the top of her head. "I told you, baby. It doesn't matter how long it takes. I'll wait for you forever."

It broke his heart to see the tears streaming down her face as she walked away from him. Cash wrapped his arm around her shoulders when she reached him. She turned back and gave Luke a weak smile. He blew her a kiss, then watched them disappear through the doors. Once they'd gone, he hurried back out to his truck.

Chapter Fifteen

Laney opened her eyes and lay there, staring at the ceiling. She wanted to believe that this was just a bad dream. But it wasn't. She was really here – back in Kentucky. She rolled over and sat up on the edge of the bed.

She should be waking up with Luke this morning. They'd faced her family, her brothers finally knew what was going on, and she was ready to start building a life with him. Instead, she was back here, and he was still there.

She got to her feet and went to make coffee. She wasn't going to get bummed out about it. There might be a couple of thousand miles between them again now, but there was no real distance between them anymore – they were closer than they'd ever been.

She went to check her phone where it was charging on the counter. She smiled when she saw that she had a new text from him.

Luke: Morning, baby. I wish that we were waking up together. Let me know when I can come visit, and I'll talk to Deacon about taking some time off.

She covered her heart with her hand as tears sprang to her eyes. He was so good to her; she wasn't sure that she deserved him. She let out a short laugh as she wiped her eyes. Deserve him or not, she wasn't letting him go now.

Laney: I'll talk to Tom today about the schedule. I'd love for you to come out here, but I'm hoping that I won't be here long enough for that. I want to come home to you.

She watched the screen, hoping that he'd reply straightaway, but he didn't. He was probably in the shower, getting ready for work. She checked her watch – she'd better do the same.

After she'd showered, and dressed, she took a mug of coffee and ran down the steps to the tack room, grateful that Tom had let her have the apartment. At least she didn't have far to go to get to work.

She settled herself at the desk and had just pulled up the schedule when Tom walked in and gave her a grim smile.

"Thanks for coming, Laney. I take it from what you said yesterday, you weren't planning on coming back."

She shook her head. "I wasn't. Things have worked out at home. I have plans there."

Tom cocked an eyebrow. "Not much racing up there in Montana, is there?"

She smiled. "Nope, but I'm out of the racing business. At least, I will be once you get Tony back."

"You have a great future ahead of you if you want it. I can pay you more next contract, if that's what it's about."

"It's not, and I wouldn't ask you for more money if I did plan to stay. You've always been fair with me, Tom, more than fair. You've always been in my corner, and I'll never forget it."

Tom shrugged. "Don't go making me out to be some kind of good guy," he grumbled. "I'm a grouchy old bastard, remember? Just ask anyone; they'll tell you, in case you've forgotten."

She laughed. "Nah, you might trade on that reputation, but I know better. It's all right, though, I won't tell anyone."

"Good. Are you okay with the schedule for today?"

She glanced at the screen in front of her. "I haven't seen it yet, but I will be. What are you up to?"

"I'm going to head over to the hospital in a little while. I want to check on Tony, see how he's doing. By all accounts, it's not as bad as it first seemed. And if you don't plan to stick around for the long haul, I'm going to start putting feelers out to see who else might be available. You good with that?"

She appreciated him asking. It was all too common in the industry that managers went behind their trainers' backs when they started looking for their replacement – often leaving the trainer blindsided to find themselves out of a job.

"I am. I can put some feelers out, too, if you want me to?"

Tom laughed. "Thanks, but no thanks. I think a couple of my potential candidates will like the idea of being headhunted to replace the best in the business."

Laney just stared at him. He was calling her the best in the business?

Tom rested a hand on her shoulder. "Yes, I mean you. I'm going to miss you, Laney. But you've got to do what you've got to do." He smiled. "And I've got to do what I've got to do, and that means appealing to some male egos. I think you know that there are a couple of guys who will be happy to think that I might be getting rid of you to bring them in. I'm hoping that it'll help me when it comes to contract negotiations – they might be prepared to settle for a lower number if they think that they're also getting the prestige of being the one to oust you."

Laney shook her head at him. "And you really want to bring in a guy who thinks that way?"

"Want to? No. I'd rather keep you, but there's going to be no persuading you, I can see it in your eyes. So, I'll have to work with what's available to me." He winked. "And you know damn well that I'll work it to my advantage."

She had to laugh. "You always do."

Tom frowned. "I hope you never thought that I took advantage …"

"Hell no! Like I said, you've been more than fair with me. You've gone above and beyond for me; I appreciate it and I'll never forget it. I do want to go home as soon as possible, but even when I'm back there, I need you to know that as far as I'm concerned, I owe you, big time. If ever there's anything I can do for you in the future, all you have to do is let me know. Anything from Montana," she added with a smile.

Tom chuckled. "Well, if you want to start a breeding program, that might be something we could talk about. Other than that, maybe you can tell me some secret spot if I come up to visit you and want to do some flyfishing."

Laney grinned. "I can tell you all the best spots. You bring your ass up there to visit me whenever you like. I'll look forward to it."

"I will too." Tom tapped at the screen. "For now, get back to work, missy. I'll check in with you when I get back from the hospital." He turned back when he reached the doorway. "And Laney?"

"Yeah?"

"Thanks for coming. I'm the one who owes you."

~ ~ ~

Luke had to circle the parking lot at the bakery a couple of times before someone pulled out and freed up a spot. He pulled in and cut the engine and then sat there for a few moments. He'd decided to stop by on his way home from work because he couldn't face the idea of going back to his house and finding it empty. He'd have to go soon; the house might be empty but there were still three horses in the barn. He just wanted to build himself up before he had to go back there.

He took his phone out and checked Laney's message from this morning again. She'd said that she wanted to come home to him. He wanted that more than anything. He'd started to type out a reply several times through the course of the day but each time, he'd stopped. He wanted to tell her that he wanted nothing more than for her to come home, but that wouldn't be fair. He hated that she'd left, but he respected the hell out of why she'd done it. No way did he want to make her feel bad for doing what was right. It felt like there was a fine line to walk between telling her how much he missed her and being supportive of what she was doing.

A knock on his window made him startle so badly that he dropped his phone. He gave Candy a sheepish grin before grabbing his phone and opening the door.

"Sorry," she said. "I didn't mean to make you jump. But when I saw you sitting out here, I had to come and make sure that you were okay."

"I'm fine."

She reached out and gently touched his cheek. "You don't look fine. I'm going to give those MacFarland boys a piece of my mind."

He chuckled. "It's not as bad as it looks, and it's a hell of a lot better than it could have been."

She made a face at him. "Why do you boys always think that you have to settle everything with your fists? And it's not as though you're boys anymore, is it? You should know better at your age."

Luke chuckled as he got out of the car and wrapped his arm around her shoulders. "I guess old habits just die hard. And to be honest with you, it was the quickest and most straightforward way of settling what was going on between us. The guys said what they needed to say with their fists, now we're all straight and everything's good."

Candy shook her head. "Everything except your face."

Luke chuckled. "Don't go saying things like that, you'll give me a complex."

She slapped his arm. "Come on, come and have a coffee with me. I was about to head home but I'd rather catch up with you first."

By the time they'd gotten settled in one of the big booths at the back of the bakery, the place had emptied out a little. Spider brought their drinks over and raised his eyebrows at Luke as he set them on the table.

"Damn."

Luke shrugged. "It's all good."

Spider grinned at him. "Yeah, I suppose it is. It could have been a whole lot worse."

Luke grinned at Candy. "See, I told you."

She shook her head at them. "You boys."

Spider chuckled and backed away from the table. "If you're here for a while, we'll come and join you when it quiets down."

"Take your time," said Candy. "I need to have a little chat with Luke."

After Spider had gone, Luke gave her a puzzled look. "What do you need?"

She took a sip of her latte and then held his gaze over the rim of her mug. "I need to make sure that you're going to be okay."

Luke smiled and brought his hand up to his face. "It's nothing, really. It looks way worse than it is."

She shook her head, looking serious. "I don't mean that, Luke."

"What then?"

"I mean Laney."

"Well, I can't say it's going to be easy waiting for her to come back. But I've waited years. A bit longer won't kill me. Is that not what you mean?" he asked when he saw the expression on her face.

"No. I'm more concerned about what will happen to you when she comes back than while she's gone."

Luke didn't get it. "What do you mean?"

"I mean, do you really think she's going to be good for you – good to you?"

Luke frowned. "Yes. I do. Why?"

Candy waved a hand at him. "Don't go getting all defensive on me. I'm worried about you, that's all. Obviously, I don't know Laney, but I've heard things about her. And what I've heard worries me."

Luke scowled. "What have you heard?"

"Just… you know… how she is, what she's like."

Luke's heart was pounding now. "What do people say that she's like? And who have you heard this from, anyway?"

She reached across the table and patted his hand. "Don't go getting upset. I just want to look out for you."

He took a deep breath and forced himself to calm down a little. "I get that, but I don't get what you've got against Laney. You don't even know her. I want to know who's talking shit about her."

Candy held her hand up. "You're right, I don't know her, and no one's talking shit about her. It's just that I've heard a few things, and I've put two and two together and I don't really like what I'm coming up with."

"Well, whatever you're coming up with, it's wrong. When you get to know her, you'll love her. And honestly, Candy, I'm surprised at you. You give everyone a fair go. Why would you judge Laney before you even know her?"

Candy sat up a little straighter at that. "I'm not judging her, Luke, sweetheart. All I'm doing is trying to look out for you."

He took a deep breath and forced himself to relax. "Tell me what you've heard, and I'll set you straight."

Candy took another drink of her coffee before she spoke again. Luke didn't feel like touching his drink.

"Wasn't there an issue between her and Janey?"

"Jesus. That was when they were eighteen years old. And it was only a misunderstanding, anyway. Janey liked a guy, and she was upset when he asked Laney out. That's all. It's not like Laney did it on purpose. She didn't even know. If she'd known that her sister liked him, she never would've gone out with him. She'd never hurt Janey on purpose."

"And what about you? Didn't she hurt you on purpose?"

Luke blew out a sigh. "No. She didn't do it on purpose. Yes, she hurt me. But I hurt her just as badly. We're both as responsible as each other for handling things poorly back then. But we were kids. That's all ancient history as far as I'm concerned. We're back together now, and I was kind of hoping that people might be happy for us."

Candy smiled. "I am happy – cautiously happy – for you. But I'm concerned as well."

"Well, there's no need for you to be. You just need to get to know her. You'll see."

Candy's smile faded. "I'd love to, but hasn't she run off, back to Kentucky again?"

Luke's hands balled into fists at his sides. "No. She hasn't *just run off.* She's gone back to help out her old boss. She's doing someone a favor – I would have thought that you, of all people, would understand that. Someone who used to rely on her needed her help. So, even though we're just getting back on track, and she really didn't want to go, she's done the right thing. Am I happy that she's gone? No. But do I admire her for doing what's right? You bet your …" He stopped when he remembered who he was talking to and gave Candy a rueful smile. "You bet I do. I respect her choice to step in and help out where she's needed. And more than that, I'm proud of her."

Candy gave him a sheepish smile. "I'm sorry. And you can bet *your* ass that I'll try not to jump to the wrong conclusion in the future. All I can say in my defense is that I was trying to look out for you."

"I know, but Laney's … People always seem to think that she's a lot harder than she is. Just because she's strong and capable, it doesn't mean that she's hard. She's way sweeter than most people will ever know."

"But *you* know, and that's all that matters."

"It's all that really matters, yeah. But at the same time, I wish other people could see past the capable cowgirl and into the heart of the sweet girl that I know."

"I really don't know her, but from what you've said, I'd guess that she doesn't want anyone else to see or know the sweet girl on the inside. She saves that for you."

Her words reminded Luke of his conversation with Cash the other night. He loved to think that perhaps he was the only one who Laney trusted enough to be her true self with. At the same time, he wished that other people could see her for who she was.

Rocket appeared next to the table and sat down beside Candy. He scowled at Luke. "What's going on here? Are you okay, Miss Candy?"

She chuckled and patted his hand. "I'm okay, Rocky. And don't you go scowling at Luke like that. We're good. If anyone was out of line, I was." She smiled at Luke. "And I apologize."

Luke smiled back at her. "It's okay. I appreciate your concern, but I hope you'll give her a chance." His smile faded at the thought that she might not. "It's important to me."

Candy nodded. "I know it is. And don't you worry. I'm going to go out of my way to get to know her just as soon as she comes home."

Rocket looked at Candy and then back at Luke. "I take it we're talking about Laney?"

"Yeah."

"You and Sierra need to get over that, Miss Candy. I know you're both protective of Janey, but Janey doesn't blame Laney."

Luke met Rocket's gaze. "Janey's told you what happened back then?"

Rocket nodded. "Yeah. And Sierra knows too. I think she feels like she needs to protect Janey."

Luke nodded. That would explain why Sierra had been frosty toward Laney.

"I'll have a word with her," said Candy.

Luke shook his head. "I think Laney might need to be the one to do that herself."

They all looked up when Deacon and Spider came to join them.

"What's going on?" asked Deacon. He leaned in to kiss Candy's cheek. "I was on my way home, but I saw that your car's still here. Why all the serious faces?" He grinned at Luke. "I know about the battered face."

Luke smiled at him through pursed lips. He wasn't about to tell him that Candy had been giving him a hard time about Laney.

He should have known better, though. Candy told him herself. "I've just been putting my foot in it."

Deacon cocked an eyebrow at her. "What have you done now, darlin'?"

She laughed. "Don't worry, Luke's already set me straight. I was worried that Laney might be taking advantage of him."

Deacon met Luke's gaze and laughed. "You've got nothing to worry about with those two. Her going back to Kentucky might be a bit of a blip, but they were always meant to be together and now they're finally on track."

Luke gave his brother a grateful smile. He loved that Deacon knew – and had always known – the truth about Laney and him.

Chapter Sixteen

Laney dismounted and handed the reins of the mare she'd just been working with on the gallops to one of the grooms.

"Walk her off and cool her down, would you?"

The girl nodded. "Tom was looking for you, he's in the office."

"Thanks."

Laney jogged past the stables to the office at the end of the row. Tom looked up when she went in. She started to back away when she saw that he was on the phone, but he gestured for her to come in.

"Yeah, that's right, I'll see you then." He ended the call and pointed at the seat across the desk from him. "Have you got a minute?"

She gave him a wry smile. "All my minutes are yours until I leave."

Tom smiled. "I wanted to talk to you about that Wagoner mare. They want to come out and use the training gate this afternoon."

Laney rolled her eyes. "They're amateurs, Tom, and you know it."

"Maybe so, but they are paying amateurs. And it's not as though I'm asking you to work with them. You can send a couple of the crew up there to work the gate. I just wanted to make sure that you weren't planning to use it this afternoon."

"No. Not today."

"Good. I'll let them know, then."

He started to scribble on the pad in front of him.

"How's Tony doing?" Laney asked.

"It's only been a week. Are you getting impatient already?"

She laughed. "I've been impatient since before I got here. But no, I'm not expecting to see him walk through the door any day soon. Believe it or not, I was actually inquiring about his well-being."

"You could go over to the hospital and see him."

"I could – if my slave driver of a boss left any free time in my schedule."

Tom looked up at her. "I know I've got you working your ass off, but it's kind of a needs must situation at the moment. That phone call before you came in? That was Jason Denny – I've set up a meeting with him later."

Laney pursed her lips but didn't comment.

"Don't look like that, missy. I know what you think of him, and I know why. I wouldn't bring him within five miles of the place if you were still going to be here. But you're not. He's one of the best." He winked at her. "One of the best available anyway, and since the very best insists on leaving me and going home to Montana, all I can do is work with what's available."

Laney shrugged. "He's good. Even I can't deny that. And I suppose, once I go, the fact that he's a misogynist pig won't matter too much, will it?"

Tom laughed. "You really think he's that bad?"

Laney nodded emphatically. "I don't just think it, I know it. But he'll be your problem, not mine." She frowned. "You're going to have to watch him with the grooms, though. Some of those girls..."

Tom frowned. "You think he's a problem in that respect?"

Laney shrugged. "I don't know. I've never heard about him having any problems with female staff. So, it's not fair of me to paint him with that brush. Maybe he only has a problem with women he sees as competition. I'm sure he's fine with them as underlings."

Tom shook his head slowly. "I've never had a problem with him. I've never heard of anyone having any kind of problem with him. Anyone other than you," he added quickly when Laney opened her mouth. "And I trust your opinion. I'll just have to play it by ear."

"Do you have any idea how long it will be until Tony can come back?"

Tom shook his head. "If it were up to him, he'd be back out here next week. He even said that he'd be prepared to hire an assistant who could push him around in a wheelchair."

Laney laughed. "He'd do it, too."

"He wasn't joking."

"I know I don't get a vote since I'm not going to be here, but if I were you, I'd rather have Tony in a wheelchair than Jason Denny."

Tom shrugged. "I would, too, but I'm trying to do you a favor here. I know you're in a hurry to go home. If we get Tony back before he's a hundred percent, I'll need you to stick around. If I can bring in an able body in the meantime – someone who can keep the program on track – then you can go."

Laney closed her eyes. "You know I'm in a hurry to get back to Montana, but I won't leave you in the lurch. I'll do what's best for you. And you know that I don't believe that Jason's the best solution, in any sense."

"I'm going to keep working on it, see what else I can come up with."

Laney went to check her phone, which was in her jacket, hanging in the tack room. This whole week had been like this – she and Luke texted each other whenever they could, and they talked at night before she went to sleep. It didn't help that she was two hours ahead of him, but it was what it was – it wouldn't be forever. She smiled when she saw the text that was waiting for her.

Luke: Get this, Tanner is coming over to my place tonight and bringing a six pack.

Laney: You mean he's willingly giving up a night on the prowl?

She was surprised when he answered straight away.

Luke: Yep. He says he can tell that I'm pining, and so he's coming to keep me company.

Laney: Aww, who knew my brother could be such a sweetheart?

Luke: Not me. Although, I'm not convinced that he won't ply me with a few beers and then suggest that we go to Chico anyway.

Laney's heart started to race. It was dumb, and she knew it. There was no reason that Luke shouldn't go out with Tanner. It was just ... She couldn't help thinking about all the times they must have done that over the years – or how those nights would have ended. The thought of Luke with another woman now, made her blood run cold. But she didn't want to be one of those pushy, clingy girlfriends.

Laney: Go if you want to.

Luke: I don't want to. What are you doing this weekend?

Laney: Working. It's what I'm here for, and the more I work, the less time I have to spend sitting around missing you.

Luke: I guess we're different in that. I'd rather sit around missing you than do anything else.

Aww. He was such a sweetheart.

Laney: I just don't want to miss you anymore. I want to come home.

Luke: Any idea when that might be yet?

Laney: Not yet, but Tom's talking to a possible replacement this afternoon. And apparently, Tony's eager to get out of the hospital and back to work.

Luke: I'm wishing him a speedy recovery.

Laney: Me too.

Luke: Sorry, baby. I have to get back to work.

Laney: Me too.

Luke: Can I call you tonight?

Laney: Please. And it doesn't matter how late it is. Have your fun with Tanner first. I've got tomorrow morning off.

Luke: I'll try to kick him out as early as I can. You know I'd rather spend Friday night with you — even if it is only on the phone. Love you. Talk to you later.

Laney: Love you, too.

~ ~ ~

Luke shoved his phone back into his pocket when he saw
Deacon coming toward his cubicle.

"You got a minute?"

Luke chuckled. "Like I'm going to say no?"

Deacon rolled his eyes at him and perched on the edge of his
desk. "Remember the burglary at the Shannon place the other
week?"

Luke nodded. "Yeah. Is she okay? Have there been any
developments?" Luke had been the one to go over and take
Mary Shannon's statement after a break in at her house. The
whole situation had really pissed him off. Mary was a widow
who lived alone. She wasn't an old lady, but she seemed
vulnerable to him. She'd been frightened by the knowledge
that someone had been in her house. Luke hated it for her.

"No," said Deacon. "But there has been another break-in.
This one was just down the road from Mary's place. I'd guess
it's the same team. Same method of entry – they broke the
glass in the back door and just let themselves right on in."

"Whose house?" Luke asked.

"Stan Joseph."

"Shit. Is he okay?" Stan had to be in his eighties, but he was
sprightly enough, and Luke couldn't imagine him backing
down from a burglar.

"He wasn't home. He's away in Glendive visiting his
brother."

"Well, that's something. I'd hate to think what might have
happened if he was there."

"Me too."

"Do you want me on it?"

"Yeah. Since you were the one on Mary's case, it makes sense for you to work at this one, too. Take Miller with you."

Luke pushed away from his desk. "On it."

"Before you go, how's Laney?"

"Missing me, but not nearly as much as I miss her."

Deacon cocked an eyebrow.

"No, I don't mean it like that. She's missing me. It's just that I miss her like hell."

Deacon smiled. "Hopefully it won't be for much longer."

"Yeah, I hope so. And did you talk to Candy about the other day?"

"Yeah. I set her straight." Deacon chuckled. "I don't mean that how it sounded. I mean, I filled here in on how it really is. It seems Sierra had gotten into her head. Although what Sierra's problem is, I'm not sure."

"Me neither, but I hope she's going to be able to get over it when Laney comes home."

"I'm sure she will."

"Anyway, sorry, I don't mean to stand around here gossiping. I'll go get Miller and we'll head over to Stan's place."

~ ~ ~

Laney lay in bed, staring at her phone. It was midnight, and it still hadn't rung. She blew a sigh at the ceiling. It might be midnight here, but it was only ten o'clock in Montana. It was hardly fair to expect Luke to get rid of Tanner this early just so that he could call her.

She grinned when her phone started to ring, but her smile faded when she saw the name on the display.

"Hey, Nixon. What's up? How did you get my number?"

"It's not Nixon, it's Buck. How you doing, pretty lady?"

Laney scowled at her phone. "What the hell do you want?"

"Hey now, that's no way to talk to me."

"I don't want to talk to you at all. What do you want? Why are you using Nixon's phone?"

"Why shouldn't I?"

Laney sat up. "No reason, just don't use it to call me again." She ended the call. She had no desire to talk to that guy. Asshole.

The phone started to ring again before she set it down, but when she saw Nixon's name on the display again, she ignored it. After it stopped ringing, it beeped with a text.

> *Nixon: Bitch. Just because you're a MacFarland doesn't make you something special. Just because your boyfriend is a deputy doesn't mean I can't get to him.*

Laney sucked in a deep breath. Where the hell did this guy get off? She'd never done a damn thing to him. Okay, so Luke had punched him, but he'd earned that, and he had to know it. That was the law of the jungle at Chico – in the valley in general – you couldn't go pawing at a woman and not expect her boyfriend to come after you.

She was tempted to reply and tell him that – and tell him a few other things about what she thought of him, too, but she stopped herself from doing it. There was a time when she wouldn't have cared about the consequences, but she was older now, wiser. She wasn't going to go stirring up more trouble just by running her mouth.

She eyed the phone suspiciously for a few minutes, expecting more messages, but none came. She got up and went to the kitchen for a glass of water. She wouldn't be able to snooze while she waited for Luke's call now.

She didn't have long to wait. Her phone rang again at quarter after midnight. She checked the screen before she answered, not wanting to get caught out by Buck again. Her shoulders relaxed, and a smile spread across her face when she saw Luke's name on the screen.

"Hey you," she answered. "I didn't think you'd be calling for a while yet."

He chuckled. "Neither did I, but Tanner took pity on me. He said to tell you that I'm like a lovelorn kid, and he couldn't stand to see it any longer, so he's taken himself off to Chico."

Laney laughed. "Is he mad at me that I've cost him his hunting partner?"

"No. It's not as though he ever really needed me. You know what he's like."

Laney made a face. She did know what Tanner was like. All he had to do was smile at a girl to have her dropping her panties for him. And there was never any shortage of girls around him.

"Anyway," Luke continued when she didn't answer, "how are you doing?"

"Okay. It's been a busy week. How about you?"

"Same."

"Anything interesting going on? Any sudden crime waves to keep you busy?" She laughed as she asked it. The valley was hardly a hotbed of crime. People were mostly civilized, even up in town. They were more likely to look out for each other than to steal from each other.

Luke didn't laugh with her. "As a matter of fact, it's not exactly a crime wave, but I'm working on two – possibly connected – burglaries."

"I'd say that constitutes a crime wave. What happened? Who – can you tell me about it, tell me who?"

"Yeah. It's public record. Do you remember Mary Shannon and Stan Joseph?"

"Aww! Really? That's awful. God, do you think it's someone who knows them? Someone who knows they live alone and aren't exactly able to defend themselves?"

"It's looking that way. Although, there was no question of them defending themselves. Both break-ins took place while they were away. Mary was gone last weekend, and Stan was out of town visiting his brother."

"Thank goodness, at least that's something. I'd hate to think…" She let her words trail off as she shuddered.

"You're going to hunt them down, right? Lock the bastards up."

"I'm going to do my best."

"Well, you are the best, so you'll manage it. I know you will."

~ ~ ~

Luke gripped the phone tighter and held it a little closer to his ear, as if that could somehow bring her closer to him. "I love that you have so much faith in me."

He could hear the smile in her voice when she answered. "I do. I… even when…"

"What?"

"Never mind."

"No, go on, tell me. What were you going to say?"

"I was going to say that even when I thought you didn't want me. All those years that I thought you just saw me –saw what we'd done together – as a mistake, I still had faith in you. I had so much faith in you, that I believed you must be right – that I wasn't worth it."

Luke's heart sank. "I never thought that, baby. Never. You were always worth it. I was just too … I was going to say too young, but that's not right – I was too scared and too stupid, that's the honest explanation. You were always worth it, and I hate that you thought you weren't."

She laughed, and he knew that she was trying to let him off the hook, but he wanted to make it up to her somehow, some way.

"I know better now. I learned my worth over the years, working here. I learned that I am strong enough and smart enough and now, now that we've figured things out, I know that I'm worthy of the future that we're going to build together."

"You're more than worthy, Laney. You're everything. I'm the one who wants to prove that I'm worthy of you."

She laughed again. "Nah. Let's not go down that road. We both know that we are. We're good people, and we can hold our own with the best of them. We can be one of those power couples if we want."

Luke frowned. "Is that what you want?"

He loved the sound of her laughter. "Hell no, I don't. I just thought it sounded good."

He laughed with her. "I have to be honest and tell you that I'm relieved."

"You've got no worries there. I might want to turn us into a trainer couple, or a breeder couple, but not a power couple."

His breath got caught in his chest. "What?" Was she talking about having kids? He'd love to, but he hadn't really thought that Laney was into kids.

She didn't pick up on his shock, and he felt kind of dumb when she explained. "I've been thinking about what I'm going to do when I come home. It's one thing to help Tanner out here and there when he needs the extra help. But that's not going to be enough for me. I want to do more training. And I've been thinking about maybe starting a breeding program, too. And as for the couple part … I'm not trying to pressure you or anything, but if ever you do decide you're done with law enforcement, I'd love if we could raise and train horses together."

His heart thundered in his chest.

"Too much? Should I not have said that?" she asked.

"No! I love that you said it. I love the idea. I don't know that I'd be able to walk away from my job anytime soon, but you've certainly given me something to aim for."

Laney yawned. "Give it some thought. I think we could be onto something good there."

Luke checked his watch. "It's late for you, baby. I should let you go."

"I know, but I don't want you to let me go."

His fingers twitched with the need to reach out and touch her. "You know what I mean. I mean let you go to sleep. I'm never letting you go again."

"That's good, because if you try, I won't go so easily this time. I know you said that it was all your fault, what happened back then, but it wasn't. I'm as much to blame. I could've stuck around and fought for you – fought for us."

"You shouldn't have had to."

She yawned again. "We don't need to rehash it. I don't think we'll make those kinds of mistakes again."

"I can't promise I'll never make any mistakes, but I won't make the same ones. Go on, go to sleep. Text me tomorrow when you get a minute."

"Okay, goodnight. Oh, wait, I was going to tell you... No, never mind. Good night. I love you."

Luke wanted to ask her what, but she sounded so tired that he felt bad keeping her any longer. "Tell me tomorrow, okay?"

"Okay."

"Good night baby. I love you more."

She chuckled. "We're not going to fight about who loves who more. I'll wrestle you for it when I get home."

He laughed with her. "You're on. I'll look forward to it. Now go to sleep."

Chapter Seventeen

Laney kept herself busy all through the weekend. Before she left to go back to the valley, she'd made it a rule for herself not to come into work unless she was called in. There was always so much going on, that it was easy to make this place her whole life. Now, she wasn't looking to try and create a life for herself here in Kentucky. She felt as though her real life wouldn't begin until she got home to Montana – home to Luke.

She was helping out with afternoon feeds on Sunday when Tom came striding into the barn.

"What are you doing here, missy? It's the weekend. You should be at home, taking a break. I need you here fresh and early tomorrow morning."

Laney shrugged. "If you think about it, this place is home for me at the moment." She pointed at the window of the apartment above the tack room. "So, if you want to get picky about it, I am at home, I'm just messing around in my backyard."

Tom chuckled. "I hope this guy back in Montana knows what he's getting himself into with you. Does he know that he'll never win an argument?"

Laney laughed. "We grew up together."

"Still, I wish him good luck."

"He'd tell you that he's the luckiest guy on earth – since he got me."

Tom laughed. "I'm glad. I hope he truly knows how lucky he is."

"Aww. Are you saying that you're going to miss me?"

"You know damn well I am. But seriously, Laney, take a break, would you? I don't need you working yourself into the ground." He met her gaze and held it. "I can guess what you're doing – you want to stay busy so that you're not just sitting around wishing you were back there with him, right?"

Laney bit down on her bottom lip. "You got me."

He patted her shoulder. "We'll get you back there just as soon as we can. Although, after talking to him the other day, I can see what you mean about Jason. I don't want to bring him in."

Laney didn't know what to say to that. She didn't know how to feel about it. On the one hand, it would be way better for her if Tom said that Jason was starting tomorrow. On the other, she really didn't like the guy, and she didn't want to leave Tom, the horses, or the grooms at his mercy.

"Do you have your eye on anyone else?" she asked.

"I have a couple of irons in the fire, and Tony called me this morning. Turns out that he's serious about coming back out here in a wheelchair."

Laney laughed. "Don't tell me you're surprised. You know what he's like."

Tom nodded.

"And I can't say I blame him," Laney added. "We both know that he was keeping his fingers crossed that I wouldn't come back. We worked well together, but it's only natural that he would jump at the chance to be your main man with me out of the picture."

"Yeah. And I'd like to have him." Tom winked at her. "Since I can't have you. I'm thinking that if maybe we give it another week or two, we might be able to get him out here and let you go home."

Laney's heart leaped. "I hope so. Not just because I want to go home, but because I think that's a win-win for all of us. You win because Tony's great, and you get some continuity. Tony wins because whoever you do bring in will be his subordinate, I imagine."

"Yeah, that's the way I think it'll work out. But will you do me a favor and call it quits for the day? We've got a busy one tomorrow and I don't want you dragging ass."

Laney rolled her eyes at him. "Okay. I'll go sit on my couch, watch TV, and eat bonbons if it'll make you feel any better."

Tom just laughed. "Go on, smartass, get out of here."

When she got up there, the apartment felt kind of claustrophobic; but that was nothing new. The place was nice enough, but she didn't want to be cooped up in here. At the same time, there was nowhere else she wanted to go – at least, nowhere in Kentucky – so she knew that she might as well just hang out. Watching TV wasn't really her thing. Although, she could've eaten bonbons if she had any. But since she didn't, she needed to find something else to fill her time.

She didn't want to call Luke. Well, she did, but he was working this weekend and she didn't want to feel like she was constantly harassing him – even more so, she didn't want him to feel that way.

She toyed with her phone, wondering if she should text him, but decided against it. She scrolled through her contacts and stopped when she got to her sister's name. She hadn't had the chance to say goodbye to Janey before she left, since she and Rocket had been away for the weekend.

She dialed her number and waited.

"Hey, sis. Sorry, I've been meaning to call you."

Laney laughed. "I've told you before, it's not always on you to call me. At least, it shouldn't be."

Janey chuckled. "I know, but it's just one of those habits that we fell into years ago, isn't it?"

"I guess, but some habits are worth breaking." Laney's smile faded. "You know what? I just realized, you broke a pretty major habit last year, didn't you? There was a time when there would have been no point in me calling you on a Sunday."

Janey sighed. "True. I still feel guilty sometimes, though, that I don't go to see him anymore. No one goes these days. He could die and we wouldn't know about it until the hospital called."

Laney pursed her lips. She knew that her sister wouldn't want to hear what she had to say – that she hoped he did.

"Anyway, we don't need to talk about him, do we?"

"Oh hell, no! As far as I'm concerned, he's already dead."

"I wish I could feel that way. I just can't … I don't know. He's our father. I wish I could feel like that means nothing, but I can't. I guess I'm just weaker than the rest of you."

"No, it's because you're a sweetheart. You're better than the rest of us, Janey. If anything, you're the strong one. The one who could handle going to see him for years and years, even when the rest of us just gave up."

"I guess. But that's enough about him. Tell me about you? When are you coming home? Isn't it just typical that I missed everything? I go away for one weekend – just one weekend – and it all goes down. You and Luke finally came clean with the brothers – and they are happy about it. I don't know how much time you had with them before you had to leave, but in case you're still worried about them, I want to set your mind at ease. They're all thrilled."

Laney had to smile. "I kind of got that impression before I left, but it's nice to hear you say it. Of course, Tan and Ty had to throw a couple of punches..."

Janey laughed. "I know. Luke's still got a bit of a shiner. But when you think about it, he got off lightly. And Cash! If I'd known that he was coming, we wouldn't have gone away."

Laney smiled. "He was awesome. I thought he'd be the worst of the lot of them, and yet he was so supportive. It turns out that he knew all along."

Janey cleared her throat.

"What's up? What are you not saying?"

"Why? Why do you think there's something I'm not saying?"

Laney laughed. "Because that's one of your tells, sister dear. When you're not sure if you should say something, you clear your throat, as though the words are stuck there, and you don't know whether to spit them out or swallow them."

Janey laughed. "Hmm. I didn't know that. I'm going to have to watch myself, aren't I?"

"Maybe. But go on, tell me what you were thinking."

"I felt bad that you didn't know that Cash knew. He told me at our wedding that he knew about you and Luke."

"Wow!"

"I didn't deliberately keep it secret from you or anything, it's just that it's never come up again since."

"It's okay. It's not a problem."

Janey cleared her throat again, and then she laughed. "Don't worry, I'm doing that on purpose. I'm trying to let you know that there's something else I need to say."

"What's that?"

"Well, I think I need to apologize to you. While we're coming clean about who knows what, I should tell you that when Sierra first came here, she was really sweet to me. She was trying to help me make more of myself – trying to make me see that Rocket might really be interested in me. I told her about what happened between us before you left – you know, about Wyatt."

Laney sighed. "I'm still sorry, Janey."

"And I've told you a million times, you don't need to be. That's not why am bringing it up. The only reason I'm mentioning it is because I think Sierra kind of holds it against you. I didn't tell the story like you were the bad guy or anything. But Sierra feels protective toward me. I'm sorry."

Laney had to smile. "First of all, don't be sorry. There's no need. As a matter of fact, I'm glad that you've told me. I wondered why Sierra didn't like me – now I know. And if anything, it makes me like her more. I like her for trying to look out for you – even if it is misguided."

"I just feel bad, because she's close with Candy, too, and I think the two of them have gotten the wrong impression of you. Sierra wants to protect me, and Candy wants to protect Luke –" she laughed "– but if it's any consolation, Luke and I have both been busy trying to protect you."

Laney's hand came up to cover her heart. "That's more than just consolation, sis. To think that the two people I love most in the world are standing up for me, even though I don't deserve it, means more than you can imagine."

"You deserve it." Janey's voice was full of tears.

Laney sniffed. "Anyway, what else is going on there?"

Janey laughed. "Alrighty then, moving swiftly on. Emmett asked me to send you his best. And the girls have been pestering, asking if they're going to get to see you when you come back."

Laney smiled to herself. She would have cried if she and Janey had continued down the same path. This was better – catching up on news in the valley, and on people who used to be a big part of her life – and who she hoped soon would be again.

They got so carried away, catching up on each other's news that an hour had passed when Laney looked up and saw the clock.

"Where's Rocket?" she asked, suddenly aware that she was keeping her sister from her husband on a Sunday, which was usually the only day the two of them had free together.

She could hear the smile in Janey's voice when she answered. "He skipped lunch with the brothers today. Candy invited him and Spider over to eat with her. It's so sweet; they do that every now and then. She's such a good mom to them."

Laney had to smile. She didn't know Candy all that well – and they hadn't exactly gotten off on the right foot, but Laney loved what she'd heard about her. She loved that she'd taken Rocket and Spider in as foster kids and that those two big, burly, tattooed guys still saw her as their mom to this day.

"Aww. That's awesome. What about Deacon?"

"I think they're kind of playing musical families today. Candy's getting time with her boys, and Deacon decided to take himself over to see Luke."

"Awesome." Laney loved that the two brothers were getting time together, but she felt a little left out that Janey was the one to tell her.

"I think they only decided that this morning," said Janey. "I think it might have had more to do with the robberies in town. There's been another one."

"Oh no. Who this time? Do you know?"

"I don't. I only heard about it because Rocket texted me when he got to their place. He told me that Deacon wasn't there. It's funny, I think Rocket's kind of rattled about the robberies. He's gotten used to thinking of this place as somewhere bad things don't happen."

"I can't blame him. I think of it that way myself. Has it changed so much over the years? I find it shocking to think that people's homes are being broken into. Even in town, I still think of it being a place where people can leave their doors unlocked."

"No, it hasn't changed. We all still think of it that way, too. This is something new. It's the talk of the town. Everyone's trying to figure out who might be doing it. I think most people want to believe that it's someone just passing through. Although, there are some old faces who've moved back recently as well."

"Like who?"

"Remember Nixon's brother, Buck?"

Laney shuddered. "Ugh. I probably wouldn't have remembered him, no. But I had a little run in with him at

Chico. And don't tell Luke, but only because I need to tell him myself; he called me here the other night."

"He did? Why?"

"I guess because he's mad at me. He was hitting on me at Chico the night that everything went down. Luke came over and punched him."

"Oh, right, Frankie told me about that. That's why it all came out, right? Because Buck said he wasn't doing anything wrong – because you were single – and Luke set him straight that you're *his*."

"That's right."

Janey chuckled. "I have to tell you – I can't imagine you letting any guy other than Luke get away with that."

"With what?"

"With saying that you're *his*. I'm pretty sure if it were anyone else, you would have turned around and punched him yourself."

"You're right, I would. I didn't even think about it. But … yeah. I've always thought that whole thing of a man talking about a woman like she's a possession was … ugh … I don't know."

"But when it's Luke saying it about you, you love it."

She had to smile. "Yeah. I do."

"Aww. But anyway, sorry, you were going to tell me about Buck. What did he call you for?"

"Like I said, I don't know. He told me that just because I'm a MacFarland doesn't mean that I'm something special. Well, shoot, I really do need to tell Luke. I'd kind of forgotten about it, but he also said that just because my boyfriend's a deputy, it doesn't mean he can't get to him."

"Wow! It sounds like he's pissed and might be out for revenge. I agree, you really should call Luke and tell him about it."

"I will."

"Well, I'd better let you go. We've been on for ages, and Achilles just came to tell me that it's dinner time."

Laney laughed. "And the furry orange master must be obeyed. Say hi to him and Boo for me, and I'll talk to you again soon."

"Will do. And let's – let's talk again soon. I've loved this, sis."

"I have, too. And I will, I'll do better at keeping in touch while I'm here. But hopefully, I'll be home again soon, and we'll be able to catch up in person."

"I can't wait."

"Me neither. Anyway, love you, sis."

"Love you, too, bye."

~ ~ ~

Luke parked his truck in the driveway and hurried out to the barn. He'd been up in town at the station all afternoon with Deacon. He'd been planning to ride the horses this afternoon, but now, all he had time to do was make sure that they were fed and watered – and spend a little time just hanging out. He'd forgotten how much he enjoyed that.

When he was done, he stood outside the palomino mare's stall, rubbing her nose. He closed his eyes and rested his cheek against hers. It felt good – right.

He hadn't been able to stop thinking about Laney's suggestion that they might become a breeder couple or a trainer couple – or both. There was no denying that he enjoyed being out here in the barn more than he enjoyed sitting in the station or trying to follow up on any leads on the robberies.

He wanted to catch whoever it was that was breaking into people's homes. He knew that he was doing an important job in keeping the community safe. But he could admit that he wasn't like Deacon. He wasn't driven by a need to see justice done. He wanted to do his part – he'd do whatever he could to help anyone out, but he would be way happier spending his days here in the barn, working with the horses – especially if it meant that he got to work with Laney.

He took his phone out to check, but there were no messages from her. She'd told him that she was going to be working today. So, he hadn't wanted to make a nuisance of himself. It would be late in the evening in Kentucky now, though. So, he figured he'd be safe to give her a call when he got back up to the house and cleaned up.

By the time he was showered, he didn't want to wait any longer. He wrapped a towel around his waist and collected his phone from the nightstand. He dialed her number and flopped back on the bed while it rang.

"Hey you," she answered.

"Hey yourself. How are you doing? How was your day?"

"It was okay. Tom kicked me out of the barn, told me that I had to take a break. But it worked out okay, I talked to Janey, and we were on the phone for hours."

"That's great. I'm glad that the two of you had the chance to catch up." He frowned, hating that he didn't even know, but then he relaxed when he realized that he finally had the right to ask. "How are things between you two these days?"

He could hear the smile in her voice when she answered. "Good. Really good. And I think that when I get back there, they'll just keep getting better."

"I love that. I hated that there was friction between you all these years."

"There wasn't, not really. But I know what you mean. I hated not feeling as close to her. And how about you? She said that you were hanging out with Deacon today."

He laughed. "I wouldn't exactly call it hanging out. We were working."

"Any breakthroughs on the robberies?"

"Not much. I have a few leads to follow up on tomorrow, but to be honest, I don't even want to think about that tonight. I want to talk to you. What I really want is to be with you, but until we can do that, I just want to hang out on the phone with you and talk about a whole lot of nothing."

"Aww. I wish we could just hang out, too. There's something I wanted to tell you, but it can wait. You know what? How about we watch a movie together?"

Luke chuckled. "How do you mean? If I could open my door and step through it into yours, I would. But since I don't know how that's possible, how are we going to watch a movie together?"

She laughed. "We can decide on a movie, and both turn it on at the same time. We can watch it together – kind of."

He reached for the remote from the nightstand. "I'm fresh from the shower, with just a towel around my waist. But if you want to watch a movie, just tell me which one and I'll find it."

"You big tease! I don't know about turning a movie on, you're turning me on. Now, all I can think about is you lying on your bed wearing nothing but a towel."

He chuckled. "I wish you could join me."

"Not as much as I do."

"Soon, baby. This isn't forever. And I'm warning you now, when I get you back, we'll be making up for lost time."

She laughed. "When I come back, you'd better book some time off work. I don't plan to let you out of bed for a week."

Luke closed his eyes. "Keep talking, I like where this is going. I'm not sure I want to watch a movie; I think I'd rather you tell me a story."

Her voice was low and breathy when she spoke again. "I can do that."

Luke rested his head back against the pillows and sighed. "No. Let's do the movie thing. I want you any way I can get you, but in the flesh. I want to save myself until we can be together again – not use my hand as a poor substitute."

She laughed out loud. "Okay, mood killer. I was prepared to use mine, but if you can wait, I can."

He chuckled. "I'll make it up to you when I get you back."

"For a whole week?"

"Either that or die trying."

Chapter Eighteen

Luke stopped into the bakery in town before he headed to the station to start his shift. He felt guilty that he hadn't stopped at Spider's place to pick up something to eat – he liked to support those guys as much as he could – but he'd spent most of the afternoon in town. He found that a lot of his work got done more easily when he was off duty. People liked to stop and chat, and they tended to give more away when they were busy gossiping than they could remember when a deputy was interviewing them.

He hadn't learned anything new, though. It seemed that most people had heard about the latest break-in, but no one had any new information.

He grabbed a cup of coffee before heading to the briefing room. He was relieved that he was there early for the shift change meeting – because it meant that he got a seat.

Deacon ran through the usual business, and they all listened to the updates, which were mostly the usual run of the mill reports.

Two of the deputies in the back were chatting about something, and Luke was just glad that it wasn't him when Deacon banged his fist down on the desk in front of him.

"Anything you want to share with the rest of us, Hawkins?"

Luke dropped his head to hide his smile when he heard
Hawkins stammer, "No, sir. Sorry, sir."

Deacon glowered at him as he continued. "We're doubling
up nighttime patrols given what's going on with these break-
ins. It seems that they're getting bolder. The first couple of
jobs they pulled, they waited until the homeowners – Mary and
Stan – were gone. This last one, Karen Jennings, was at home.
Fortunately, she slept through the whole thing. But you don't
need me to tell you how ugly things could have turned if she'd
woken up and gone to investigate."

An angry murmur rippled its way around the room. Luke
scowled. He knew everyone in the room was of the same
mind; they hated to think what might happen to a woman
home alone if she'd interrupted the intruders.

"So," Deacon continued, "we're doubling up on the
investigation during the day shift and, like I said, doubling up
on nighttime patrols. Any questions?"

Luke sipped his coffee and sat back and listened as a couple
of the deputies who'd just come back from leave asked
questions. He loved that Deacon worked hard to ensure that
everyone always felt like they could ask questions – no one was
ever made to feel stupid for not knowing something. And
although everyone was expected to bring themselves up to
speed after any time off, they were also encouraged to speak
up in these meetings while everyone was together and could
share information.

After they were all dismissed, Luke hung around, not
because he had anything in particular that he needed, just to
check in with Deacon.

Deacon frowned when he saw him waiting. "Don't tell me
that you're pissed that I've moved you to nighttime patrol."

Luke laughed. "Okay then, I won't. And just so we're clear –
I wasn't going to. We both know that I'm better on the street
than sitting at a desk trying to piece things together."

Deacon nodded. "That's the way I see it. For a minute there, I was worried that you might disagree."

"Nope. And if you want to know the truth, I'm glad to be working nights."

"Any news on when Laney might be coming back?"

He blew out a sigh. "Not yet. She's hopeful. The other trainer – the one who was in the car wreck – is doing better than anyone hoped, but I think it's still going to be a while before he can return to work."

"She'll be back before you know it, and when she is, the two of you can start getting on with the life you should have always been living."

"Yeah. Did Cash say anything to you?"

Deacon chuckled. "Only that he was happy that he can finally admit that he knew."

Luke cocked an eyebrow. "He surprised me with the way he reacted – that he was happy about it. I think I'm even more surprised that he didn't say anything before now."

"That shouldn't surprise you. He plays everything close to his chest. I know everyone thinks that he'll come barging in and take charge, but he does his best to hang back and let the rest of them live their lives the way they see fit."

"I guess."

"Anyway, get your ass to work, Deputy."

"Sir, yes sir." Luke grinned at him and headed to his cubicle to gather his things before heading out for the night.

~ ~ ~

Laney lay in bed, staring at the ceiling. She'd sent Luke a good night text a little while ago, but she hated this. She knew that he worked the night shift often enough, she felt like the only thing that had gotten her through the time since she'd been back was being able to talk to him every night and say good night before she went to sleep.

She was tempted to send him another message now, but that wouldn't be fair – he'd told her that he was on patrol. The last thing he needed was her distracting him. She smiled as she pictured him in his uniform, sitting in his patrol car. That made her think about the day that she'd arrived home, when he'd pulled her over for speeding.

When her phone beeped with a text, she rolled over to grab it. Maybe it was a slow night, and he was sitting in his car just as she'd pictured him.

Her smile evaporated when she saw the notification. It wasn't Luke, it was a message from Nixon – or at least, Nixon's phone. It was probably that damn Buck again. She didn't know what his problem was, but she sure as hell planned to set him straight when she got home.

She set her phone back down. Whatever he wanted, she didn't want to know about it tonight.

Some people counted sheep when they couldn't sleep; Laney counted horses. Usually, it worked well, too. Tonight, it didn't help at all. She tried to focus her mind on the schedule for the rest of the week, but even that didn't help. It was a trick she'd learned when her mind used to race about everything that she needed to get done – just thinking about the schedule made her feel so exhausted that she fell asleep.

She smiled to herself. Perhaps it wasn't working tonight because she knew that exhausting schedule wouldn't last for much longer. It wasn't her whole future; it was just the next little while. She couldn't wait for Tom to figure out what he was going to do. She was really hoping that he'd hold out for Tony, and that Tony would make a miraculously speedy recovery. But whatever happened, she just wanted it to happen quickly so that she could go home.

There was no way that she was going to be able to get to sleep anytime soon. She rolled out of bed and went to get her laptop from the dining room table. She'd told Luke that she would love to start a breeding program. Since right now she couldn't be with him – couldn't even talk to him – the next best thing she could do was start looking into what sires might be coming to market.

She froze with her hand above the keyboard when she realized another key aspect of a breeding program that she could maybe start looking into while she was here. She couldn't stop smiling as she took her laptop back to bed. She might be tired when it was time to get up and go to work in the morning, but right now, she was wide awake.

~ ~ ~

Luke took another pass down Second Street. He'd crisscrossed all the residential streets on either side of Main a couple of times already. It appeared that everything was quiet, but that was the way it went. Everything *was* quiet – until it wasn't.

When he hit the end of Second Street, he took a left and headed out of town a little way, passing the exit from the interstate, and carrying on to the gas station. He liked to check in with whoever was working there. Usually, they were more likely to encounter trouble than anyone else in town – given that most of their traffic was travelers passing by or through.

He took a minute to stretch his back and legs when he got out of the car. He stopped in surprise when he opened the door to the gas station and saw Brooke behind the counter.

"Hey, Brookie. What are you doing here, girl? I thought you weren't working the night shift anymore." He gave her a stern look. "At least, that's what Blaine said."

She looked up at him with wide eyes. "Don't tell him, Luke!"

Luke smiled through pursed lips. "You think I'd set the big brother brigade on you?"

She gave him a tight smile. "I hope not. Believe me, I wouldn't be working the night shift if I didn't have to. But we both know I'm safe. Blaine just likes to overreact."

"First of all, why do you have to? I thought you were watching the girls for Emmett these days."

"I am. And he pays me really well. It's just that I'm trying to save up. I'm taking all the hours I can get, anywhere I can get them."

"What are you saving up for? Trying to get out of here?"

She let out a short laugh. "No. I don't ever want to leave. That's part of the problem. If I wanted to leave, I could probably start my business much more easily somewhere else."

Luke frowned. "Your business? Are you still doing that clothes thing?"

She laughed. "Oh my God! You're such a guy. Yes, I'm doing the *clothes thing*. But never mind me; what about you? What's happening with Laney? She's coming back, right? Please tell me she's coming back. I always thought that the two of you would make a great couple."

"You did?" Luke asked in surprise. Brooke had been one of their gang of friends growing up. She was the same age as Laney – he thought – maybe a couple of years younger. Her older brother, Blaine, was good friends with Deacon and Cash, and that whole group of older guys. But for some reason, Brooke had always kind of been on the outskirts of the group.

"Yeah." She smiled. "I think maybe I'm just a closet romantic. But I always thought the two of you were going to get together. Then, she left. But you never really got with anyone else – not for real. So, I always held out hope."

He had to smile. "So did I."

"Aww. Well, don't let her get away again this time, will you? Although…" She frowned. "She already did get away, didn't she?"

"No. She had to go back to Kentucky for a little while, but she didn't get away." Luke smiled. "This time, I'm not letting her go."

"Good. Anyway, sorry, I'm getting as bad as the rest of the gossips in town. What can I get you? And is there anything going on that I should know about? It seems like there have been a lot more patrols tonight."

"You know about the burglaries, right?"

"Oh. I do. Have there been more?"

"Yes. And this time the homeowner was home."

"Oh no! Are they okay? Did they get hurt?"

"No." Brooke really wasn't as bad as most of the gossips in town. So far, the first question that most people asked was who the homeowner was. Brooke's first concern was that they were okay – whoever they were. "They're fine. But we're concerned that whoever's committing these break-ins is getting braver."

"I'll be damn sure to double lock all my doors and windows."

"You do that. And you know my number. If you hear anything, do not go to investigate. You barricade yourself in your room and you call me, you hear?"

She grinned. "I hear you loud and clear. And thanks, Luke."

Cash: How's it going, honey?

Laney: Meh. It's going. I'm ready to go home again now.

Cash: About damn time. I'd started to wonder if you'd ever come to your senses.

Laney: Haha. I can't believe that you knew about me and Luke all this time and never said anything.

Cash: Contrary to popular belief, I'm not into interfering in people's lives.

Laney sat there staring at her phone. Although, now that she thought about it, he didn't interfere. He just made his opinions known – he didn't really try to force anyone to comply with them. It was just that she – and her other siblings – respected him so much that they tended to do what he suggested without question.

Cash: What's up, honey? Did I stun you into silence?

Laney laughed.

Laney: Nope. Just made me stop and think. You might not "interfere," but you can't deny that you "guide" or maybe "steer" people.

Cash: Maybe so – but have I ever steered you wrong?

Laney: Okay. No, you haven't. What's up anyway?

Cash: Just checking in. I wanted to see how you're doing. What's going on there – are you signing up for another contract?

Laney: Hell no! I'm here to help Tom out. I'm covering for Tony while he's laid up but I'm outta here the first chance I get.

Cash: Good.

Laney: Were you planning on doing some steering if you didn't like my answer?

Cash: Maybe.

Laney: Thanks.

Cash: You're welcome. And let me know when you're ready to go. I could take another trip home myself if it's in the next few weeks. I could probably persuade Mav to come along, too.

Laney: That'd be awesome – and it WILL be in the next few weeks. The sooner the better as far as I'm concerned.

She looked up when one of the grooms popped her head around the office door.

"They're ready for you in the arena."

"I'll be right out."

Laney: I've got to go. Duty calls.

Cash: Ok. Be good. And try to give me some notice when you're ready to go.

Laney: Will do. I appreciate it. Flying with you guys makes that trip a lot more bearable.

Cash: Yeah. I'm over the days of flying commercial into Bozeman with the tourists. Talk soon.

Laney smiled to herself as she made her way out to the arena. She couldn't imagine Cash standing waiting at the baggage claim, listening to the tourists talk about the snow like she'd had to when she arrived home.

She took her phone back out of her pocket and sent him one last message.

Laney: Any chance you might move back to the valley? Kolby said he was thinking about it last time we spoke. If the three of us all moved back, the clan would be complete.

She watched the screen wondering if he'd reply before she had to put her phone away and get back to work.

Cash: When the old man's gone. Not before. But Kolby might be back sooner than you think. And Mav's been making noises about it too.

Laney: Damn! I want to ask you so many questions right now, but I've got to get back to work.

Cash: Me too — no peace for the wicked, right? We'll talk soon.

Laney didn't have the time to think about what Cash had said for the rest of the afternoon. She was too busy working. But when she finally got back up to the apartment, she took her phone out and reread their conversation. Mav was making noises about maybe moving back to the valley? And Kolby might be there sooner than she expected? Wow.

Mav was Frankie's older brother, Laney's cousin. But he was more like another big brother. He and Cash had grown up like brothers – and they still acted like brothers. They'd left the valley years ago when they signed up for the military.

Mav had been married back then – to Libby. They were divorced now, and Laney had believed that Mav wouldn't ever move home – because of Libby. She'd also believed that Cash wouldn't move back either – because of their father. But she shouldn't be surprised that he'd said not until the old man died – there'd be nothing to keep him away then.

She'd said the same thing – that she wouldn't set foot on the ranch while their father was still alive, but she'd relented. She hadn't relented for the old bastard's sake – she still hadn't seen or spoken to him, and she didn't plan to – she'd gone back to the ranch for Janey's wedding. And once she was there, she'd realized that staying away was only cutting off her nose to spite her face. The old man had been lying in a private hospital for almost two years. He wasn't on the ranch, and he most likely never would be again.

After her shower, she made herself a salad and topped it with strips of chicken breast – she wasn't the world's greatest cook, but she did okay.

Once she was sitting at the table to eat, she took her phone and scrolled through her contacts. She hadn't spoken to Kolby for a while. She'd deliberately been putting it off since she and Luke had gotten together. She hoped that he'd be okay with it – and it was time to find out.

She dialed his number and waited.

"Laney-Lou!"

"Hey, you. How are you doing?"

"Busy. Well, less so now. It's been a hectic few months, though. This private hire stuff can get crazy. What about you?"

"I'm good."

"Any news?"

She swallowed. She'd have to tell him – she couldn't keep quiet now, not when everyone else knew.

Kolby laughed. "If you're trying to figure out how to tell me about Luke, you can relax. Ty told me. I think it's awesome."

"You do?"

"Yeah. Why wouldn't I? He's a great guy."

Laney had to laugh. "He is."

"Were you worried that I was going to give you shit?"

"A little bit."

"Nah. I can see why the others would. I mean Ford, Wade, and Tan are your big brothers, so they have the whole *look out for their little sister* thing going on. And Ty ... well, Ty's just Ty. But me? You were always the one who looked out for me. I trust your judgment, and, like I said, Luke's a great guy. I'm happy for you."

"Thanks."

"You're welcome. But now you're back in Kentucky and stuck there for a while?"

"Hopefully not too long. I'm headed home as soon as I can. And I talked to Cash today; he said that you might be headed home, too?"

"I dunno yet. I've been crazy busy, and I'm thinking about taking a break, but it's not as though I could do much in my line of work at home, is it?"

"Does that matter? I mean, don't you go wherever your clients are when you're working?"

"I do."

"So, why can't you move home and just go away for work whenever you need to?"

"I suppose I could."

"I'd love it if you moved back. It'd be nice to live in the same time zone as you again."

Kolby laughed. "Yeah, I don't think we've done that since you left home, have we?"

"Nope. You should think about it. I'm excited about being back there, but they all have these lives that they've built while I've been gone. If you came back too …"

"You don't need me. You'll fit right back in – especially since you're with Luke."

Laney laughed. "Who said anything about needing you? I *want* you there. That's different."

"Yeah, it is. I'm going to have to go in a minute, but I'll tell you what – let me know when you're going back and – unless I'm working – I'll come out for a visit. Maybe even think about sticking around."

"Awesome! I should warn you – I plan to get back there just as soon as I can."

"I figured as much – so let me know."

"Will do."

"Listen, I've gotta run. Talk to you soon."

"Okay. Love you, little brother." She'd gotten into the habit of calling him that when he was twelve and had a growth spurt that had him towering over her.

Kolby laughed. "Love you too, big sis."

Chapter Nineteen

Luke shoved his hands in his pockets as he walked out of the afternoon briefing. Another week had gone by, and nothing much had changed. Everyone in the sheriff's department was still on high alert, although there hadn't been any more break-ins. He was still working nighttime patrols – but that was mostly because he was hoping that Deacon would give him a break from working the night shift once Laney came home.

He was hoping that she would be coming home soon. When he talked to her last night, she'd said that Tony was supposed to be getting out of the hospital tomorrow. Luke didn't know the guy, but he'd never rooted so hard for someone to make a speedy recovery.

He looked around when he got back to his cubicle and then took out his cell phone. He really shouldn't be talking to her while he was working, but with each day that went by, he missed her more. There was no harm in shooting her a quick text.

Luke: I'm about to start my shift so I won't be able to call you later. I miss you, baby. Love you.

He watched the screen for a few moments but there was no reply – he hadn't really expected one.

He gathered his things and headed out to his patrol car. He'd been working with Miller for the last few nights, but he was by himself tonight. Normally, he didn't mind, but lately he preferred to have company. When he was by himself, he tended to get distracted, thinking about Laney.

He pulled his phone back out when it buzzed with a message.

> *Tanner: Do you get a night off anytime soon? I was thinking I could come and hang out.*

> *Luke: I'm off for the next two days. Come over whenever you like. It'd be good to hang out. And if you want to come during the day, I can show you how the horses are coming along.*

He'd reached the patrol car and got inside before he checked to see what Tanner had to say about that.

> *Tanner: That'd be great. I can come tomorrow? I was going to ask if you wanted me to take the horses back. I know it can't be easy while you're working nights.*

> *Luke: Hell no! I love having them.*

> *Tanner: Awesome. And besides, you should probably get used to having horses on the property, ready for when Laney comes home, right?*

> *Luke: Yeah.*

> *Tanner: Any word on when she'll be back yet?*

> *Luke: I'm hoping to know more tomorrow. Tony's getting out of the hospital.*

> *Tanner: I'll keep 'em crossed.*

Luke: Thanks, bud. I'll see you tomorrow.

Tanner: Just give me a shout when you're up.

Luke slid his phone back into his pocket in a hurry when he saw Deacon striding across the parking lot toward him.

He put the window down and asked, "Everything okay?"

Deacon frowned. "Nothing's wrong. Well... Nothing except in my gut. I just ... Don't go laughing at me, but I've got a bad feeling. You be careful out there tonight, okay?"

"Hey, I wouldn't laugh. I trust your gut. I'll be extra alert."

Deacon nodded. "Is anyone else solo tonight? I'd rather have you all out in pairs."

Luke shook his head. "No. Tennyson called in sick, so there's an odd number of us tonight."

Deacon rubbed his chin. "I could ride with you."

Luke waved a hand at him. "I'll be careful, I promise. You're supposed to be on your way home. Can you honestly tell me that you'd rather spend the night sitting in a patrol car with me than at home with Candy and Clawson?"

Deacon smiled through pursed lips. "I..."

Luke could tell that he was about to say that he'd rather ride with him to make sure he was safe, and that Candy would understand. "I'll be careful, I promise."

Deacon blew out a sigh. "Okay, but if you run into anything that even looks suspicious, you call it in and you wait for backup, you hear me?"

"Yes sir."

"Okay. Oh, and Candy wants to know if you want to do one of our family reunion things at the bakery tomorrow – about this time. You're off duty tomorrow, right? And everyone else will be finishing about this time."

"Sure. Tanner's coming over to hang out tomorrow afternoon, but I'm sure he'd be happy to come over to the bakery, too."

Deacon smiled. "Tell him to ask his brothers, too."

Luke grinned back at him. "Will do."

"The way I see it, our family circle just keeps getting bigger. The MacFarlands have always felt like family – to both of us – and I reckon you might make it official one of these days soon, huh?"

Luke's heart pounded in his chest. It hadn't occurred to him before, but if he and Laney were to get married, those guys would be his brothers-in-law.

Deacon grasped his shoulder through the open window. "The look on your face tells me just how much you like that idea. I wouldn't waste any time about it if I were you."

"No? You don't think I should take it slow?"

"I don't. You've known pretty much your whole life that she was the only girl for you. I'd guess that she's known for just as long, if not longer, that you're the guy for her. You've wasted enough years as it is, it's time you made up for it."

Luke liked the sound of that, he just hoped that Laney would, too. They'd have to talk about it when she got home. They'd only had a couple of weeks together before she left again – and most of that time they'd been keeping their relationship a secret. He didn't want to do anything to screw things up between them going forward, and he'd already promised himself that he was going to try and make communication one of the strengths of their relationship. He couldn't deny that it had been a failing before.

"Go on," said Deacon. "Stop sitting there grinning like an idiot and get to work."

Luke laughed. "Okay, I'll see you tomorrow. Say hi to Candy for me."

"Will do. And you be careful out there."

~ ~ ~

Laney opened her eyes and sat up quickly at the sound of a car door slamming shut outside. She'd fallen asleep on the sofa after her dinner. She hurried to the window to look out, but it was just a couple of the grooms, chatting in the parking lot.

She made a face. They'd asked her if she wanted to join them when they all went out for dinner. She'd said no because she'd been hoping to hear from Luke. Damn! She went and grabbed her phone from the coffee table. Shit. She'd missed his text.

Luke: I'm about to start my shift so I won't be able to call you later. I miss you, baby. Love you.

She knew that he wouldn't be able to answer her now – he'd sent that a couple of hours ago – but she sent him one back.

Laney: I'm so sorry I missed your text. I fell asleep. I miss you, and I love you, too. I'm so sick of this now. All I want to do is come home to you and start getting on with our life.

She stared at the words before she hit send. Then, she deleted the last one and changed *life* to *lives*. She didn't want to freak him out. She stared at the words a little longer before changing her mind and changing it back to *life*. It wouldn't freak him out. He'd made it clear that was what he wanted. It was what she wanted, too. So, she wasn't going to go messing things up by overthinking. The plan was that they were going to build a life together. And from now on, she wanted to make sure that everything she said and did let him know that she was all in.

That thought made her smile, and she went to grab her laptop to see if she'd had a reply to the email she'd sent. If Haley and Walt were open to her proposal, that should make it pretty damn clear, to Luke and to everyone else, just how all-in she was.

She grabbed her phone again when it beeped with a text.

Luke: That's all I want, too, baby. I can't chat now; I'll call you when I finish in the morning. I know you'll be at work, but I just want to hear your voice for a minute. Love you.

Laney: I love you, too. Call me whenever you can.

She smiled as she set her phone back down and cracked open her laptop, excited to see if she'd heard back from Haley and Walt.

Luke put his cell phone away again. He really shouldn't be texting while he was working, but he had a feeling that even Deacon would understand.

He'd been sitting in an alley behind the cinema on Main Street – there was sometimes trouble back here when people started making their way home from the bars. It had been quiet tonight, though, and he figured that all the stragglers would have made it home by now.

He started up the car and radioed in. Usually, they were only expected to check in if they had anything to report. Deacon really must have a bad feeling tonight because he'd ordered that all the patrols should check in every two hours.

From what Dolores in the radio room told him, it seemed that Deacon's fears might be unfounded. She said that no one had had anything to report tonight, so far.

Luke told her that he was going to check out the east side of town and he'd check back in in a couple of hours.

As he drove down Maple Street, he looked up at the upstairs apartment in the big house on the corner. It made him sad – it was where Libby lived. Libby had been a part of his life for as long as Luke could remember. She'd been married to Mav, and they'd lived on the other MacFarland ranch down at the south end of the valley. Luke didn't know the whole story, but he knew that theirs had been a stormy relationship. They were divorced now and had been for a couple of years. But it still felt wrong to think of Libby living in an apartment in town. She was a rancher. She always had been.

He shook his head as he drove on by. He couldn't do anything for Libby and Mav – even though he wished he could. Everyone knew that they were still in love – they just couldn't make it work. All he could do was take theirs as a cautionary tale and do everything in his power to make sure that he and Laney didn't go down the same path. He was under no illusions; theirs could well turn out to be a stormy relationship, too. Laney was as independent as they came, and he could admit that he was probably a bit too set in his ways, after having lived alone for most of his adult life.

As he turned the corner, he was so caught up in his thoughts that he almost missed it. It took his mind a couple of seconds to register what he'd just seen; the window on the side of the house was broken, and the door stood slightly ajar.

He pulled the car over and got out, closing the door quietly behind him. His heart was pounding at the thought of someone making their way upstairs to Libby's apartment. That was the only place they'd be able to get to if they'd gone in through the side door. He knew the layout of the place.

Libby was not the kind of woman who would cower in her bedroom if she heard intruders. If he knew her, she'd come out shooting. That was the last thing anyone needed. He'd reached the gate and started to open it before he remembered that he'd promised Deacon he wouldn't go in alone.

He looked up at the apartment again, pressed his radio, and spoke quietly.

"Requesting back up. I'm at 27 Maple. There's a broken window next to the side door." He smiled grimly. "Can you put it on record for Deacon that I'm sorry, but I'm going in. It's Libby's place."

He reached the door by the time he finished speaking and turned the volume down on his radio. The last thing he needed was for that thing to start squawking and alert the intruders that he was there.

He took out his pistol and made his way up the stairs as quietly as he could. He stopped to listen when he reached the landing. The door to the apartment was standing open, but he couldn't hear anything. His heart was pounding; he was scared that Libby might hear something at any moment and come out to investigate.

He pushed the door open with his foot but couldn't see a thing inside. It was dark, and quiet. He edged his way inside but froze when he spotted a man with his back to him, rummaging through the drawers in the entertainment center.

He widened his stance as he raised his weapon. "Stop! Hands in the air."

It happened so quickly that Luke didn't have time to think, he simply reacted.

The man turned around and aimed a pistol at him. When he grinned and said, "Gotcha!" Luke knew he was in trouble.

"Lower your ..." were the only words he managed to get out before the man fired, and Luke fired back.

He watched the man drop his weapon and fall to the ground. He'd aimed to disarm, not to kill – the man grasped his hand, which was pouring with blood.

Luke tried to raise his pistol again, but suddenly became aware of searing pain in his shoulder. Shit! The bastard had shot him. He took a step backward, suddenly feeling lightheaded.

He thought he might be hallucinating when he heard someone say, "Give me the gun, I need to finish him off."

Luke did his best to stay on his feet as he swung around to see who else was in the room.

The guy on the floor made a grab for his gun. "No way. We need to get out of here. Leave him. Come on."

Luke's vision blurred as he saw a second man coming at him from his left. He staggered backward when he saw a tattooed arm fly through the air toward him. Then, his head felt as though it exploded with pain, and his vision faded to black.

Chapter Twenty

"Luke! Luke, wake up! Can you hear me?"

He struggled to do as the voice asked, but he couldn't quite come to the surface. His head hurt, and it felt as though someone was sticking a red-hot poker in his shoulder, but he couldn't figure out why.

"Luke, come on man!"

That voice... It sounded like Miller. But what the hell was one of his fellow deputies doing here, trying to wake him up? Luke didn't get it, and he couldn't hold onto the thought. It drifted away as Luke drifted back into the darkness.

"I need an ambulance," was the last thing that he heard.

The next time he came near the surface, he tried to open his eyes, but they wouldn't cooperate. It had to be late in the day already; he could sense the bright light beyond his eyelids. Then, he let himself sink back into the darkness. He was okay to sleep – he'd been working nights, that must be why it was so hard to wake up.

~ ~ ~

Laney rolled over onto her shoulder. She was lingering in that place between sleep and awake. It was her own damn fault. It was because she'd taken a nap on the sofa after dinner. She tried to sink back down into sleep but couldn't quite manage it. Although, maybe she had drifted back off – the alarm on her phone was going off now, so it must be time to get up. Wait. No. That wasn't her alarm. The phone was ringing.

She bolted up right and fumbled around on the nightstand. She cursed when she knocked the phone to the floor, and it stopped ringing. She took a deep breath as she turned on the bedside lamp. She needed to calm down. Her hands might be shaking, and her mind might have immediately jumped to the fear that something had happened to Luke – but that didn't make it so. Then again, she'd never had a phone call in the middle of the night that brought good news.

She retrieved her phone from under the nightstand and checked the screen. It was Cash. Her hands shook even harder as she pressed the button to call him back.

He answered on the first ring. "Are you up, honey?"

"I am now. What is it? Is it Luke?"

"Yeah. Get your shit together. We're on our way to the airport now. We'll be with you in a couple of hours. As soon the guys file a flight plan, I'll let you know what time we'll be landing; you can meet us at the airfield."

Laney wanted to scream at him. He needed to stop talking arrangements and tell her what had happened. Instead, she sucked in a deep breath and went to the closet to pull out her bag. When she knew that she wasn't likely to either scream or cry, she asked, "What's happened?"

"He's going to be okay, honey."

"That's not what I asked," she snapped.

"I know. But it's what I want you to have in your head when I tell you what happened. He was investigating a break-in and he caught them in the act."

"Oh my God! What did they do to him?"

"Well, it sounds like there were two of them. One of them shot him. And the other knocked him out with one of Libby's brass horses."

Laney squeezed her eyes shut to keep the tears in. "He's really going to be okay, isn't he?"

Cash let out a low chuckle. "That's why I told you that first, honey. It might take a while, but he's going to be okay. They got him to the hospital, and Trip is on his way. My question is – are you going to be okay? Are you going to be able to get your shit together and get to the airport?"

She sucked in a deep breath and stood up straighter. "You really need to ask?"

"That's my girl."

Laney frowned. "Wait a minute, you said they hit him with one of Libby's brass horses? Does that mean it was Libby's place they broke into?"

"Yeah."

"Is she okay?"

"She wasn't there. From what Deacon told me, it sounds like Luke went in without waiting for backup because he was worried about her. It turns out that she's over in Billings."

Laney nodded. She didn't know what to say – or how to feel. She was glad that Libby was safe, proud of Luke that he hadn't given his own safety a second thought because he wanted to protect her, and she was also mad at him for going into a dangerous situation alone.

She heard muffled voices in the background before Cash came back on the line. "As long as you're okay, I'm gonna let you go. We're almost to the airport."

"Okay. Is Mav with you?"

"He is."

"Okay. I'll see you when you get here. I'm packing now, and I'll head straight out to the airport and wait for you there."

"Don't do that! The last thing I need is you sitting around alone in your car in the middle of the night – the airport isn't staffed at night. Wait until I send you our ETA. You'll still have plenty of time to get there."

Laney blew out a sigh.

"Promise me, honey?"

"Okay."

"Thanks. I think Luke just proved that you can't go overlooking your own safety just because you're concerned about someone else's."

Laney made a face at her phone.

"I'll see you soon."

"Not soon enough," said Laney. She hated knowing that it would be at least a couple of hours before he would land here, and another couple of hours after that before they'd get to Montana.

She set her phone back down on the nightstand and started throwing her things into her bag. When it was full, she looked around; she was taking everything. Whatever condition Luke was in – however good or bad it was – when she got to him this time, she wasn't leaving again.

She'd have to let Tom know, but there was no point waking him in the middle of the night. Instead, she went down to the office to start writing out instructions for the grooms for the day. They could do without her presence for a day or two if she left them a detailed program to follow. After that, hopefully Tony would be back. If not, Tom would just have to figure it out.

She felt like she owed Tom her loyalty, but now her priority had changed. Luke was everything. She was trying to keep herself as busy as possible until she could head to the airport –

but only so that she didn't go out of her mind with worry until she knew more, until she could see him.

Once she got home to him, nothing else would matter. She wouldn't have a thought to spare for Tom, this place, or anything else. She checked her watch and murmured, "Come on, Cash."

She grabbed her phone off the desk when it beeped.

Cash: Landing at 05:25am. Don't get there too early – the guys will have to refuel the plane before we can take off again.

Laney shook her head. She didn't care what he said, she was leaving right now.

Laney: I'll be there.

Cash: Drive safe.

~ ~ ~

"I brought you coffee."

Deacon took the Styrofoam cup from Candy with a grunt of thanks and leaned back against the wall.

"You should sit down," she said as she rested her hand on his arm. "You've been standing there like that for hours."

He almost snapped at her that he would continue to stand there until his brother regained consciousness, but he remembered just in time that it was Candy he was talking to and managed to reel himself in.

"I'm okay, darlin'."

She gave him a sad smile. "No, you're not. But you will be. You'll be fine just as soon as he wakes up. And he's going to wake up soon. I know it."

Deacon closed his eyes and took a sip of the coffee as he willed her to be right. He couldn't stand this – couldn't stand seeing Luke looking so pale. The gunshot wound to his shoulder was one thing. From what the doctors had told them, it wasn't too serious. It wasn't ideal – gunshot wounds never were – but it hadn't done any major damage. It'd put him out of action for a while, but that didn't matter.

Deacon was more concerned about the head injury. The doctors were more concerned about that, too. They were monitoring him for swelling and internal bleeding – but so far, so good.

He turned when the door opened, and Trip came in.

"How's he doing?"

Deacon scowled. "You're the damn doctor. I was hoping you'd tell me."

Trip smiled at him through pursed lips. "I just arrived, Deacon. From what I've been told, the shoulder isn't too bad and as far as his head goes…" His smile faded. "We have to play the waiting game."

Deacon nodded. "Well, there's nothing that I can tell you to add to that. He looked like he might be coming around a little while ago, but it didn't happen."

"It might take a while. You guys should think about going home."

"No!"

Trip smirked at him. "I know. But as his doctor, and yours, I had to suggest it."

"I'm going nowhere." He went to Candy and put his arm around her shoulders. "Sorry, darlin'. I'm going to live up to your old name for me until I know that he's going to be okay."

She smiled up at him. "Don't you go apologizing. You have every right to be grumpy. I understand. He's going to be fine, though. I know it."

Trip nodded. "Do you want me to let anyone know?"

"I called Cash. I figured it was best to let him get ahold of Laney and tell her. Other than that, I figured that the grapevine would do its thing."

He looked up and smiled through pursed lips when the door cracked open, and Ace popped his head around it. "Looks like I was right."

Ace stepped inside and raised his eyebrows. "Right about what? How's he doing?"

"Right that the grapevine still works well enough to get people here, and…" Deacon looked at Luke again, hating to see him so pale and still. "As for how he's doing, we're still waiting to see."

"What can I do?" Ace asked. "Do you need to get back to work?"

Deacon shook his head. "I'm not going anywhere. Undersheriff Townsend is heading up the investigation. He'll do a better job than I would at this point."

"Do we have any idea what happened?"

"He saw signs of forced entry at Libby's place."

"Libby's place? Is she okay?"

Deacon nodded. "She wasn't home. She's over in Billings at some equine therapy conference."

"I'm guessing Luke didn't know that?"

"Nope. I told him before his shift last night that he wasn't to go into anything without backup." He smiled through pursed lips. "The damn fool even left a message for me – said to tell me he was sorry, but he was going in because it was Libby's place."

Ace and Trip exchanged a smile.

"Don't give him too hard a time about it when he wakes up, huh? You know damn well that any one of us would have done the same thing."

"Yeah. I won't be giving him a hard time. I just want him to wake up."

Trip cocked an eyebrow at him. "And what did you tell Cash?"

Deacon smiled through pursed lips. "That he was investigating a break-in at Libby's place when it happened."

Ace chuckled. "Let me guess – Mav's coming with him?"

"He didn't say as much, but I'd put money on it. I'd imagine that Mav marched right out to that plane of theirs with him, and they flew straight to Lexington to get Laney."

Candy looked at her watch. "Do we have any idea when they'll arrive?"

Deacon shook his head. At this point, his only focus was Luke. Yes, he was concerned about Laney, but Cash was with her.

Ace took his phone out of his jacket pocket and stepped back toward the door. "I'll go see what I can find out."

~ ~ ~

As Luke became aware of the darkness, it started to recede. He'd slept hard, and he had one hell of a headache. The closer he came to the surface, the more aware he was of the bright light shining in. He must have forgotten to close the curtains before he went to bed.

He couldn't remember even coming to bed. There were other thoughts just on the edge of his awareness, but the more he reached for them, the further away they moved. He should check the time – he'd said that he'd call Tanner to hang out this afternoon. His eyes didn't want to cooperate, but he forced them open. The moment he did, he regretted it. The light was blinding, and this headache was a bitch.

"Luke?"

He closed his eyes again. Now he was hearing things. That had sounded like Deacon. He must be really groggy because he felt like he was back in high school. He used to struggle to get up in time, and Deacon used to come into his room to make sure he was awake.

"Luke? Are you awake?"

He groaned. He didn't want to get up.

"Maybe we should leave him be? Or do you think we should call a nurse?"

That was weird. That was a woman's voice. Luke replayed the sound of it in his head until he realized that it was Candy. What the hell was going on?

He squinted, only opening his eyes a little crack this time. Bright overhead lights shone down at him, and the smell … He knew that smell – hated it. It was… the hospital? What the hell was he doing in the hospital?

He tried to turn his head when he heard Deacon speak again, but the pain stopped him. It felt as though someone was tightening a vice, crushing his skull. He tried to reach up to touch it, but that just sent searing pain through his shoulder. What the hell?

"Deacon?" His voice came out as a croak. "What's going on?"

His brother's face appeared in front of him, the lines around his eyes etched with concern. "How are you doing? Nice of you to finally join us."

"I feel like shit. What happened?"

"You don't remember?"

Luke closed his eyes again. He remembered talking to Deacon before he went out on patrol. He'd texted with Tanner to make arrangements for this afternoon. Other than that … He'd sat behind the cinema, but everything had been quiet. Then…

"Libby!" He tried to sit up but didn't get far.

Deacon put a hand to his shoulder. "Take it easy, bud. Libby wasn't home."

"Thank fuck for that."

"What do you remember?"

"The door to her stairs was open. I had to go in. You know what she's like. She would've confronted them."

Deacon nodded. "What else?"

Luke peered at him and gave him a rueful smile. "I may have disobeyed orders."

Deacon chuckled. "Yeah, you did. But I can't give you too much shit for it. I got the message. And even though this is the result of you not waiting for backup, I can't tell you that I would have done any different."

"Thanks. There were two of them."

"That's what the guys figured. What do you remember?"

Luke squeezed his eyes shut as his head pounded. "I thought the first guy was alone. He was going through Libby's drawers." He replayed the scene again in his mind. "There was something weird about it, though."

"What kind of weird?"

"It was almost as though he was expecting me. When I drew my weapon and told him to turn around, he drew a pistol of his own. But... The weird thing was that instead of just shooting – and he could have ..." Luke swallowed as he understood just how lucky he was to be lying here in a hospital bed.

Deacon's hand came down on his good shoulder. "I know."

"But he didn't just shoot. He smiled, and said, *gotcha*."

"You didn't recognize him?"

"No. I don't think I've ever seen him before."

"Description?"

Luke sighed. "My height, maybe an inch or two shorter. Light brown or dirty blond hair. I'd guess mid-thirties. Denim jacket, shearling collar. Medium build." He tried to think of anything else, but nothing came.

"Don't you think you should let him rest?" asked Candy.

Luke cracked one eye open, and she smiled at him. "It's good to see you awake."

"Wish I could say that it's good to be awake – but it hurts like hell."

"I imagine it does," said Deacon. "What about the other guy?"

"I didn't see him. Well, I saw an arm swinging for me. He was holding something." He reached up to touch his head again, remembering to use his left hand this time.

Deacon pursed his lips. "Yeah, you've got one of Libby's brass horses to thank for that."

"Damn."

"You're lucky that he only hit you once."

Luke's heart pounded in his chest. "I am. And as strange as it may sound, I'm grateful to the guy who shot me, because the one who hit me asked for the gun before he hit me. He said he wanted to finish me off."

All the color drained from Deacon's face, and his jaw set. "And you can't give me any description of the second guy?"

"No. Like I said. Just an arm swinging for me – holding something."

Deacon straightened up. "You stay right here with Candy."

Luke had to smile. "Okay then. If you insist. I mean, I was planning to get up and go for a run but ..."

Deacon scowled at him. "Very funny. I'm going to call Townsend. I'll tell him what you've told me and get him to send someone over to take a statement. The sooner the guys know who they're looking for, the more chance we'll stand of running them down."

"Well, I guess one detail that might come in useful is that I shot the first guy – the one I described – in the hand. That's not going to be easy for him to hide."

"I'll tell him. And you see if you can remember anything at all about the second one – about that arm you saw."

"Yeah." Luke tried to dredge up the memory. He felt as though there was something, but as he tried to chase the thought, it just led him back into the darkness. His head was pounding, his shoulder screaming. The darkness offered a little reprieve, and he let himself slide away.

Chapter Twenty-One

The next time Luke opened his eyes, he had a better idea of what was going on. There was nothing dull about the pain in his head or his shoulder, and he was fully aware of where he was – in the hospital.

"There he is."

He turned his head slowly and saw Tanner and Tyler sitting beside his bed.

"Hey, guys."

Tyler chuckled. "Hey, yourself. How are you feeling? It's a good thing you've got such a hard head."

Luke rolled his eyes at him. "I've had better days."

"Seriously," said Tanner, "how are you feeling? The nurse said we should call for her as soon as you wake up."

Luke smiled. "Did she say that, or did you volunteer to do it just to get her back in here?"

Tanner scowled at him. "I'm not joking. You've had us all worried."

"Sorry."

"Dammit, don't say sorry – that just makes me worry even more."

"No need to worry. I'm fine – or I'm sure I will be in a day or two. What are you guys doing here, anyway?"

"What do you think? When we heard what had happened – and that you were in the hospital – Wade and Ford are on the way up as well. Deacon and Candy have been here the whole time. Trip pretty much had to drag him out of here and make him go and eat something."

Luke was listening, but he didn't like what he was hearing. He didn't like being the cause of any worry to anyone.

"Laney!" he said when it hit him. "Make sure no one tells Laney. I don't want her worrying."

He rested his head back down on the pillows when the guys both laughed at him.

"Too late," said Ty. "She'll be here soon."

"What? How?"

Tanner smiled at him. "The big brother brigade – what do you expect? Deacon called Cash, he and Mav hopped in the jet, and they stopped in Lexington to pick Laney up on the way." He checked his watch. "And I reckon they'll be landing right about now."

Luke closed his eyes. "Shit. I don't need people turning their lives upside down for me."

Tyler cocked an eyebrow at him. "Are you saying you don't want her here?"

Luke had to smile. "Hell no! I can't wait to see her. I just hate to think of her being worried about me, and that she's been yanked away from her job just because I went and got myself shot."

Tanner chuckled. "Not just shot. By all accounts, you did a pretty decent job of getting your head bashed in, too."

"It'll be fine in a day or two."

"Let's hope so," said Tyler. "But from the way Trip's been in and out of here, and the way he's had nurses checking on you every half hour, I'd say they think it's a bit more than a bang on the head that will heal in a day or two."

Luke stared at him. "Nah, they just have to be careful with head injuries." He was sure that he was going to be fine. He still felt a bit groggy, and the pain shot through him whenever he moved, but the news that Laney would be here soon went a long way to making him feel better.

"And you didn't recognize either of the guys?"

He looked at Tanner. He knew what he was thinking. "Even if I did, I wouldn't tell you. Let Deacon and Townsend do the police work. I don't want you guys going getting yourselves in any trouble."

Ty scowled at him. "Even Deacon says that the law and justice aren't always the same thing."

"Yeah, but your kind of justice could land you in trouble with the law. I appreciate it guys, I do, but I don't want you going out trying to hunt them down."

"You think they were out-of-towners?" asked Tanner.

"I have no idea. I didn't recognize the one guy, and I didn't see the other. Well, I saw his arm."

"No identifying marks?" Ty asked.

Luke closed his eyes. "I feel like I should say yes, but I don't know. When I close my eyes, I can see the guy with the gun. I know that another guy was there. I heard him speak." He shuddered when he remembered the words that the second guy had spoken – *Give me the gun, I need to finish him off.*

"What is it? What did you just remember?"

He opened his eyes and looked at them. "Before he hit me, the second guy said that he needed to finish me off." He shuddered involuntarily. "It doesn't make any sense. The guy who'd just shot me refused. He grabbed the gun with his good hand and said that they needed to get out of there. If he was okay to shoot me once, why wouldn't he want his partner to finish me off?"

The brothers stared back at him. "Do you think they were after you – I mean, you in particular? Deacon told us how the first guy said *gotcha* when he saw you. Do you think …" Tanner shook his head. "Am I being paranoid? It sounds like a set up to me."

Luke stared back at him. "It was weird the way he said that. But why would someone want to lure me into Libby's place to shoot me but not kill me? It makes no sense."

Ty folded his arms across his chest and leaned his head back against the wall. "Have you pissed anyone off lately?"

Luke thought about it. "Not that I can think of." He tried to focus, working his way through the people he'd interviewed in relation to the break-ins. "I talked to the usual suspects about the burglaries. You know, the guys who pull the usual petty stuff in town. But there was no one that I thought I could tie to the break-ins. I don't think I was getting too close for comfort with someone."

Ty drummed his fingers on his forearm. "How about other people? Is there anyone who's got it out for you? It doesn't necessarily need to be the burglars. If someone had it in for you, they could have used the break-in as a cover."

Luke just stared at him. It all seemed too far-fetched. He couldn't think of anyone he'd crossed – not anyone who would try to pull something like that, anyway. He closed his eyes and ran his tongue over his lips; they were parched.

"Leave it, Ty," said Tanner. "We're wearing him out, and he looks like he could use a drink. I'll get the nurse."

Luke smiled but didn't open his eyes. He wanted to joke about Tanner only being here for the nurses, but he was drifting away again.

~ ~ ~

Laney willed the time to go faster as she rode in the back of the Suburban that Cash had rented at the airport. She just wanted to get to Luke, and this journey had felt like it had taken forever already. Right now, she felt like a little kid again – riding in the back seat while Cash and Mav sat up front.

She leaned forward when Mav's phone beeped, wanting to know what he had going on. Of course, he'd want to be here if something had happened to Libby – but she hadn't even been home. He wasn't much of a talker at the best of times, but he hadn't done much more than grunt since they'd picked her up in Lexington.

She couldn't see his screen, and she knew that she shouldn't be reading, so she sat back in her seat. Cash met her gaze in the rearview mirror and cocked an eyebrow at her. Of course he knew what she was up to.

"Not long now. We'll be there soon."

She nodded and took her own phone out. "I know, but I think I might explode with the waiting. I'm going to call Tanner."

"Hey, Laney-Lou. Where are you?"

"About twenty minutes out, I reckon. What do you know? Have you heard anything?"

"Yeah, we were talking to him until just a little while ago. He's gone back to sleep now."

All the air rushed out of her lungs, and her eyes pricked with tears. "How's he doing?"

Tanner chuckled. "He asked us not to tell you."

Laney's heart slammed to a halt. "He did *what?*"

Cash glanced at her again in the rearview mirror and cocked an eyebrow. She shook her head at him. If he told her to calm down … She didn't know what she'd do.

Tanner laughed again. "Take it easy, sis. He just didn't want you worrying. That's all. I thought it was kind of sweet that even in the state he's in, he was more concerned about you."

Laney slumped back in the seat. Of course Luke was thinking about her.

"Hey." All the laughter had left his voice. "Come on, Laney. He's okay. He's gonna be okay. Relax."

"Thanks, Tan."

"Do they have any leads on who did this?" Mav had turned in his seat and was looking back at her.

If Laney hadn't grown up with him, if she didn't know what a big teddy bear he was underneath the tough exterior, she'd be scared silly of him and the look on his face right now.

"Did you hear that?" she asked Tanner.

"I did. Tell him that … In fact, no – why don't you put me on speaker?"

Laney did as he asked and then held her phone up in between the two front seats so that they would all be able to hear him.

"You're on."

"What do they know?" Mav asked.

"Luke was able to give them a description of one guy. And if he's still around, he shouldn't be too hard to spot – given that Luke managed to shoot his hand. The other guy – the one who clobbered him – is a mystery. Luke didn't see anything but his arm."

"No identifying marks?" Cash asked.

Tanner chuckled. "You taught Ty well; he asked the same question. Luke said he feels that there's something, but he can't remember."

Laney covered her heart with her hand and sucked in a deep breath. "Is that, like, just a detail that he can't remember… Or …?"

"Just that one detail. Well, maybe others. But in general, he remembers everything. Don't worry. It's not like he has amnesia and won't remember you."

Laney scowled at her phone. "Jesus, Tan. Give me a break, would you? I'm worried sick here."

"Sorry, Laney-Lou. I was just trying to lighten things up."

"Yeah, well, I don't think anything will feel very light to me until I see him with my own two eyes."

"Is Deacon still there at the hospital?" Cash asked.

"He is. He's on the phone all the time with Townsend, and checking in with the deputies, but I don't think he'll go anywhere until he knows for sure that Luke's okay."

Laney's heart started to hammer again. "I thought you just said that he was okay!"

"He is. Just… Tell her, Cash. You know what I mean."

Cash chuckled. "Come on you guys, I thought we were beyond this. Do you really need me to referee your fights anymore?" He winked at Laney in the rearview mirror, and she had to smile.

"Sorry, Tan. I'm just worried."

"That's okay. I get it. Listen, I just saw the nurse and I'm going to …"

Cash laughed. "That right there tells me what I need to know. If you were really worried about Luke, you wouldn't be chasing nurses."

Tanner's laughter filled the cab of the SUV. "There you go, Laney. You remember how Cash could always figure out if we were telling the truth or not when we were kids? I think he just proved it to you right there that Luke really is okay."

She smiled through pursed lips. "I hope so. You'd feel like a real shit if he went downhill while you were out chasing nurses around."

Tanner sounded much more serious when he spoke again. "Damn straight I would. I'll talk to you later."

~ ~ ~

Luke woke himself up when he tried to turn over. He groaned at the pain that shot through his head, neck, and shoulder.

"Oh my God, he's awake!"

He opened his eyes in a hurry. He knew that voice. "Laney!"

Her face appeared, hovering over him. Her hazel eyes shimmered with tears.

He smiled. "Hey."

"Hey yourself." She smiled, even as the tears ran down her cheeks. "What have you been up to? I can't leave you alone without you getting into trouble, can I?"

"I did okay for a while, but I was missing you. I had to do something to get you back."

She chuckled. "You could have just said something. You didn't need to do something this dramatic."

He reached for her hand and squeezed it tight. "Seriously, I'm sorry. You didn't need to come back."

She crushed his fingers. "Yes, I did. What, you think I'd be okay just to hang out there in Lexington knowing that you were lying here in the hospital?"

"I guess not."

She leaned in and pressed a gentle kiss to his lips. "I hate the reason that I came, but I'm glad to be back – and I'm not leaving you again this time."

"You can stay? Is Tony back?"

She shrugged. "He's getting out of the hospital today. I've left them a plan to follow for the rest of the week. After that, Tom will just have to figure it out – either with Tony, or whoever else he can bring in. I'm done." She met his gaze and held it. "My place is here – with you."

A rush of warmth filled his chest. "I'm not going to argue with that."

"Good. And besides, even if you don't want me, the horses need me."

He smiled. "I've been taking good care of them; you can ask Tanner."

Her smile had faded. "I believe you, but it'll be a while before you can get back to them, won't it?"

He sighed. "Hopefully not. I'm hoping that Trip will say I can go home soon."

She raised her eyebrows at him. "You've been shot and had your head bashed in. I think you might be stuck here for a little while, Deputy."

He still didn't like it when she called him that, and it must have shown on his face.

"What? What did I say?" she asked.

"Just the deputy thing."

"You don't like me calling you that? What would you rather I call you?"

He held her gaze for a long moment, a variety of answers running through his mind. He didn't dare tell her the name that he hoped she would be calling him before too long, so he went with "Luke? Baby? Honey, maybe?"

"I can't call you honey – that's what Cash has always called Janey and me. You call me baby; it'd be weird for me to call you the same thing." She smiled. "Luke has always been my favorite name in the whole world – but I want to have a special name for you, too."

She stood back when the door opened behind her, and Trip came in.

"How are you feeling, Luke? It's good to see you awake."

Luke smiled at Laney. "I'm feeling way better now."

She squeezed his hand again, and Trip laughed. "I mean your head and your shoulder – although, I have to tell you that it makes my heart happy to see the two of you together."

"It does?" Laney asked.

Trip nodded. "It really does. But anyway, enough of the mushy stuff. Can you move over Laney, honey? I need to get a look at your man here."

Laney chuckled as she moved a little farther away from the bed and rolled her eyes at Luke. "See what I mean about the *honey* thing?"

He chuckled with her, but then had to give his attention back to Trip when he started prodding and poking him and shining a light in his eyes.

"Can I go home, then?" he asked when Trip stood back.

"Not only no, but hell no! You're going to be in here for a while, buddy." Trip chuckled. "And before you start, Laney, I'll arrange to have a cot brought in here for you – but only in the hope that it will stop you from crawling up on the bed with him."

Laney laughed. "I'd be too scared of hurting him, but thanks. A cot would be great; I wasn't looking forward to sleeping on the floor."

Luke looked up into her eyes. "You don't need to sleep here. You can go home and ..."

The look she gave him cut his words off. "I've told you – I'm going nowhere. We can both go home when you're ready."

Trip grinned at him. "You know this is Laney you're talking to, right? You should probably get it into your head here and now that she's never going to thank you for trying to make life easier for her."

Laney laughed and slapped his arm. "I want to think that's a compliment, but it kind of feels like you're having a dig at me."

Trip winked at Luke. "Take it any way you want to, Laney. I'm just setting your man here straight. I need him to get as much rest as he can for the next few days; he doesn't need to be using up his energy trying to look out for you, when we all know that you won't let him."

Luke reached for Laney's hand again, and she came to stand right next to the bed as she took it. "I might suggest things for you – but I know better than to argue when you say no."

Trip smiled as he looked down at their joined hands resting on the bed. "I'll leave you guys to it."

Chapter Twenty-Two

Laney stuck her hands in her pockets as she walked back down the corridor from the cafeteria. She'd barely left Luke's bedside since she arrived two days ago. She'd been sleeping on the cot that Trip – true to his word – had arranged to have put in Luke's room.

This morning, Cash and Mav had stopped by, and along with Deacon, they'd run her out of the room. She knew that they wanted to talk to him about what had happened – the big brother brigade was on the warpath, determined to hunt down whoever had done this to Luke. But she didn't see why she couldn't have stayed. She wouldn't have gone if Luke hadn't asked her to. He'd said that he was concerned about her, and he wanted her to go and eat. So, she had.

Those guys had better be finished by the time she got back – they might be able to run her out, but they wouldn't be able to stop her from returning.

"Laney!"

She turned when she heard someone calling her name. She was surprised to see Sierra waving at her. Sierra wasn't someone she particularly wanted to talk to, but she forced herself to smile. After what Janey had explained to her – about

Sierra being protective – Laney was more prepared to give her the benefit of the doubt, even though Sierra hadn't exactly been welcoming when Laney first came home.

She waited, and Sierra hurried toward her. "Hi. I hope you don't mind me coming. The kids are at school, and Wade wanted to come up and see Luke." She dropped her gaze before looking back up at Laney. "He's in there with them now. I asked if I could come with him because... I'd like to talk to you ... I'd like to apologize."

Laney shrugged. "There's no need. Janey explained it to me."

Sierra met her gaze. She was a couple of inches shorter than Laney, and she seemed kind of... delicate. Laney figured that it took some courage for her to straighten her shoulders and lift her chin and say, "I feel like there is. I want to say I'm sorry. I wasn't very nice to you when you first came back and that was wrong of me. I just ... it's no excuse ... I felt protective of Janey – and I won't apologize for that."

Laney had to smile. "Good. I'm glad that you won't. I reckon that you feeling protective of her at least puts us on the same side."

Sierra nodded. "It does, but I should have taken the time to figure that out before deciding that you were the bad guy. I really am sorry."

"It's okay. It's behind us now."

"I hope so. I'd like for us to be friends." Sierra smiled. "And I have to tell you, that Maya wants to be your friend, too. She hasn't stopped talking about you – she thinks you're amazing. She wants to be a cowgirl, just like you."

"I'm not much of a cowgirl these days."

Sierra looked her up and down. "Your hat, your boots – pretty much everything about you says that you are."

"Maybe to you. But to me, cowgirl isn't defined by what you wear, it's what you do – who you are. It's a way of life, a state of mind even, not an image that you portray. I've still been working with horses all the years I've been gone, but even that's not the same as living and working on the ranch."

"Well, you still portray the image; you might not have been living the life, but I'd put money on the fact that you still have a cowgirl state of mind."

Laney nodded. "I guess I do."

"Well, if you wouldn't mind, Maya would love to spend some time with you." Sierra smiled. "I think it would do her good to be exposed to that cowgirl state of mind. I think you'd be a good influence on her and be able to give her something that I can't."

"I don't see how I could do that. It seems to me that you can give her everything she needs." Sierra was a freaking billionaire; Laney didn't see how she would have anything to offer the little girl that Sierra didn't.

Sierra bit down on her bottom lip. "I don't mean in a material sense. I mean ... We're different people, you and I. I'm doing better since I met Wade, but I don't mind admitting that I was kind of ... weak-willed ... if you want to call it that, in my old life. I mean, I let people push me around. Like I said, I'm doing better now, but I'm never going to be ..." She smiled. "I'm never going to be like you. And I'd love to think that Maya could pick up a little of your strength and determination by hanging out with you. If you wouldn't mind."

Laney nodded slowly, then she chuckled. "I don't think anyone's ever called me strong-willed and meant it as a compliment before. Stubborn maybe. But I know what you mean. I have to warn you that I'm no good with kids – I've never spent any time with kids. I like Maya but ... Aren't you worried that I might be a bad influence?"

"No."

"Well, that makes one of us." She smiled. "She asked me about teaching her to rope, but I thought Wade might want to do it."

"I'll talk to him. He might want to be the one to teach her, but even if that's the case, I'm sure there are lots of other things that you could teach her – we both know that it's different for girls."

"Yeah. There's no denying that."

They both turned when the door to Luke's room opened, and Wade came out. He smiled when he saw them and came to put his arm around Sierra's shoulders.

"There you are. I see you found her, then."

Sierra nodded.

Wade met Laney's gaze. "Are we good?"

She had to smile. Wade was the most easy-going of all her brothers, and she imagined that he must've felt pretty uncomfortable, knowing that his fiancée had an issue with his sister.

"We're good." She looked at Sierra. "We've straightened things out, and we were just talking about me maybe spending some time with Maya."

Wade grinned. "That would be awesome. She's been talking about you. She wants to be a cowgirl like you. And I'll tell you what, if you want to teach her to rope, I'll be forever in your debt."

Laney exchanged a smile with Sierra as she asked, "You wouldn't mind?"

"Mind? I'd love it."

"Then, I'd be glad to." She glanced at Luke's door again. "Of course, it won't be for a while yet. Not until I get him home and settled in. Are they all still in there with him?"

"Yeah. Although, I think the interrogation's over now. He might appreciate you getting back in there so that they give him a break."

Laney scowled and started toward the door. Wade laughed. "Don't go storming in and reading them the riot act, Laney-Lou."

She looked back at him and Sierra and smiled. "I don't plan to. I'm not as bad as people think. I just want to be there with him. We know how intense the big brothers can get. I wouldn't try to stop them – there's no point – but I do want to be right by his side. I'll see you guys soon."

~ ~ ~

Luke reached up to touch Laney's hand, which was resting on his shoulder as he sat in the wheelchair. "I cannot wait to get home."

"And I can't wait to get you there."

Luke looked up at the nurse who was pushing the chair. "I promise you, we can take it from here."

The nurse chuckled. "And I promise you that I'd let you if I could, Luke. But you know it's protocol. We have to wheel you out and wait with you until you're in a vehicle and on your way."

Laney grinned. "And here's the vehicle."

Tanner pulled up next to them at the curb and climbed out of Luke's truck. It had been sitting in the parking lot at the sheriff's department since he'd parked it there when he arrived for his shift on the night everything went down. Ty had given Tanner a ride into town so that he could collect the truck and drive them home.

Tanner grinned at them and offered Luke his hand. Luke took it and let his friend help him to his feet. Once he was settled in the passenger seat, he grinned at the nurse. "Thanks for everything, Mike. Nothing personal, but I hope I don't see you again anytime soon."

Mike laughed. "Also nothing personal, but ditto."

Once Laney was settled in the back seat, and Tanner was behind the wheel, they set off.

"Did you manage to do everything, Tan?" Laney asked.

"I did. Well, I didn't do it all myself. I have to tell you that Candy stocked the fridge for you, and Sierra dropped off a bunch of stuff this morning."

Luke smiled to himself. He was glad that those two were making an effort. It might be more for his sake than for Laney's, but it was a start.

"All I've been doing is keeping an eye on the horses." He glanced over at Luke. "Are you sure that you still want them around?"

"I am. If anything, I was thinking about asking if you want to send any more over."

Laney leaned forward between the seats. "You're supposed to be taking it easy for at least the next few weeks."

Luke leaned in and pressed a kiss to her cheek. "And I will. I won't be able to ride for a while, but I figured ..." He brought his hand up and probed his shoulder with his fingers. "Yeah, I guess I wasn't thinking straight. I figured that since I'm going to have all this time off work ... but I'm not going to be much use in the barn either, am I?"

Laney grinned at him. "You are. You can hang out with me while I'm out there. You might have to stick to light duties, but you can keep me company."

Tanner laughed. "Don't talk like that, Laney. You'll have him desperate to get back to work as soon as he can."

"What?" Laney asked. "It'll be nice – won't it? The two of us being able to hang out together?"

"It will be nice to be able to hang out," said Luke. "But I think what Tan means is that I'm not going to enjoy feeling useless and watching you do all the work."

"But —" she started to protest, but he stopped her with a look.

"Think about it, Laney. If the roles were reversed, how would you feel about sitting on a hay bale watching me do all the work?"

She pursed her lips. "Oh. Right. I'd hate it."

He chuckled, but didn't feel like he needed to say anything more.

They rode down the valley in silence for a while. Luke was just glad to be out of the hospital. It felt good to be able to see the sky — the window in his room had looked out on a brick wall.

"What's the news on the investigation?" Tanner asked. "I've been crazy busy in the barn the last couple of days, I haven't spoken to Deacon."

"He wouldn't have had much to tell you if you did. It's like those two guys just disappeared into thin air. Maybe they were just passing through."

"What about what he said, though?"

Luke's heart hammered in his chest as he glared at Tanner. He'd asked the guys not to say anything to Laney about what had actually gone down that night. He didn't know for sure that the two men had been after him in particular — even though Deacon and the others seemed to believe that might be the case. He didn't want Laney worrying about it.

"What who said?"

Luke closed his eyes. He didn't want to lie to her, but he didn't want to get into explaining it all to her, either. He couldn't see how any good could come from telling her that the one guy had said *gotcha,* or that the other guy had wanted to finish him off before they left. He wanted to believe it was just because he was a deputy – that it didn't have anything to do with him personally. Despite Deacon, Bill Townsend, and a couple of the deputies having questioned him repeatedly, he couldn't think of anyone who would have it in for him – anyone he might have pissed off.

He was grateful that Tanner caught on and covered for him. "Deacon said at one point that he thought they must be locals."

That wasn't a lie. Deacon was like a dog with a bone, and he was convinced that whoever it was had lured Luke to Libby's place that night.

Laney scowled. "I kind of hope that they are. That way, you know damn well that they'll be found and brought in at some point – and then they'll be at Deacon's mercy, and I doubt that he'll show any."

He and Tanner both laughed at that. Deacon might be the sheriff, his job was to uphold the law, but he was pretty ferocious about protecting his own.

When they got back to the house, a sense of ease swept over Luke. It might just be from getting home after all that time in the hospital, but it felt like something more than that. It wasn't just coming home; it was coming home with Laney. He couldn't know for sure where things would go for them from here, but he was hoping with all his heart that this was the beginning of the rest of their life.

Tanner helped him down from the truck, and Laney wrapped her arm around his waist as they walked up the porch steps to the front door.

"Thanks, guys. I hate that I need your help, but I'm more grateful than you know that I have it."

Tanner met his gaze as Laney unlocked the front door to let them in. "Don't start saying thanks. We've always had each other's back, and we always will."

Laney came and took Luke's hand and led him inside to the sofa. "Here, sit down. Do you want a drink?"

He laughed. "I'm not a freaking invalid."

She narrowed her eyes at him. "I didn't say you were. I asked if you wanted a drink." She turned to Tanner. "Do you want a drink? You won't get offended if I offer, will you?"

Tanner laughed. "I'd love one, thanks, Laney-Lou. I'd bet that Candy made sure that there's beer in the fridge."

Luke watched Laney go to the fridge. He knew he was feeling better when he realized that he was watching her ass as she bent over. He looked away quickly when he realized that Tanner was watching him. That was something he was going to have to get used to.

He gave Laney a hurt look when she came back with two beers and handed one to Tanner. "Don't I get one?"

She laughed and handed him the second one. "You can have this, but no more. When the nurse went through your list, he said no alcohol. When Trip ran through everything before we left, he knew you wouldn't go for that, so he told me that you could have one – and only one."

Luke grinned. "That'll do for me."

Laney came and settled on the sofa beside him, and Tanner sat on the loveseat and swung his legs over the arm.

"So, what happens now?"

Luke and Laney looked at each other. "In what respect?" he asked.

"In every respect. I mean, you don't have a job or a place to live, Laney."

Luke tightened his arm around her shoulders. "Yes, she does."

Tanner chuckled when she smiled up at Luke. "I figured as much, but since neither of you had officially told me, I wanted to see what you'd say."

Laney made a face at him. "I thought you were smart enough to figure it out for yourself."

"And what about work?"

Luke looked at Laney. He was glad that Tanner was asking the question; it had been worrying him what she was going to do back here in the valley. She'd spoken to Tom a couple of times, and from what she said, Tony was back at work and things were going okay. She had no intention of going back to Kentucky – she was here to stay, and he couldn't be happier about it.

She smiled at him. "I'm not entirely sure yet, but I have plenty of ideas, and I don't need to worry about it for a while. Not until Luke's better."

Tanner looked at him. "And what about you? How long do you think you're going to be out for?"

"I don't know. Until whenever Trip gives me the all-clear to go back."

Laney rested her head against his shoulder and looked up into his eyes. "I think you should take as long as you can get."

He frowned at her. They hadn't talked about it yet, but he'd been thinking the same thing. It'd be a while before he could go back to anything but desk duty – and he wasn't looking forward to that.

Tanner drank down the last of his beer and got up. "I'm going to take that as my cue to leave – looks like that's something you need to talk about. It's good to see you home, bud. If you need anything, just give me a shout." He grinned at Laney. "And when she gets busy or goes out, give me a call, and I'll come rescue you."

Laney made a face at him. "I'm just glad to have him home. That's all. I'm not going to go hogging all his time, and don't you go talking about me like I'm one of those clingy girlfriends, you hear me?"

Tanner laughed. "I wasn't talking about you that way. I was thinking more along the lines of calling you wifey."

A rush of warmth spread through Luke's chest when Laney's eyes grew wide, and she shot a quick look at him. He kept hoping that he'd get to call her that, too.

Tanner laughed again. "And now that I've dropped a bombshell, I'll be on my way. See you guys."

Chapter Twenty-Three

Laney opened her eyes and tightened her arm around Luke's waist. He'd only been home for a couple of days, but she'd already grown used to waking up with him. If she got her way, she'd be waking up beside him every day for the rest of her life.

She smiled when he pressed a kiss into her hair. "Good morning, baby."

She looked up and kissed his lips. "It is. Every morning's a good morning with you."

He chuckled. "I won't argue that they're good, but I'm hoping that this morning might be even better than the last few."

She raised her eyebrows. "What do you want? Tell me, and I'll make it happen."

He caught hold of her hand and brought it down beneath the covers. She smiled when he cupped it over his hot, hard cock. "I was hoping that you might be able to help me out with this."

"Yeah? What would you like me to do with it?"

She loved seeing such a happy smile on his face as he said, "I thought you might have some ideas of your own."

She propped herself up on her elbow and smiled down at him. "I have lots of ideas, but remember what Trip said?"

Luke rolled his eyes. "He said that I need to be careful." He chuckled. "We can use a condom if that counts?"

She slapped his arm. "You know damn well that's not the kind of careful he was talking about. He doesn't want you over exerting yourself."

Luke shrugged and went to fold his arms behind his head but had to bring his right arm back down again – that shoulder was giving him trouble, even though he wouldn't admit it.

"I wouldn't need to exert myself if there was a cowgirl around who wanted a ride. I could just lie back and ..."

Laney didn't need telling twice. It had been so hard to lie beside him the last few nights and not make love to him, but she could deny herself anything if it helped his recovery. She wasn't about to deny him, though. She straddled him and sat up with a smile.

"It's funny you should mention that; I happen to know a cowgirl." She closed her eyes when his hard length pressed into the heat between her legs. "And I can tell you, without a shadow of a doubt, that she would love to go for an early morning ride." She opened her eyes and met his gaze. "As long as you're sure you're up for it."

He chuckled. "I swear to God, baby, it'll be good for my health."

She laughed. "Good for your health?"

"Yeah. I'm serious. My head might just explode if I have to go through another day without making love to you. It's been like a special kind of torture to have you back and not be able to have you. To sleep naked with you and not be able to do anything about it." His hands rested at her hips as she closed her fingers around him.

"Are you sure?" She had to ask, but she knew that it was just a formality at this point. He was throbbing in her hand, and she was already wet for him.

He slid his hand over her stomach and strummed her clit with his thumb. "So sure. Take me, Laney."

She lifted her hips and positioned him at her entrance; he was hard, so hard, and the way his thumb was teasing the bundle of nerves between her legs was taking her toward the edge all too fast. She lowered herself onto him slowly, taking him inch by inch until they both moaned when he was seated deep inside.

"You feel so damned good."

She nodded, unable to form words.

When he started to rock his hips, she moved with him. "Take it easy," she murmured.

His fingers dug into her hips. "I can't. I've waited so damn long. I …"

She tried to keep the pace slow and steady, but it wasn't working. He grasped her ass and pulled her down to receive his thrusts. She sat upright and rested her hands on his thighs behind her.

"So fucking beautiful," he gasped.

"I love you, Luke," she breathed. "I'm going to …"

"Come for me, baby!"

She felt him tense as she let herself go, moaning his name as her orgasm crashed over her.

With a few more hard thrusts, he followed her over the edge, giving her all that he had.

When they finally slumped together, breathing hard, she turned her head and pressed a kiss to his cheek.

"I love you, Luke."

"I love you, too, baby."

"Do you feel any better for that?"

He chuckled. "Better than I've felt since the day you left."

"Aww."

"In fact, that might turn out to be the best medicine."

She laughed. "Don't tell me, you need it to be administered twice a day?"

"Yeah. Maybe three."

She raised her eyebrows. "You could take it three times a day?"

He chuckled. "I don't know, but I reckon we could have fun finding out."

She shook her head at him and slid down to his side. He curled his good arm around her and held her tight.

"What do you have going on today?"

She shrugged. As far as she was concerned, there wasn't anything that she needed to do until he was back on his feet properly. "I'll go out to the barn in a little while and see to the horses before I make us some breakfast."

"Why don't I make breakfast?"

"You know why."

"I know why you haven't been letting me do anything so far. But remember that Trip said to ease back in."

She cocked an eyebrow at him. "I thought that was what you just did."

He laughed. "You know what I mean. Into doing things."

"Things other than me?"

His smile faded. "Yeah. Part of me would love nothing more than to stay in this little bubble like this – you and me in the house, not doing much of anything other than being together. But that's not life, is it? It sure as hell isn't the kind of life that we want to live. You're not cut out to be a caretaker, and I'm not cut out to be someone who needs taking care of."

"Yeah. I want to stay in the bubble, but I know what you mean. So, what are you thinking? What do you want to do?" Her heart started to hammer in her chest. "You're not saying that you want to go back to work, are you?"

"No."

"Good."

His eyes looked stormy when he met her gaze. "How would you feel if I didn't go back?"

She couldn't help the smile that spread across her face. "I would absolutely love it. I mean, if you don't want to. I just … I got the impression when we talked about it before I left that you don't love your job, and I hate that for you."

He pressed a kiss to her forehead. "Thanks, baby. I don't know what I'm going to do with myself instead, but this whole deal has made me stop and think." His eyebrows drew together as he continued. "I don't want to sound dramatic or anything, but I'm lucky to still be here. This…" He reached up and touched his shoulder. "If this had gone a couple of inches the other way? I wouldn't be here."

Laney swallowed. "I know."

"I don't want you to think that I'm a coward or anything, but I had to live without you for all those years. Now that I've got you back, now that we can have a life together, I don't want to do anything that might risk ending mine."

She tightened her arms around him. "I don't think you're a coward. I could never think that — because you're not." She lifted her head so that she could look into his eyes and smiled at him. "I actually think that you're being very smart. And I'm relieved that I won't have to try and persuade you to give it up — I'm not sure that I'd want to do that. You know what I mean. I'd love to talk you into giving it up, to keep you safe. But I wouldn't want to be the kind of person who would nag you into it."

He chuckled. "I don't ever see you being a nag. And you can relax, it's my choice — it's what I want. I want a long and happy life with you, not one that gets cut short by a stray bullet on the job. I don't want to make you a widow until you're in your nineties."

All her breath caught in her chest. She didn't know what to say. She loved the idea of them still being together in their nineties, but the thought of him dying even then broke her heart.

He stroked his hand over her hair. "Did I say too much?"

"No."

"What then?"

"Just … can you try to not make me a widow until I'm at least a hundred? We have a lot of lost years to make up for."

"I'll do my best. But for now, what do you say we get up and start getting on with the day?"

"Sounds good to me. You can come out to the barn with me if you want. Then, over breakfast, maybe we can talk about what you plan to do when you're no longer a deputy."

She was glad that he smiled at that – he looked relieved. She just hoped that he might be open to what she had in mind. When they were kids, he'd always loved to spend time in the barn with the horses. He might have joked before that he wasn't like Tanner and her, but Laney had a feeling that if he could spend his days riding and training, he'd realize just what a natural he was.

~ ~ ~

They were sitting on the deck, enjoying the sunset the next evening and both turned at the sound of a truck coming up the driveway. It was Deacon.

Laney smiled at Luke and got to her feet. "You stay there, I'll go and bring him around."

Luke made a face at her. "I can go. I'm doing better, in case you hadn't noticed."

She wagged a finger at him. "I know you are, but you've done a lot today already. It won't do you any harm to sit there and wait. And besides, you know Deacon will only give you shit."

He had to laugh; she was right. "Okay." He couldn't feel too bad about it – he got to watch her ass as she walked away.

A few moments later she reappeared around the side of the house with Deacon at her side.

"No Candy?" he asked. He was happy that Candy had made an effort to help get the house ready for when he came out of the hospital, but he'd been hoping that she might come around now that Laney was here.

"No. This is her night out with Libby."

"How is Libby?" She'd come straight to the hospital to see him when she got back from Billings. She felt terrible about what had happened, since it'd happened at her place. But he hadn't seen her again since.

Deacon pursed his lips. "She's lying low. She feels bad about what happened, and Mav didn't help things."

Luke leaned forward. "Shit! I must've been really out of it. It didn't even occur to me … He came back with Cash." He looked at Laney. "They brought you. But Mav was here because of Libby, wasn't he?"

"Yeah." Deacon blew out a sigh. "I can understand why he came, but by the sound of it, he didn't handle things too well. He left with Cash, but before he went, I think he made things worse instead of better."

Laney shook her head. "I wish the two of them could figure it out."

"Don't we all," said Deacon. "But if they do, they'll do it by themselves. None of us are going to be able to help."

"True," said Luke. "And is that what brings you out here? Candy's gone out, and you'd rather come and hang out with us than spend the evening with Clawson, the demon cat?"

Deacon chuckled. "He's not a demon."

Luke laughed. "Maybe not, but he is a vicious little bugger – you can't argue with that, I have the scars to prove it."

"He's just picky, that's all. He's fine with Candy – and with Rocket."

"Make me feel bad, why don't you? Are you saying that it's just me he hates?"

"No. He hates most people. Just not everyone. Anyway, I didn't come to talk about him. I came to talk about you. How are you doing?"

Luke smiled at Laney. "I'm doing great."

"I can see that – that the two of you are doing great. And I know I've said it before, but I'll say it again – I couldn't be happier for you." He gave each of them a stern look. "Just don't screw it up this time, okay?"

"We won't," they said in unison.

Deacon laughed. "It's good to see that you're both on the same page at last."

"We are," said Laney. "Is there any news on the investigation?"

Deacon shot a look at Luke before he answered. "Nothing new to report, I'm afraid."

Laney blew out a sigh. "Do you think that they were out-of-towners, then? That they've moved on?"

Luke didn't like the way Deacon's eyebrows drew together as he shook his head. "I don't know." He met Luke's gaze. "I don't mind telling you that I'm getting frustrated as fuck. There haven't been any more break-ins, so that's something. But at the same time, it makes me wonder …"

"Wonder what?" Laney asked.

Luke had a feeling that he knew. Deacon was probably thinking the same thing that he was. That the burglars were local and were lying low. At least, that the second guy was a local. Luke had gotten a good look at the first guy, and if he were local, he would have recognized him. He closed his eyes, trying to catch hold of a detail that danced at the edge of his memory. There was something about that arm coming through the air toward him. He hadn't recognized at the time what it was holding. He knew now that it was one of Libby's brass horse figurines – she had a whole collection of them.

He opened his eyes again when he felt Deacon watching him. He was holding his hand up to quiet Laney.

"Sorry, honey. Is anything coming back to you, Luke?"

He blew out a sigh. "Sometimes, like just now, it feels like it's right there. I don't even know what. Some detail. Something about that arm."

Laney looked at him. "You think you recognized it?"

He stared at her. He didn't want to lead her down the path of thinking that whoever it was, was someone he knew. If she started thinking that way, she'd worry about him, and worse than that, she'd probably start trying to find the guy herself – looking for revenge.

Deacon saved him when he asked, "Try a different angle. You said you heard him speak. Did you recognize his voice? He said *gotcha*, right?"

"No, that was the first guy." He glanced at Laney, not wanting her to know what the second one had said. He closed his eyes and conjured up the words he'd heard. *Give me the gun, I need to finish him off.*

He shuddered, and Laney reached out to touch his arm. "Are you okay?"

"I'm fine."

She narrowed her eyes at him. "Why don't I give you guys a minute? Do you want a beer, Deacon?"

"That'd be great, thanks."

Once she'd gone inside the house, Deacon cocked an eyebrow at him. "You remember something?"

"Just that the voice was familiar."

Deacon blew out a sigh. "Familiar like someone you know? Or familiar like a local accent?"

Luke shrugged and regretted it immediately as pain shot through his shoulder. "Both maybe? I don't know."

"Maybe it'll come back to you."

"Maybe," said Luke. "But it's frustrating as hell." He glanced at the door that Laney had disappeared through. "I still haven't told her that there's a possibility that it might be about me – not just because I interrupted a break in."

Deacon scowled at him. "I want to ask why the hell not, but I know. You don't want to worry her."

"Yeah. She's been worried sick about me as it is."

Deacon chuckled. "I get it. Candy was madder than a wet hen at me when I almost got myself shot up in town that time. Laney's just as fierce as Candy – and you actually did get shot."

Luke laughed with him. "Rub it in, why don't you? You managed to dodge the bullet; I took it in the shoulder."

Deacon's expression softened. "I wasn't rubbing it in. If I could change things around, if I could take a bullet to save you from one, I would."

"I know."

"I guess all I can tell you at this point is that we're still searching for them. And I want you to keep searching through your mind. Maybe that detail will surface." Deacon jerked his chin toward the house. "And how are you two?"

Luke grinned. "We're doing great."

"What do you think? Are you going to make her the next sheriff's wife, after Candy?"

Luke's smile evaporated.

"What?" Deacon gave him a puzzled look. "You're not going to tell me that you don't plan to marry her, are you?"

Luke swallowed. He had to tell him – he didn't want to hide it from him. "I do. I haven't asked yet, haven't even brought it up yet. I want to make her my wife, but I don't want to make her the sheriff's wife."

Deacon's puzzled look slowly morphed into a smile. "You never wanted to be sheriff, did you?"

Luke felt the tension leave his shoulders. "No. You knew?"

"Not for sure. But I've wondered for a while." He met Luke's gaze. "Tell me that you didn't do it for me."

Luke knew exactly what he meant. "I didn't. Don't worry. I did it for me. I wanted to be in law enforcement. Yeah." He smiled. "I had a pretty awesome example to follow. I wanted to be like you. But I joined the force because I wanted to be a deputy – I didn't do it for you."

Deacon rested his elbows on his knees and clasped his hands together between them as he leaned forward. "And you're not just saying that you don't want to be sheriff, are you? You're saying that you want out?"

Luke's heart pounded as he nodded. He hadn't lied – he hadn't become a deputy just to please his brother. But at the same time, he hated the thought of disappointing him by leaving.

Relief washed over him when Deacon smiled. "Good for you. Any idea what comes next?"

They both looked up when Laney came back out with their drinks. "Did I leave it long enough?" she asked with a smile. "I can go away again if you like."

They both laughed, and Luke held his arm out to her for her to come and sit beside him. "No, baby, we're good. I was just telling Deacon that I want out."

Her eyes widened. "You were?"

He nodded happily. "And he was asking what I'm going to do next." He smiled at his brother again. "I don't know for sure, yet. But I can tell you that whatever it is, it will involve horses, and this lady right here."

He knew that was the right choice for him, and the way they both smiled told him that not only did they agree, but they were thrilled for him.

Chapter Twenty-Four

Laney braced her hands on the counter in the kitchen and stared at Luke.

He cocked an eyebrow at her. "What's up?"

"Are you sure you're up to going? Are you going to be okay?"

He chuckled. "I'm sure I'm sure. What about you? Are *you* going to be okay? I can stay here if you'd prefer."

She let out a short laugh. "No. Thanks, but I can't do that to you. You're going to have fun."

"You'll have fun, too. If you just relax a bit."

"Maybe. It's just, that relaxing thing? I don't know if I can."

Luke had been doing better for the last couple of days. He had more movement in his arm and the wound was healing. She was more relieved — and she knew he was — that the headaches weren't as bad now. Trip had stopped by to check on him yesterday and he'd been happy to hear that. He hadn't said as much, but Laney knew that he'd been concerned.

And since Luke was doing better, Tanner was coming over this morning to pick him up and take him to the ranch. She was pleased for him, she really was. But since he hadn't been out of her sight much since he came out of the hospital, she was nervous. Although it was stupid, and she knew it. Tanner would keep an eye on him.

Luke came to stand behind her and slid his arm around her waist. He kissed her neck, sending a shiver running down her spine. "Which is it? Are you more worried about me going over there with Tanner, or about Maya coming over here with you?"

She made a face at him. "You, of course. Although … I can admit that I'm nervous about little Maya, too. I mean, she seems like an awesome kid, but she's still a kid. I don't know what to do with her. What if … I don't know. What if I upset her or something – if I mess up and make her cry somehow? Sierra will never forgive me, she'll hate me."

Luke laughed, and the sound of it vibrated through his chest and into hers, making her want to cancel their plans for the day and take him back upstairs instead.

"You'll be fine. She thinks you're amazing. You're not going to upset her."

"But I don't know the first thing about kids, Luke!"

He turned her around and tucked his fingers under her chin, making her look up into his eyes. "Then forget that she's a kid. Don't think of her like some little alien. Just think of her as another cowgirl. At least, a wannabe cowgirl. Do you remember how it felt to be her age?"

Laney looked away. She wasn't even sure how old Maya was – five or six maybe? And she did remember how it felt to be that age. She looked back at Luke. "All I can say to that is, I hope that my experiences at her age mean that we won't be able to relate to each other at all."

Luke's smile faded. "Well, I hate to break it to you, but I think those experiences are more likely to be just another bond that the two of you can share. You know her history, don't you?"

Laney closed her eyes as she nodded. She did. How could she have forgotten? Maya and her brother Mateo had an even rougher start in life than she and Janey and their brothers had. They'd lost their mom and their dad within a year of each other. And not just lost them, but had seen them murdered.

"Did Wade tell you that Maya didn't even speak for the first few weeks that she was here?"

"That just makes me even more nervous, Luke. What if I traumatize her somehow?"

He laughed. "You won't. Relax. I think you're going to do great together. I honestly expect that by the time I get home tonight, you'll be raving about how awesome she is." He met her gaze, and his eyes shone a brighter blue when he added, "Maybe you'll even start talking about wanting one of our own."

Laney's heart thudded to a halt. "You want one?"

He laughed and ran his hand over her hair. "Maybe someday. But don't panic; I don't want kids anytime soon. I want you to myself for a couple of years before we even think about it. And it won't bother me if you decide you never want kids. I want you – everything after that is just details."

She relaxed against him and tightened her arms around him. "I can't say that I don't ever want them." She looked up into his eyes. "But I can't promise that I will, either. Are you sure that you'd be okay with that? Because if not…"

He leaned in and stopped her with a kiss – a deep, hard kiss. When he lifted his head, his gaze was intense as he said, "Like I just told you. I want you. That's the only detail that matters – that we're together."

"Together here?" She had to ask – she'd grown to love this house and the property. And she was hoping that he felt the same way about it.

"Here in the valley?"

"Yeah, but I thought that was a given – for both of us. What I meant was here in this house."

He nodded slowly. "If we can swing it, I'd love to make this place ours. Would you?"

She tried to hide how happy his answer made her, but she knew that she was grinning like an idiot. "I would. I think it's perfect for us – and for whatever kind of business we decide we want to build."

"We should talk about it." His smile had disappeared. "I'd love to think that we can pull it off somehow but… I'm still on full pay for now – while I'm out, due to injury." He frowned. "But I don't know…"

She put a finger to his lips. She didn't want him to start worrying about it – especially when there was no need. She was relieved when she spotted Tanner's truck pulling up outside. "We can talk about it later. Tan's here."

Luke pecked her lips. "Okay, but even if it's not this place, we'll figure something out. I promise."

She felt bad – it seemed that he was concerned about whether they'd be able to afford it. She didn't want him worrying, but at some point – soon, she was going to have to explain to him how things were for her. She just smiled and gave him one last kiss.

"I know we will. I'm not worried."

"Do you want me to hang around – wait until Sierra and Maya get here?" He winked at her. "I don't want you to feel like I've abandoned you in the face of the enemy."

She laughed. "No. It's okay. I know Sierra's not the enemy now. And thanks to your little pep talk, I'm kind of looking forward to hanging out with Maya. I can only imagine how thrilled I would have been to have had a grownup cowgirl to hang out with at her age."

"Yeah. That's a better way to look at it. I have a feeling that the two of you are going to get along just great."

~ ~ ~

Luke watched in the wing mirror as Laney stood on the front porch, watching them drive away.

"Man, you've got it bad," said Tanner with a laugh.

"I do. And I don't mind admitting it." He dragged his gaze away from the mirror when Laney disappeared from sight and turned to look at his friend. "I'm sorry that I never told you the way I felt about Laney before."

Tanner glanced over at him. "You know, I've had a lot of time to think about that since it all came out. And to tell you the truth, I'm glad I didn't know. I'm glad that no one knew. I think it might have changed the course of things. I mean, look at the way Ty and I reacted when we found out. We're supposed to be grown men now, and we still needed to punch you. I can only guess that if we found out about the two of you back then, we'd have beaten the shit out of you and never spoken to you again."

Luke gave him a rueful smile. "I imagine you would have."

"See, so it all turned out for the best in the end. You've been my best bud all these years, and now, I reckon I'll end up getting you as my brother-in-law." He shot another glance at Luke before turning his attention back to the road.

"I reckon you will."

"Yes!" Tanner took one hand off the wheel to punch the air. "I was hoping like hell that was where you guys were headed. Have you talked about it?"

"Not in so many words, no. But whenever we talk about our plans, we're talking about the rest of our lives."

"Awesome. Do I get to be your best man?"

Luke had to laugh, but he sobered when he remembered that Deacon had asked him to be *his* best man. He frowned.

"Is that a no?" Tanner asked with a laugh. "It can't be. Who else would you ask?"

"Deacon."

"Oh, well shit! I didn't even think about that. Yeah, that makes sense. Sorry. I shouldn't have jumped the gun like that. I didn't think … I … Sorry."

"I didn't either. I just … Shit! I want it to be you. But I want it to be him, too."

Tanner shrugged. "It doesn't matter. It should be Deacon. I get it. I mean, he's your brother, but he pretty much raised you. It's always been the two of you."

"Yeah. And he's already asked me to be his best man."

Tanner grinned. "That's awesome! And it's only right that he should be yours, too. Forget that I brought it up, would ya?"

"I don't think I can forget it, no."

"Well, maybe you just need to have a big bridal party. Deacon can be your best man, and I'll be your chief groomsman — how about that?"

Luke laughed. "I like that. We'll figure it out. But can you believe this?"

"What?"

"That the two of us are riding around in your truck making arrangements for a wedding?"

Tanner laughed out loud. "It's a bit of a change, huh? But I like it. Hey, and while we're making arrangements, do you have the ring yet?"

"No. It's not as though I've just been able to hop on in my truck and run up to town lately, is it?"

Tanner grinned at him and pulled his truck over to the side of the road. Luke didn't need to ask what he was doing when he made a U-turn.

"Are you good with this?"

"Good? It's awesome!"

"I think so. And it's probably best if your chief groomsman helps you pick the ring rather than your best man. I mean,

Deacon's great and everything, but he's getting on a bit. You need a younger guy to help you choose – and the ladies always like my style."

Luke laughed out loud. "They like your style in the bedroom, I'm sure. But I doubt there's a woman out there who could vouch for you style – or your taste – in jewelry. You're not a jewelry kind of guy."

Tanner shot him a disgruntled look. "You don't know that. I could be. It's just that I haven't met a jewelry kind of girl yet."

Luke chuckled. "And I doubt you will anytime soon, either."

Tanner laughed with him. "I'm not going to argue with you about that one. And this is different, anyway. I know Laney. I know what she likes – what her style is."

Luke just smiled. So did he.

~ ~ ~

Laney leaned her elbows back against the fence as she watched Maya practicing. The little girl was amazing; Laney couldn't get over it. She'd brought the roping dummy out into the corral in front of the barn, but she hadn't expected that they'd get around to it in this first session. She'd thought that Maya would need the whole time just to get the hang of throwing the rope.

But the little girl had surprised her. She was sharp. She listened intently to everything Laney told her, and she watched with a quiet intensity in her big brown eyes when Laney demonstrated what she meant.

They'd only been out here an hour and Maya was roping the dummy with every other throw.

As she went to retrieve the rope, the little girl smiled up at her. "I am doing good, no?"

Laney grinned at her. "You're doing amazing. You're going to make a great cowgirl."

Maya nodded at her happily as she looped the rope over her arm and came back to where Laney was standing. "I know. Mateo – my brother – he says that he's going to be the sheriff. And some days he says that he will be a chef. Some days he says he will be a cowboy like our daddy." She looked up at Laney. "He wants to be them all. I don't. I want to be a cowgirl – like you."

Laney's hand came up to cover her mouth, and she tried to blink away the tears that pricked behind her eyes. This kid! She loved her!

"You'll be the best cowgirl around if you want to be. But you don't need to be like me, you just be you. That's the best thing you can ever be."

Maya gave her a puzzled look. "You don't want me to be like you?"

"I didn't say that. It's just … You want to be like me because it's easy for you to see who I am. As you grow up, you'll have a better idea of who you are. And if you already have it fixed in your head that you want to be like someone else …" She winked. "Even if that someone is as awesome as me, it can get in the way of you being the person *you* are meant to become."

Maya stared at her for a long moment. "I understand."

Laney wasn't sure that she did; she wasn't sure why she'd gone telling the kid that. "I'm flattered that you want to be like me."

Maya smiled. "It's okay. I understand. I will be like you while I learn. Then, I'll be old enough to know how to be me."

Laney grinned at her. "Yep. That. You explained it better than I did. Do you want to go up to the house for a drink?"

Maya looked back at the roping dummy. "Yes, but we should put our things away first. And maybe we can say hello to the horses?"

"We can. And after you've had a drink, maybe we can get you up on one of them."

Maya's eyes lit up, and she tugged at Laney's hand. "Come on. We must hurry. Sierra will be back to get me, and I want to ride before she comes."

Laney grinned to herself as she followed the kid, who started pushing the roping dummy back toward the barn. She was going to be a cowgirl, all right.

When they came back out of the house after Maya's drink, a shiver ran down Laney's spine. She looked around, feeling as though there were eyes on her, but she couldn't see anything. She was hardly likely to out here. She looked up the driveway, wondering if a vehicle might be approaching, but there was nothing.

Maya tugged on her hand. "We must hurry!"

"Okay. Let's go." She checked her watch. "Have you ever ridden bareback?"

Maya's eyes grew huge. "Without a saddle?"

Laney nodded.

"No! But I want to. Can I?"

"Sure you can. We'll put you on Billie, she's the little palomino."

"I know. She's pretty."

Laney laughed and touched the end of Maya's nose. "So are you."

Maya giggled and pushed at her leg. "So are you."

When they got to the barn, Laney got that weird feeling of being watched again, but she brushed it away. She didn't have time to go creeping herself out. If she was going to get Maya up on Billie, she needed to be quick about it. Sierra would be back to collect her soon.

Maya trotted ahead of her, down the aisle between the stalls. She looked back over her shoulder at Laney with a grin. "I'm not running – just walking fast."

Laney had to smile. Wade had no doubt taught her not to run inside the barn. She hurried after her but stopped in her tracks when someone stepped out from the empty stall on the end of the row and grabbed Maya.

"Gotcha."

Maya screamed, and Laney rushed forward, but another figure stepped out of the stall and grabbed her. She yelled and stamped down on his foot, as she struggled to break free. She managed to get one arm out of his grasp, but couldn't break away from him before his fist came flying through the air into the side of her face. She saw stars as she staggered forward.

"Maya!" She had to get to her, had to get her away from here. Had to keep her safe. Sierra would never forgive her … It was no good, she couldn't stay on her feet. She stumbled forward and landed on her hands and knees. The back of her head felt like it exploded with a second blow, and everything faded to black.

~ ~ ~

Sierra was surprised not to see Laney and Maya in the corral when she arrived. She parked her SUV and ran up the steps to the front door. She knocked and waited, but there was no answer.

Laney had said that they might still be out in the barn when she came to collect Maya. She trotted back down the steps and followed the path past the corral to the barn.

"Hello?" she called when she got there.

They weren't there, she could tell. The horses were the only presence in there. And they were restless.

She went to the first stall and stroked the palomino's nose. "What's the matter, Billie? Do you know where they are?"

Not surprisingly, the horse didn't speak, but she did nod her head. Sierra laughed. She was being silly, getting freaked out because she couldn't see Laney and Maya – and talking to horses.

She walked down the aisle between the stalls, all the way to the end. When she got there, she opened the door that led out to the pasture. There was no sign of them out there, either.

She turned around to go back. They were probably in the house, and just hadn't heard her knock.

She froze when she spotted something on the floor inside the empty stall at the end of the row. It was Laney's cowboy hat. Her heart started to race. She might not know much about being a cowgirl, but she knew full well that Laney wouldn't leave her hat lying on the floor like that – especially brim side down.

She pulled her phone out of her back pocket to call Wade, but hesitated before she hit the button – wondering if she was still being silly. Wade was busy at the lodge. She shouldn't go worrying him for nothing. She hit Laney's number instead and waited.

She gasped when she heard it ringing – not just on her phone but … she hurried back to the door and out to the pasture. Her heart started to hammer when she spotted Laney's phone lying on the ground, ringing.

Now, she *really* needed Wade!

Chapter Twenty-Five

Luke held his head between his hands as he paced back and forth in the kitchen. His headaches had been easing up, but right now it felt like that vice was back and was clamped tight around his skull. He couldn't believe it – this could not be happening.

He and Tanner had been on their way back from town. He'd had a stupid grin on his face as he kept opening up the little box to stare at the beautiful ring that he'd just bought for Laney. It had cost more than he should have spent, but he didn't care. It was perfect; it was her. It was a simple, bold design – a square cut diamond set in a wide, smooth, platinum band. But then, his phone had rung, and his stomach had lurched when he saw Wade's name on the display.

Wade didn't often call him, and the fact that he was calling while little Maya was hanging out with Laney made all the hairs on his arms stand up.

That had been over two hours ago. And they still had nothing to go on. It was as though Laney and Maya had just disappeared into thin air. He'd told Laney this morning not to think of Maya as a little alien, and now, it felt as though aliens could have just beamed the two of them up – leaving only Laney's hat and phone behind.

Tanner came and put a hand on his arm, but he shook him off and kept pacing. Deacon had every available man out searching for them, but they had nothing to go on. He couldn't give a description of who had taken them, or even of a vehicle that they might be traveling in.

He reached the fridge and turned around again before he finally stopped. The scene before him broke his heart. Sierra was clinging to Wade, crying. Little Mateo was sitting on the sofa, his arms wrapped around his middle as he rocked back and forth. The kid was beside himself; after everything that had already happened to them in their short lives, he'd cast himself in the role of his sister's protector. And now, she was gone, and there was nothing he could do.

Luke went and sat down beside him. He wanted to put his arm around him, try to comfort him, but he knew there was no point. The kid was feeling the same way that he was – and *he'd* just shaken off his best friend because, until they had them back, there was no comfort to be found.

"We'll find them," he said.

Mateo turned big solemn eyes on him. "Before it's too late?"

Luke's heart cracked in two as he nodded. He had to believe that they would, but it killed him that this little kid, who'd already suffered through so much, was no doubt fearing the worst. No one had gotten to his mom before it was too late – and he'd seen his dad executed in front of him.

"We have to believe it, kid. Deacon's got everyone out there looking for them."

Mateo frowned. "Why aren't we out looking?"

Luke had been asking himself the same thing. Deacon had insisted that they should stay right here. Luke had only agreed once he'd made his brother promise to call as soon as he had any information. "Because we don't even know where to start. Until we have something to go on, we could be going in the opposite direction of where we need to be."

Mateo's eyebrows drew together but he nodded.

They both scrambled to their feet at the sound of a vehicle approaching. Mateo shook his head and went back to the sofa when he saw that it was Ford and Tyler.

Luke went out onto the porch to greet them. It wasn't as though they would have any news, but he couldn't just keep sitting there.

"Anything?" asked Ford.

"Not a damn thing."

Tyler scowled. "This shit just doesn't happen here. I mean, if we were in a big city or something, then yeah, I could see a woman and a little girl being grabbed. But out here? It just doesn't make any sense."

Ford nodded. "It feels personal."

Luke closed his eyes. He'd been thinking the same thing. "The only thing I can come up with is that maybe the burglars showed up to finish me off, and when they didn't find me here, they took Laney and Maya." His heart was pounding as he finished speaking. He hated the thought that he might be the cause of this. Little Maya would no doubt be scared to death. Laney didn't do scared, at least not for herself, but she'd be madder than hell and desperate to protect Maya.

Ford shook his head. "Do you really think that's a possibility? If they were going to come after you again, wouldn't they have done it before now?"

"I don't know. I have no idea. I've been racking my brain, and that's the only thing I can come up with."

They all turned to watch another truck make its way up the driveway. It was Rocket, and he'd brought Candy and Spider with him. Luke turned away. He wasn't up for answering the same questions over and over again. He took his phone out and walked away to call Deacon. Deacon had promised he'd call as soon as he had any news, but Luke needed to feel as though he was doing something.

"Talk to me," Deacon answered.

"Nothing to report. You?"

Deacon blew out a sigh. "Not a damn thing. Candy should be showing up at your place any minute now."

"Yeah, they just arrived."

"I called Cash as well."

Luke closed his eyes. He should have thought of that.

"Don't sweat it. He and Mav were already on the way to the airport; Ford called him."

"It's good that they're coming. It's good that everyone's here. But with no leads to go on, there's nothing we can do."

"We're working on it."

"I keep thinking that it's the guys who shot me."

"I've been thinking the same thing myself. I don't suppose you've had a breakthrough on the details you couldn't remember?"

"No. The more I try to chase the memory, the further away it moves."

"Well, I'm not going to say relax and let it come. You're probably better off trying to remember than getting caught up in the other thoughts I know are in your head right now."

Luke closed his eyes. "I can't afford to think that way."

"No. You can't. We'll catch a break. We'll find them."

"Janey's just arrived. I'm going to go and talk to her."

"Do that. Maybe she'll have some insight."

"On what?"

"The hell if I know. But they're twins, and Janey will have a different perspective from everyone else anyway. She always does. Just talk to her."

"Okay. Keep in touch."

"Will do."

~ ~ ~

Laney reached up and touched her head gingerly. Damn, that hurt. She felt bad for Luke, with all the headaches he'd been having. She knew that the punch she'd taken to her head couldn't compare to what had happened to him, but she felt like she had a little insight into what he'd been through now.

She still felt woozy as she pushed herself up into a sitting position. Wherever she was, it was dark. By the feel of the floor, she guessed that she was in a barn. Her breath caught in her chest when she heard a whimper not far away. Shit! Maya!

"Are you there, sweetie?" she whispered.

"Yes," Maya whispered back. "I'm scared, Laney."

Laney crawled in the direction of her voice, and soon found her, curled up in a little ball. She wrapped her arms around her and hauled her into her lap. "I am, too. But it's going to be okay. We're going to get out of here."

She could just make out Maya's eyes shining at her in the darkness. "I thought cowgirls didn't get scared."

Laney leaned down and pressed her forehead against Maya's. "Since you're a cowgirl now, I need to let you in on a secret."

"What's that?"

"We get scared, and it's okay. We just don't let it show to anyone but each other. Whenever a cowgirl looks mad, she's probably scared." She was kind of telling the truth, but more than that, she was hoping that her words would give the kid some strength when those bastards came back.

She sensed, rather than saw, Maya nod. "When they come back to kill us, I'll be brave."

Laney closed her eyes. "They're not going to kill us, sweetie. I told you; we're going to get out of here."

Maya was trembling in her arms. "The bad men came and took my mamá, and they killed her. They killed my papá, too."

"I know, sweetie. But those were really bad men. These guys? They're not the same. They're weak, and they're stupid. We're going to get away from them. And besides, your daddy, and Mateo, and my Luke, and all my brothers are going to be looking for us. We're stronger and smarter than these bad guys, and we're not on our own."

Maya took a deep breath, and when she slowly blew it out, she seemed a little calmer. "Uncle Rocket says that Mateo and me are the bravest, smartest kids in the world."

Laney silently thanked Rocket. She'd heard him say those words to the kids before, and she'd loved that he was trying to build them up to believe in themselves. Now, she just had to hope that he'd instilled enough self-confidence in Maya that she'd be able to get through whatever was about to come at them.

"Uncle Rocket is a smart guy, and he's right."

Maya's voice wavered. "But Mateo is braver and smarter than me, and he's not here."

Laney closed her eyes to keep in the tears that threatened to fall – she felt so bad for the little girl; she knew that her brother did his best to shelter her. It took her a moment, but then she knew what she could say. "He's not braver and smarter, he's just a little bit older. That's all. And all those times he's protected you? He's been teaching you how to protect yourself if ever he's not there – because he can't always be there, can he? And now that you're a bit bigger, I think you're old enough to know another cowgirl secret."

"What's that?" Maya whispered.

"Us cowgirls? We can take care of ourselves. It's nice that the boys and the men who love us want to take care of us and protect us – and we let them when we can. But when it comes down to it – when it's just us, we can do it for ourselves. And cowgirls never give up. Give me a fist bump?"

Maya nodded and bumped her fist against Laney's, and Laney pressed a kiss to her forehead.

"We've got this. You and me, okay?"

"Okay."

At that moment, a crack of light flooded the barn as the door slid open.

"Wakey, wakey, Laney. You can't go sleeping in the barn all afternoon."

Her arms tightened involuntarily around Maya, who let out a little squeak and did her best to burrow her way under Laney's arm.

Laney's mind was racing. She recognized the voice, but she couldn't place it ... Not immediately. And then it hit her.

It all clicked into place. When that asshole had grabbed Maya, he'd said *gotcha*. That was the guy who'd shot Luke. And now that she'd heard his voice, she knew who the second man was.

She looked around, desperately searching for a place she could tell Maya to run and hide. She spotted a couple of musty old hay bales near the bottom of the steps that led up to the loft.

"What's the matter, bitch? Surprised to see me?"

She was about to tell Maya to make a run for it when the figure in the doorway turned to look back over his shoulder.

"Fuck! What's he doing here?"

Laney's heart was pounding as the door slid shut again. Whoever had just shown up had bought her some time, and she didn't intend to waste it. She pushed to her feet and grabbed Maya's hand. "Come on, sweetie we've got to move."

She hurried as fast as she could in the darkness in what she hoped was the direction of the hay bales. When they reached them, she couldn't believe her luck. The bottom of the wooden boards of the wall had rotted away. There wasn't much of a gap, but there was enough to let in a little light, and more importantly, enough room for Maya to get out.

She had to get her out of here. She'd been worried before that they might be dealing with a predator who wanted a woman and a little girl. Now, she knew that he had no interest in Maya – Laney herself was the target. She was so mad at herself, but there was no time for that. She could beat herself up later. For now, she got down on her stomach on the ground and got as close as she dared to the gap in the boards. She was hoping that she'd be able to spot a safe place that she could tell Maya to run to and hide. She doubted that he'd go after her.

~ ~ ~

Janey came running up the steps to Luke. "I came as soon as I heard. I was down in Gardiner. Is there any news?"

"No. We don't have a damn thing to go on."

Janey rubbed her hand across her forehead. "Do you think it's Buck?"

Luke inhaled sharply. "Why would I think that?" It felt so out of left field that he couldn't process it. But then ... ever since that night at Libby's place, Deacon and the deputies had been questioning him, asking him if there was anyone who might have a grudge against him.

His heart started to pound. He'd forgotten about punching Buck. He'd been so mad at him when he saw him pawing at Laney. But that whole thing had been overshadowed by coming clean with her brothers.

"Fuck!"

Janey put a hand on his arm. "Tell me she told you about him?"

He closed his eyes. "Told me what?" He knew Laney. If she had a problem with someone, she wouldn't come asking for his help. She'd deal with it herself. This was it; he knew it. "In fact, come inside, and you can tell the others at the same time you tell me."

He hurried back into the house, where everyone was sitting and standing around, the air filled with palpable tension.

Luke dialed Deacon and put him on speaker. "What have you got?" he answered.

"It's Buck."

"Give me a minute while I get some cars on the way out to their place."

Wade came striding toward him. "It's Buck? What makes you think it's Buck?"

Luke looked at Janey, who in turn looked at his phone.

"Don't wait for Deacon," said Luke. "We can fill him in when he comes back on."

Janey nodded, looking pale. "She told me that while she was back in Kentucky, he'd texted her and called her."

"And said what?" Luke's voice came out as a growl.

"Something about how her being a MacFarland didn't make her anything special, and that ... Oh my God, Luke! He said that just because her boyfriend was a deputy, didn't mean he couldn't get to you. Do you think that he was the one ...?"

Luke didn't just think it; he knew it. The memory that had been on the edge of his awareness all this time finally came into focus. He'd known that it was a tattooed arm that had swung toward him – holding what he now knew was one of Libby's brass horses. Now, he recognized the tattoo. It belonged to Buck. It was a snake, and it had registered in Luke's mind that night at Chico. When Buck had his hands on Laney, Luke had been intent on getting that snake away from her.

He turned away, needing to find his keys. He needed to get in his truck and get out to ... He didn't know where Buck lived.

Deacon came back on the line. "I've got cars on the way. Talk to me."

"On the way where?"

"The Hofstetter place. Their folks passed on a few years ago, but Nixon's been keeping the place up. If Buck has Laney and Maya, I reckon he's more likely to take them out there than to bring them into town to wherever he's staying."

Luke met Wade's gaze, as he headed for the door. Wade shook his head. "I'm not waiting."

Ford was close on his heels as they ran for Wade's truck.

Tanner touched Luke's arm as he and Ty made for the door.

"We're on our way out there," Luke told Deacon.

"I thought you'd already be on the road. I am."

Luke climbed into the passenger seat, and Ty jumped in the back seconds before Tanner's truck sent gravel flying as he sped up the driveway.

He rested his elbows on his knees and held his head between his hands. He couldn't wrap his mind around it yet. Buck had threatened Laney – and threatened him? And she hadn't told him? He blew out a sigh, remembering that there had been a couple of times when they talked on the phone that she'd said she had something she needed to tell him, but he'd distracted her.

He couldn't be mad at her. He hadn't been completely honest with her, either. Perhaps if he'd told her his suspicions about being lured to Libby's place – about being attacked because of who he was, not just because he'd interrupted a burglary – it might have jogged her memory. She might have put two and two together. But hell, none of that mattered now. All that mattered was that they got her and Maya back before Buck hurt either of them.

"Nixon!"

Luke swung around to look at Tyler, who had his phone to his ear.

"Do you know if your brother has a problem with Laney and Luke?"

Ty scowled as he listened to whatever Nixon was saying.

"Put him on speaker," said Tanner.

"… got some kind of problem. I just got home. I've been over in Butte the last couple of days, and to say Buck wasn't happy to see me back, is an understatement."

Luke could feel the blood pounding in his temples.

"What did he do?"

"It was weird. He looked like he was about to go into the barn when I arrived. I don't think he's set foot in there in twenty years."

"Fuck!" Luke exclaimed.

"Can you go in there?" asked Tyler.

Nixon sighed. "Shit. You think he's been stealing again? What am I looking for? I'll go look, but not until he leaves. I'll be honest with you, he scares me. And that guy with him, he's one crazy fucker."

Luke clenched his jaw. He couldn't stand to think of Laney in the clutches of Buck and some crazy fucker. This was getting worse by the minute.

"Where is he now?"

"He's in the house. He came inside when I arrived. Now that you mention it, he closed the barn back up in a hurry when he saw me – no doubt he didn't want me to see what he's got stashed in there."

"What he's got stashed in there," Luke said through gritted teeth, "is Laney and little Maya."

"What the fuck? Seriously? Shit. I need to …"

Luke hated to say it, but he knew that he had to. "Stay put, Nix. We're almost there. Deacon and the deputies will probably get there right around the same time that we do. If you go out there, it'll only set him off."

"Fuck! Shit, Luke. I'm so sorry,"

"It's not your fault. Tell me one thing – the guy who's with him, have you seen both of his hands?"

Nixon was quiet for a moment before he said, "No. I mean, I've seen his hands, but only in gloves. Why?"

"Because I think he's the fucker who shot me."

"Shit. I'm sorry, Luke."

"Just hang tight. Are they both in the house together?"

"Yes."

"Then you stay put."

"I'm going nowhere."

"Right. But keep an eye on the barn – distract him if he looks like he's going back out to the barn. We'll see you soon."

Chapter Twenty-Six

Laney watched through the gap in the boards as Buck and his friend stood talking to Nixon. Shit. She wished that she could get Nix's attention, let him know somehow that she was here. But she couldn't risk it. She couldn't believe that Nix knew what Buck was doing; he'd always known that his brother was an asshole. But trying to get Nix's attention without alerting Buck was too risky.

She let out a breath as she watched the three of them go inside the house. Then she scanned the area, looking for somewhere that might be a safe place for Maya to hide. If she was out of the way, she doubted that Buck would go after her. But if she was still in here, she didn't trust him not to hurt her.

She shuddered. He'd shot … Oh wait, no. His friend, the one who'd said *gotcha*, was the one who'd shot Luke. Her blood ran cold. That meant that Buck was the one who'd tried to bash his head in. She had to get Maya out of here. There was a small shed, just beyond the house, but she couldn't know if it was unlocked. She couldn't send Maya running to it, only to find that she couldn't get in it when she got there.

There were some bushes behind the shed, but she wasn't sure they would provide enough cover. She looked back at

Nix's truck. Would he have locked it? Again, it wasn't a risk worth taking. She strained her neck in the other direction and spotted a tractor. Would Maya be able to climb up into the cab and hide there? She didn't know. She looked back over her shoulder at the little girl who was sitting beside her, shaking.

"Come here, sweetie."

Maya got down on her stomach next to Laney and peered out of the gap in the boards.

"Can you see that tractor?"

Maya nodded.

"Do you think you could climb up into the cab and hide?"

Maya nodded again, but she didn't look very sure of herself.

"You can tell me if you don't think you can do it."

"I can do it."

Laney hoped to hell that she wasn't just telling her what she wanted to hear. She looked at the tractor again.

"Cowgirls always have a backup plan, too."

Maya looked at her with big, round, scared eyes.

"I want you to run to the tractor. Run around the other side, so that no one can see you from this side. If you can, I want you to climb up into the cab and hide in there. Your backup plan, if you can't climb up, is you get underneath the tractor and hide behind the tire."

Maya looked out at the tractor. "Where are you going to hide?"

Laney swallowed. "I need to stay here."

"Then I stay, too."

"No, sweetie. I need you to go. That bad man? He's angry at me, he's not angry at you. If you can get away, he'll let you go. If I go with you … He'll come after both of us. And besides …" She pulled at the rotted board. You can fit out of this gap; I can't."

Laney's heart melted in her chest when Maya wrapped an arm around her neck and pressed a kiss to her cheek. "I love you, Laney."

She held the little girl against her as close as she could as they both lay there in the dirt. "I love you, too, Maya. What do you think? Can you do it?"

Laney had no clue how long it would be before Buck came back out. Perhaps, after she got Maya out of here, she'd risk making some noise by trying to bust out more of the rotted wood, but her first priority was getting Maya somewhere that was hopefully safer.

"I can do it. I think I can climb up. If I can't climb up, I will hide underneath."

"That's my girl." As she said it, it gave her an appreciation of how Cash must feel when he said those words to her.

She looked back out through the gap again. Everything was quiet.

"Okay, are you ready?"

Maya nodded bravely. "I can do it."

Laney kissed her cheek. "I know you can, sweetie. And when you get there, you hide, and you wait. I'm hoping I'll be able to come for you soon. But if I don't, Luke or Wade will show up soon." She had no idea if that was true, but she had to hope it would be.

Maya nodded. "They will find us."

"That's right."

Laney checked outside again. There was no sign of movement anywhere. "Okay. It's time to go."

Maya wriggled forward on her stomach until she was under the boards and out the other side. When she was clear, she lay there for a moment, and met Laney's gaze. "We are cowgirls," she whispered. "We're brave, and smart, and strong."

Laney's eyes pricked with tears as she nodded back at her. "That's right, we are. Now go. I'll see you soon."

She held her breath, her heart pounding in her ears, as she watched Maya run at a crouch until she rounded the other side of the tractor. Her heart leaped into her mouth when the front door of the house opened. Her fingers balled into fists. If Buck had spotted Maya, Laney was going to kick her way through the boards to get out there to stop him.

She let out the breath she'd been holding when she saw that it was Nixon coming out. She frowned as she watched him hurrying in her direction. Had he seen Maya?

As he approached the spot where she was lying, she made a decision.

"Nix!" she called in a whisper shout.

He stopped and looked around.

She stuck her hand out through the gap and waved. He spotted it and took two steps toward her before he stopped.

Shit. Was she wrong about him? Was he going to go and get Buck?

"I'm just going to stand here, and get my phone out, Laney. If he sees me, he'll think that I'm talking on it – and not to the barn wall."

"Good thinking. While you've got your phone out, can you call Luke?"

"I already did. He's on the way. It sounds like all your brothers and the entire sheriff's department are hot on his heels."

Some of the tension left Laney's shoulders. "Awesome. Does Buck know that you're out here?"

"I don't know. I don't think so."

"Then, can you go and get Maya?" She turned to look but couldn't see her. "She's either in the cab of the tractor, or underneath it."

"That's where I was headed."

"Thanks. Get her, tell her that you're my friend and Luke's friend – otherwise she might not go with you. But you get her, and you take her as far away from here as you can, you hear me? Run up to the road – that'll probably be the safest if everyone's on their way."

Nix froze when they heard voices coming from the house. He pressed his phone to his ear as if he were talking into it rather than to her.

"I'll do my best. I think you should do the same, though."

She nodded. As soon as he had Maya safely away, she planned to start kicking out boards, and taking her chances with making a break for it herself.

She watched Nix walk to the tractor and squat down beside it. Maya's little head appeared around the back tire. She looked over at Laney, and Laney held her thumb up. That did the trick. Laney breathed a sigh of relief as she watched Maya scramble out from under the tractor and take hold of Nixon's hand as they started to run.

Then, the front door of the house flew open. Shit! Had they seen him leave? Apparently, they had, but they hadn't seen that he'd taken Maya with him.

"Jesus, I thought he was never going to leave," Buck's friend said.

"Well, he's gone now. But we can't stay here. Not with him around. He always was a little snitch. We'll have to put them in the truck and take them up the road."

Laney's heart thudded to a stop. *Up the road* could be anywhere, and if they took her away from here, Luke would have no way of finding her again. She had to hold out until he got here. She could do her best to fight, but there were two of them and she wouldn't stand much of a chance. She'd do better trying to run and hide. She scrambled back into the barn and looked up the steps that led to the loft. It was probably dumb to go to a place with no exit, but if she could pull the steps up after her, it might be her best bet.

~ ~ ~

They were almost to the Hofstetter place. Luke gripped the dashboard when they saw Wade's truck pulled off the road up ahead. Wade and Ford were running across the field.

"What the fuck?"

Tyler's phone rang and he answered it quickly. "What's going on, Nix?"

Luke didn't need to ask; Ty put the phone on speaker as Nix replied.

"I've got Maya. Your brothers have spotted us, but can you please do me a favor and call them and tell them that I'm rescuing her, not kidnapping her? The look on Wade's face says I'm about to die."

"On it." Ty ended the call.

A moment later, Ford's voice filled the cab of the truck. "What's up, Ty? We found Maya. Nixon's got her."

"I know. Nixon just called me. He's on our side. Try to stop Wade from killing him."

"Shit! Wade!" Ford shouted.

The call ended and the three of them watched Ford catch up to Wade. The two of them slowed their pace when Nixon appeared with little Maya at his side. He let go of her hand and she and Wade ran to meet each other.

Luke had to clear his throat as he watched his brother scoop up his little girl and hold her tight. He was hoping that he'd have a similar reunion with Laney in just a few more minutes. Tanner braked hard when they reached the driveway, and the truck fishtailed around the corner.

Luke's heart stopped when he saw smoke rising from the barn.

"Holy shit!" exclaimed Tanner. "What the hell's going on?"

Luke held his head between his hands, willing the truck to go faster so that they could get there and find out. By the time they were half way up the driveway, they could see flames licking the walls of the barn. Nixon had told them that Buck had Laney and Maya in there.

Luke prayed silently that Laney had gotten out. Maya had. But if Nixon had been able to get her away, why hadn't he been able to get Laney out, too?

As Tanner brought the truck to a screeching halt outside the barn, Buck and his friend – the guy who'd shot Luke – came running out.

Tanner, Tyler, and Luke all piled out of the truck and started running toward them. Buck reached his own truck before they could get to him. His friend scrambled into the passenger seat, and the truck came barreling toward them and they had to jump out of the way.

"You've got a choice, Wallis," Buck shouted out of the window. "You can either come after me, or try to save your girlfriend from the loft."

There was no choice. Not in Luke's mind. He ran toward the barn.

He heard Tyler shout, "Give me your keys," to Tanner, who was running after Luke. Luke didn't bother looking back. Ty, or Deacon and the deputies, would catch up with them. His only thought was getting to Laney.

"Laney!" he shouted as soon as he was in the barn.

He could hear her coughing. If she was in the loft, she was in the worst place. There was no way to escape from the smoke up there.

"Laney! It's me. I'm here. Is there a hay door?" He looked around desperately. He couldn't see a ladder. There was no way to get up there to her. The flames were already licking around the posts that supported the loft.

His voice cracked when he called again. "Laney! Talk to me!"

"I'm okay." The way she coughed after she said it made a liar out of her.

Tanner came up behind him. "Laney, can you get to the hay door, honey?"

She coughed harder, but they heard her call, "I will."

Luke and Tanner ran outside. The hay door was on the far side of the building. Tanner pointed up at it, and Luke looked around. Even if she could get to the door, it was a hell of a long way down. It was typical for a barn like this to have a hay loft. The bales were tossed across from the trailer in through the hay door.

Luke spotted a tractor, but there was no trailer – no means that he could see of getting up to the door. Even if she made it to the door, if she jumped from that height, she was looking at broken bones at the very least.

He shook his head at Tanner. "I'm going in."

Tanner stared at him. "I don't like it, but I think you're right. If you can get her to the door, I'll have a way for you to get down by the time you get there."

Luke nodded and hurried back into the barn. He pulled his shirt off as he went and wrapped it around his face. The smoke was thick now. He could still hear Laney coughing, but it was getting weaker.

"Hang on, baby. I'm coming up." He had no idea how he was going to get up there to her, until he spotted the ladder lying on the ground – that bastard, Buck, must have pulled it down after she climbed up. The sick fucker had left her to burn to death up there.

The smoke burned his eyes, and the heat seared his skin as he climbed higher. Then, he was at the top. He started crawling in the direction of her coughing.

"I'm here, baby. I'm here. Come on, let's get you out of here."

She could barely lift her head; she had to have inhaled in a lot of smoke, but her eyes met his and she smiled.

"What took you so long?" she asked in a weak voice before she started coughing again.

He was coughing so hard himself now, that he couldn't reply. He took his shirt off his face and covered hers with it. Then, he wrapped his arm around her and started moving them toward the hay door. He panicked when it wouldn't open, until he spotted the latch and flipped it. A rush of fresh, cool air swept in when he kicked the door open. He looked down when he heard Tanner shout his name.

"You're going to have to jump."

He looked down and saw that Tanner had positioned his truck underneath the door. Even under these circumstances, Luke had to laugh when he saw that Tanner had laid out his notorious mattress in the truck bed.

Laney coughing beside him, and the heat and smoke behind them reminded him that this was no time for laughing. He caught hold of her hand and tugged for her to join him.

"Are you good to jump? Do you trust me?"

She met his gaze and nodded. "With my life," she croaked.

He swung his legs out so that he was sitting on the edge and helped her do the same. It still looked a long way down, but it was the only option they had.

"Ready?"

She nodded, and he heaved them both over the edge.

As soon as he landed, he rolled over to check that she was okay. She was still coughing, her eyes were streaming, but she smiled. "You might need to ask my brother about more subtle ways to get a girl into the back of a truck."

He laughed and pressed a kiss to her lips. "I never had you down as the kind of girl who appreciated subtle."

She wrapped her arms around him, and he hugged her to his chest. They lay that way for a long few moments, both coughing, until Tanner cleared his throat beside the truck.

"It sounds like you're both okay in there, but I should warn you that we're about to have company."

Luke slowly sat up, and Laney pushed herself up onto all fours beside him.

Deacon jumped out of a patrol car and came running toward them. "Are you guys okay?"

Luke nodded and wrapped his arm around Laney as she leaned against him. "We're okay."

"Maya?" Laney croaked.

Deacon grinned. "Wade's got her. And from what I hear, you managed to save Nixon from a beating."

"He deserves a medal, not a beating. He got her out of there," said Laney.

Deacon held her gaze. "The way he tells it, you got her out of there. He just assisted."

Laney smiled. "As long as she's okay. That's all that matters."

Luke tightened his arm around her shoulders. "And you. As long as you're okay."

Deacon rolled his eyes at Tanner. "Do you think you can move them along? Maybe leave them on your mattress back here and just drive them down the road a little way till we can get an ambulance here?" He looked up at the burning barn. "We don't want that damn thing falling on us after all this, and the fire crew is going to want us out of the way."

Chapter Twenty-Seven

Two weeks later

Laney wrapped her arm around Luke's waist as they stood on the front steps, waving at Tanner as he left. He was hauling the trailer that he'd used to bring three more horses over for them.

Luke smiled down at her and pressed a kiss to her forehead. "I think we're going to have our work cut out for us with this bunch."

She nodded happily. "I agree. I asked him to bring us the ones that need the most work."

Luke raised his eyebrows, but she just shrugged. "You're fully recovered now – well, I know your shoulder still gives you some trouble. But Trip gave you the all-clear on your head after that last scan. So, I reckon that you need to start stepping it up. Do some real work around here," she added with a grin.

He laughed. "Are you challenging me, cowgirl?"

She laughed with him. "Have I ever been anything but challenging?"

He closed his arms around her and drew her closer. "You're so much more than a challenge to me."

"Aww. You say the sweetest things."

He met her gaze, his blue eyes holding an intensity that surprised her. "I've got something I want to say to you, and I'm hoping that you'll think it's sweet. Well, more than sweet. And actually, it's something I want to ask you."

She sucked in a deep breath "There's something that I want to ask you, too. I was going to ask you that day – when everything happened. And since then, … I just … I wanted to make sure that everything was okay. That you were okay – that we were."

He gave her a puzzled look. "Why wouldn't we be okay?"

She took his hand and led him back into the house. "Let's get a glass of wine and sit out back while we talk about it. Do you want to?"

"I do. Except the wine part. I'll get you one, but I'll have a beer."

She rolled her eyes at him. "You're such a guy."

"Whatever."

While he got their drinks, Laney went to get the papers that she'd been worrying about for the last two weeks. When she'd done it, she thought it was a great idea. Now, she was feeling a little unsure of herself. Well, unsure of how Luke would feel about it. She hoped that he'd love it, but …

She gave him a puzzled look when he came out to join her on the deck. Instead of beer and wine, he was carrying two glasses of champagne. "What's that all about?"

He gave her a mysterious smile. "You'll have to wait and see. You said that you want to ask me something. I think we should get that out of the way before I take my turn. Then, hopefully, you'll want to drink a glass of this bubbly stuff with me."

"Okay." She cleared her throat. Damn, she shouldn't be nervous. She held up the envelope. "This is what I want to talk to you about."

He raised his eyebrows. "About an envelope?"

She rolled her eyes. "About what's inside it."

He chuckled. "Go on, then. What's inside it?"

"You have to promise that you won't be mad at me."

He pursed his lips. "I won't be mad."

"Promise?"

He laughed. "Just tell me, baby."

She handed him the envelope, but he shook his head. "Don't make me read it, just tell me."

"Okay. I want to give you seventeen different explanations, but I'm not going to. I'm just going to say it. I bought this place."

His head snapped back as his gaze flew up to meet hers. "You what?"

She swallowed. "You heard me. I got in touch with Haley and Walt. I asked them if they wanted to sell. They did. So, I bought it." She held her breath as she waited for his reaction.

"Damn!" He ran his hand over his face. "Whatever I was expecting, it wasn't this."

"Are you mad?"

She relaxed when he reached out and stroked her arm. "Mad? Hell no. I'm just... surprised, I guess. I mean, I thought ... I was kind of hoping that *we* might buy it."

She nodded rapidly. "We did. I didn't buy it for me, I bought it for us. We're going to be together, right?"

"We are."

"Then, does it matter who bought it? If we live here. If it's our place. I even waited to register title – since I want both of our names on there." She smiled when she remembered what he'd said. "Didn't you tell me that as long as you get me, all the rest is just detail?"

He chuckled. "I did."

She leaned in and pressed a kiss to his lips. "Then welcome home, baby."

He raised his eyebrows, and she laughed. "Ever since we talked about it, about what I might call you, I've been thinking about it. I tried a bunch of different names out in my head. But it kept coming back to *baby*. I know it's the same as what you call me. But it works. I'm your baby, and you're mine."

He grinned. "I love it."

She sucked in a deep breath. "And it's my way of telling you something else, too."

He chuckled. "What else did you buy?"

She laughed with him. "Nothing. I promise that I will consult with you on all major purchases in the future, how about that?"

"I'd appreciate it. So, what else are you trying to tell me when you call me baby?"

She bit down on her bottom lip. "That I think that someday... Not too soon, but someday, I'd like to have babies with you."

He'd said that it didn't bother him, but the way his smile lit up his face told her how important it was to him. "Yeah? What made you change your mind?"

She grinned. "Maya. She's amazing. And you were right – when I started to see her as a fellow human being, I started to see things differently."

He took hold of her hand and squeezed it. "I'm glad. I'm not in any rush, but I'm glad that you see it as an option."

He stuck his hand in his pocket and fiddled with something there. She raised her eyebrows at him. "What are you up to?"

He laughed. "I can't get away with a damn thing with you, can I?"

She shook her head happily. "Nope."

~ ~ ~

Luke closed his fingers around the little box in his pocket. This was it. The moment had finally come.

"What I'm up to, is figuring out how best to do this."

"Do what?"

"Do my part, I guess, is the honest answer. Do what I wish I'd done years ago. You've already taken care of the house, and the babies, by the sound of it. All that's left for me to do is this."

He slid off his chair and got down on one knee in front of her as he took hold of her hand.

"Will you marry me, Laney? I wish I asked you years ago. But we can't change the past. All we can do is enjoy every moment that we get and build ourselves a future."

"Yes. Yes, a hundred times, yes. I don't even want to talk about what's gone. We've got so much ahead of us, so much to look forward to. And I'll look forward to it all even more, knowing that you're my husband, and I'm your wife."

He hooked his fingers around the back of her neck and pulled her down into a long, lingering kiss. "I can't wait to call you wifey."

She laughed. "Tanner will be thrilled when he hears you call me that. He said you would."

Luke held up the box and flipped it open. "He's been on board ever since he found out – well, at least since he punched me and got over it. He even came with me to pick this out for you."

A rush of warmth filled his chest when her eyes grew wide. "Oh my God, Luke! It's beautiful! I love it."

He took it out of the box and slid it onto her finger. "I knew you'd love it. It's just like you: bold, strong, no-nonsense, and beautiful."

His heart felt as though it might explode with happiness as he slid the ring onto her finger – and it fit.

She held her hand out to admire it. "I love it."

He pressed a kiss to her lips. "I love you."

"I love you, too."

He handed her a glass of champagne and tapped his against it. "Let's drink to us."

"To us," she said, then held his gaze as she downed the whole thing.

He had to laugh as he did the same.

"What do you think, baby? Want to take the next glass upstairs and seal the deal?" she asked.

"I'd love to, but I was thinking that maybe we should call the brothers – yours and mine – to tell them the good news."

Her eyes grew wide. "Please tell me that you already told Cash – or better yet, that you asked him?"

He laughed. "Of course, I did. I've had enough brushes with death lately. I wasn't going to risk having him come after me because I didn't ask for his blessing. I asked all of them."

She made a face, but she couldn't keep the smile off her face. "I feel like I should be mad about that. It's not up to them."

"I know. It's up to you. But after the way I handled things in the past, I wanted to do this right."

"It's okay. I get it." She pressed a kiss to his lips. "I even like it. And I know that they were all okay with it." She looked down at the ring. "I wouldn't be wearing this if they weren't."

"I wouldn't have let them stop me."

He relaxed when she smiled. "I know. But we both wanted to do it right this time and I know you would have gotten them on board one way or another before you asked."

"Yeah. They're happy about it, though – all of them."

"What did Cash say?"

He laughed. "He said that it's about damned time – that he's always believed it was inevitable that we'd end up together."

"Inevitable?"

He chuckled. "Yeah. I think he's right. However many ways we messed it up over the years, I think we were always meant to end up together."

She nodded and held up her empty glass. "Pour us another so that we can drink to our inevitable love before we call our family and get roped into the inevitable gathering that they'll insist we come over for."

Luke rested his forehead against hers and looked into her eyes. "That's the only reason we're not upstairs yet. They're all waiting at the ranch to hear if you're comfortable to go over there and celebrate, or if they're bringing the party here."

She laughed. "They are?"

He gave her a sheepish smile. "When I talked to Cash, he insisted that everyone would want to celebrate together."

"It's a pity he's not here then, isn't it?"

Luke raised his eyebrows, and she laughed. "Oh my God! He is?"

"Yeah. And Kolby is, too."

"Then give them a call and get them over here already. The sooner we get this party started, the sooner they'll leave, and I can take you upstairs to seal this deal."

Luke smiled as he took his phone out. "I already told them that you might not want to go to the ranch – so they're prepared to bring food and drinks over here."

She nodded. "I think I'm over that. The ranch is just the ranch. The old man doesn't factor into any of it for me anymore. Being back here, seeing the way everyone's moved on with their lives – even Janey." She shook her head. "The past is the past, he's a part of it. I can leave him there."

"I'm glad."

She nodded. "I'd be okay to go over there, but I want them to come here. This is where we live – our home. The place where we're finally going to build our life."

Luke pressed a kiss to her forehead. "Finally. I still haven't figured out what I'm going to do for a job but …"

Laney's eyes twinkled as she grinned at him. "I have. We're driving out to Oregon next week to look at brood mares."

He had to laugh. "Okay, boss lady."

Her smile faded. "No. Not boss lady. Partners – in everything."

She leaned in to kiss him and he spoke against her lips. "Partners in life, in love, and in business."

She held up her hand to show him the ring. "For the rest of our lives."

"Forever, baby."

She laughed and pulled away from him. "Go ahead and call the brothers – let's get this party started."

Luke smiled to himself as he called Cash's number. He couldn't wait to get this party started – not just the one tonight, but the one that he planned to make last for the rest of their lives;

;

A Note from SJ

I hope you enjoyed Laney and Luke's story. The next MacFarland Ranch book will be Kolby and Callie's story. You can get more details as they become available on my website at The Cowboy's Undeniable Love. I can't wait to share that one with you!

I'm still rotating through the series so the next book to be published will be Slade and Willow in Whiskey and Willow.

If you're holding out for more Summer Lake, the next Silver story is called Meet Me Where the Stars Fall — and it's Lucky and Dee's story. I thought that Davin and Zoe were up next, but after showing up in Dalton and Taryn's story with his dog, Echo, Lucky has elbowed his way to the front. Davin says he's fine to wait a while longer — he's a bit more laid back.

Check out the "Also By" page to see if any of my other series appeal to you — I have the occasional ebook freebie series starters, too, so you can take them for a test drive.

There are a few options to keep up with me and my imaginary friends:

The best way is to Sign up for my Newsletter at my website www.SJMcCoy.com. Don't worry I won't bombard you! I'll let you know about upcoming releases, share a sneak peek or two and keep you in the loop for a couple of fun giveaways I have coming up :0)

You can join my readers group to chat about the books or like my Facebook Page www.facebook.com/authorsjmccoy

I occasionally attempt to say something in 140 characters or less(!) on Twitter

I love to hear from readers, so feel free to email me at SJ@SJMcCoy.com if you'd like. I'm better at that! :0)

I hope our paths will cross again soon. Until then, take care, and thanks for your support—you are the reason I write!

Love

SJ

PS Project Semicolon

You may have noticed that the final sentence of the story closed with a semi-colon. It isn't a typo. <u>Project Semi Colon</u> is a non-profit movement dedicated to presenting hope and love to those who are struggling with depression, suicide, addiction and self-injury. Project Semicolon exists to encourage, love and inspire. It's a movement I support with all my heart.

"A semicolon represents a sentence the author could have ended, but chose not to. The sentence is your life and the author is you." - Project Semicolon

This author started writing after her son was killed in a car crash. At the time I wanted my own story to be over, instead I chose to honour a promise to my son to write my 'silly stories' someday. I chose to escape into my fictional world. I know for many who struggle with depression, suicide can appear to be the only escape. The semicolon has become a symbol of support, and hopefully a reminder – Your story isn't over yet

Also by SJ McCoy

Summer Lake Silver

This series features couples in their fifties and older. Just because a few decades—or more—have skipped by since you were in your twenties it doesn't mean you can't find love, does it? Summer Lake Silver stories find happily-ever-afters for those who remember being thirty-something—vaguely.

Marianne and Clay in Like Some Old Country Song
Seymour and Chris in A Dream Too Far
Ted and Audrey in A Little Rain Must Fall
Diego and Izzy in Where the Rainbow Ends
Manny and Nina in Silhouettes Shadows and Sunsets
Teresa and Cal in More Than Sometimes
Russ and Ria in Like a Soft Sweet Breeze
Adam and Evelyn in When Words Are Not Enough
Dalton and Taryn in Can't Fight The Moonlight
Coming Next
Lucky and Dee in Meet Me Where the Stars Fall
Davin and Zoe

Summer Lake Seasons
Angel and Luke in Take These Broken Wings
Zack and Maria in Too Much Love to Hide
Logan and Roxy in Sunshine Over Snow
Ivan and Abbie in Chase the Blues Away
Colt and Cassie in Forever Takes a While
Austin and Amber in Tell the Stars to Shine
Donovan and Elle in Please Don't Say Goodbye
Coming Next

Tiffany and Brayden in What's A Guy To Do?

Summer Lake Series
Emma and Jack in Love Like You've Never Been Hurt
Holly and Pete in Work Like You Don't Need the Money
Missy and Dan in Dance Like Nobody's Watching
Smoke and Laura in Fly Like You've Never Been Grounded
Michael and Megan in Laugh Like You've Never Cried
Kenzie and Chase in Sing Like Nobody's Listening
Gabe and Renée in Smile Like You Mean It
Missy and Dan's wedding in The Wedding Dance
Ben's backstory in Chasing Tomorrow
April and Eddie in Dream Like Nothing's Impossible
Nate and Lily in Ride Like You've Never Fallen
Ben's Story in Live Like There's No Tomorrow
Smoke and Laura's wedding in The Wedding Flight
Leanne and Ryan in Fight Like You've Never Lost

The Hamiltons
Cameron and Piper in Red Wine and Roses
Chelsea and Grant in Champagne and Daisies
Mary Ellen and Antonio in Marsala and Magnolias
Marcos and Molly in Prosecco and Peonies
Grady and Hannah in Milkshakes and Mistletoe
Jacob and Becca in Cognac and Cornflowers
Coming Next
Bentley and Alyssa in Bourbon and Bluebells
Slade and Willow in Whiskey and Willow
Xander and Tori in Vodka and Violets

Remington Ranch Series
Mason
Shane
Carter
Beau
Four Weddings and a Vendetta

A Chance and a Hope Trilogy
Chance Encounter
Finding Hope
Give Hope a Chance

MacFarland Ranch Series
Wade and Sierra in The Cowboy's Unexpected Love
Janey and Rocket in The Cowgirl's Unmistakable Love
Deacon and Candy in The Sheriff's Irresistible Love
Laney and Luke in The Cowgirl's Inevitable Love
Coming Next
Kolby and Callie in The Cowboy's Undeniable Love
Ace and Ari in The Rancher's Inescapable Love

The Davenports
Oscar
TJ
Reid
Spider

Love in Nashville
Autumn and Matt in Bring on the Night

Standalone Novella

Sully and Jess in If I Fall

About the Author

I'm SJ, a coffee addict, lover of chocolate and drinker of good red wines. I'm a lost soul and a hopeless romantic. Reading and writing are necessary parts of who I am. Though perhaps not as necessary as coffee! I can drink coffee without writing, but I can't write without coffee.

I grew up loving romance novels, my first boyfriends were book boyfriends, but life intervened, as it tends to do, and I wandered down the paths of non-fiction for many years. My life changed completely a few years ago and I returned to Romance to find my escape.

I write 'Sweet n Steamy' stories because to me there is enough angst and darkness in real life. My favorite romances are happy escapes with a focus on fun, friendships and happily-ever-afters, just like the ones I write.

These days I live in beautiful Montana, the last best place. If I'm not reading or writing, you'll find me just down the road in the park - Yellowstone. I have deer, eagles and the occasional bear for company, and I like it that way :0)

Made in United States
Orlando, FL
01 September 2023

36616506R00198